*Alan McMonagle*

# LAURA CASSIDY'S
# WALK OF FAME

PICADOR

First published 2020 by Picador
an imprint of Pan Macmillan
The Smithson, 6 Briset Street, London EC1M 5NR
Associated companies throughout the world
www.panmacmillan.com

ISBN 978-1-5098-2988-0

The lyrics on p. 250 are a slightly tweaked version of
'The Streets Of Galway' by Padraig Stevens.

Pan Macmillan does not have any control over, or any responsibility for,
any author or third-party websites referred to in or on this book.

1 3 5 7 9 8 6 4 2

A CIP catalogue record for this book is available from the British Library.

Typeset in Sabon by Jouve (UK), Milton Keynes
Printed and bound by CPI Group (UK) Ltd, Croydon, CR0 4YY

Visit **www.picador.com** to read more about all our books
and to buy them. You will also find features, author interviews and
news of any author events, and you can sign up for e-newsletters
so that you're always first to hear about our new releases.

*for fionnuala*

# BARBARA STANWYCK

July 16, 1907 – January 20, 1990
aka Phyllis Dietrichson aka The Lady Eve

**Inducted:** February 8, 1960
**Star address:** 1751, Vine Street
Orphaned at four. Screen debut at nineteen
Heavy smoker, husky voice
Three Emmys, a Golden Globe, four Oscar nominations
**Real name:** Ruby Stevens

*'Just be truthful – and if you can fake that,
you've got it made.'*

# I

Some day you're going to be a star. Your name is going to be written in bright and dancing lights. Mark my words, daddy said, people will see your face and smile. Speak memorable lines from the movies you appear in. A legend in your time, that's what you will be, daddy said, and I was happy to hear him say it.

At that hour it was just the two of us, we had just finished watching the late-night movie together, and daddy was keen to hear my thoughts. I wasn't slow giving him my verdicts. *Sunset Boulevard*. Best movie ever. When I grow up I'm going to be Norma Desmond. *The Big Sleep*. Don't ask me what was going on but I loved it. *The Postman Always Rings Twice*. Great story but no way would I end up in a jam like that. *In a Lonely Place*. Gloria Grahame – so good.

I lost count of how many movies daddy and me watched. Mother and Jennifer and everyone else on the street were in bed, and I only wanted to watch them with him. And with the lights out. That way no one could interrupt us with stupid questions like what's with the mysterious woman or why is that fellow so obsessed, or could they switch the channel because they were fed up. I never got fed up. Damsels-in-distress movies with moody strangers who came to the rescue. Dark and grainy and hard-to-figure-out-what-was-happening movies with men that were all the time looking for something, women that were too good to be true, and storylines that would bring them fleetingly together before they were ripped apart from each other forever. Film noirs, daddy called those ones. *They Live by Night. Kiss Tomorrow Goodbye. The Asphalt Jungle. Laura.* I loved watching that one because I thought it had been named after me. It's the other way around, daddy said when I asked him, and then offered me that half-smile of his that he saved for whenever I said something clever. Until the night of the accident, I used to watch films with daddy all the time. He knew everything about them. All the actors, and who made the film, and when the film was made. That film is older than me and you put together, he'd say. He knew all the lines and loved rewatching his favourites. I was convinced he must have seen all the movies ever made.

'What are we watching tonight?' I'd ask him.

'*To Have and Have Not*,' he said, patting the cushion and beckoning me onto the sofa beside him while checking the guide to make sure. 'Bogart and Bacall are in this one. Wait until you see this pair go. It's nearly as good as *The Maltese Falcon.*'

'Bogart is in that one too,' I said, remembering.

'The stuff that dreams are made of,' daddy said, and I figured that must be another movie line.

I wasn't long getting my own set-pieces going. Daddy sat on the sofa and watched my performances, applauded when I finished and called out for more. At first I did lots of damsels in distress and wet-faced maidens falling in love with the last man they should be looking at, but I quickly tired of these drippy characters and moved on to the tough-talking ladies. These quickly became my favourites. They were daddy's favourites too. And the two of us would sit up together and watch as many as we could. *I Wake Up Screaming. The Lady from Shanghai. Fallen Angel. All About Eve.* 'Fasten your seatbelts, it's going to be a bumpy night,' I squeaked, puckering my lips and gripping the edge of the sofa. And daddy laughed so much he nearly choked on his drink.

Daddy let me stay up later and later, and watch whatever was on. I saw Alan Ladd and Veronica Lake in everything they were in together. 'Every man has seen you, somewhere,' Alan tells Veronica. 'The trick is to find you.' Veronica smiled her coy smile and later I tried to do my hair in the peekaboo style she wore. I watched Barbara Stanwyck run rings around Fred MacMurray in *Double Indemnity. You're not smarter, Walter, you're just a little taller.* Lana Turner did the same to John Garfield. Lauren Bacall gave Bogart as good as she got. And Gloria Swanson gives William Holden a lot more than he bargained for. Watch out, here comes Jane Greer, daddy said one night. She is going to stop Robert Mitchum dead in his tracks and believe me when I say it, if she can stop Mitchum she can stop any man.

I could never wait to do my newest productions for him. Encore! Encore! he bellowed every time I did my finish-up bow and curtsy, and daddy was the last person I was going to disappoint, and so I did my little acts all over again. Start to finish. Tweaking them here and there, for extra effect. And he was off. Stardom. Shining lights. My name along the Walk of Fame. He asked me did I know what the Walk of Fame was and I shook my head and he smiled and cleared his throat and told me all about the famous boulevard in Hollywood and the two and a half thousand stars along it, every one of them named after someone from the world of movies. It goes on for over a mile and everyone you can think of is there. Marilyn Monroe is there. And Marlene Dietrich. Joan Crawford. She's there. And so is Bette Davis. And Greta Garbo, the greatest of them all. And when the time comes, you'll be next. They are going to put your name on a star for everyone to see. And do you know what *that* means? he asked, and again I shook my head. Immortality, daddy said, with a quiver in his voice. That's what it means.

Then he hauled me outside the front door of our house, not stopping until we had crossed the road, passed the boathouse and were standing side by side in the chill of night on Nimmo's Pier. Look, he said, hunkering down beside me and pointing to the blurry lights along the pier. Can you see it? Hollywood. Starry lights. The Walk of Fame. Just you wait, Laura. One day it will be your turn, he said. Then he stretched out his arm and, with the penknife fetched out of his pocket, he scratched into the pier wall the words A STAR IS BORN.

I wasn't going to disagree with him. And I could see it. Could see myself up there, on the silver screen, effortlessly jousting with my co-stars, moving with serene calm through my scenes, gliding with slick abandon into my close-up. Come opening night, I saw myself taking to the red carpet. The snap-happy photographers. The screaming fans. The journalists shoving their mics in my face, eager for my words. Come award season, I heard my name called out at every prize-giving in the land. At parties, I was an extraordinary person. Brilliant and illuminating. Wherever I went everybody wanted a piece of me. They couldn't wait to announce my name.

From an early age that was me, then.

Laura Cassidy: The movie world's leading light. Star of the silver screen.

Isn't that right, Laura?

Yes it is, Laura. Indeed it is.

## 2

So far, things haven't panned out as daddy and me had foreseen. My name hasn't even left the ground, let alone appeared in shining lights. Adulation and fame have offered themselves as little more than a woebegone squawk. There is still time, though. That's what I tell myself every day when I wake up, ready and eager to offer myself to the waiting world. After all, I am not long past my twenty-fifth birthday, a mere child according to one or two of mother's friends. Remember what daddy said, I remind myself when it all threatens to get away from me, the world is a place of possibilities. A place containing moments set aside just for you.

There are several small reasons, and one or two big reasons, that have delayed my progress. Among the small reasons has been the lack of parts befitting someone of my talents, hold-ups with the construction of the new theatre, and the outgoing director in our town. His name is Mitchell, but for some time now I have been referring to him as the Imbecile. The Imbecile who wouldn't know how to direct traffic. The Imbecile who seems to have a huge amount of trouble recognizing genuine talent when it is standing in front of him. The Imbecile who would only know an actress if she wiggled her ripe rump in his face and said her name was Zsa Zsa Gabor. The big reasons I try not to think about.

Because sometimes – and by sometimes I mean all the time – I think it is the little things (Mitchell the Imbecile is a good example) that cause all the trouble. It is not heart attacks or machetes or remote control bombs that zap the life out of a person. It's the way people look at you and laugh, think they are always a step ahead. That's what I told them during my brief stint in St Jude's when invited to share something with the group. So many people, so few bullets. That's something else I said, and they laughed. The scourge of the street, mother calls me when I am in this kind of mood. I am not the scourge of the street, I am fast to reply. I am the most dangerous person in the country.

Dear brain, please shut up. That's what I really ought to be telling myself. If nothing else it might do my acting career some good. Get me on the path to stardom before I reach my use-by date, am put out to pasture once and for all time. Hey, Laura, I tell myself when I sense a little impudence kicking in, last time I checked, Rome wasn't built in a day. And, hey again: better late than dead. That is another of the little pieces of philosophy that keeps me going. That, and the fact that Mitchell the Imbecile – unable to harness my talents – has moved to the other side of the country.

I'm skimming through this week's *Advertiser* from my perch on the boathouse rooftop, taking turns at dragging on my cigarette and hissing at a posse of terrorists (tourists is far too kind a word for this nuisance species) snapping shots of the harbour and Spanish Arch, when I alight on this interesting piece of information. It is included in a pull-out feature detailing what makes our little city the most get-here-this-instant little city in the world. Oh yes. The city I live in is going places. Anybody who's anybody wants to be here right now. Especially right now. It's all happening. Dance, film, spectacle. Festivals for everything from the harp to the harmonica. Our very own television station. A famous all-the-way-round-the-world boat race wants to finish up in our ancient harbour. Whatever it is you are after, look no further. This is what I am reading. This is what the bigwig people in the know are saying. Most interestingly of all, as far as I am concerned, at long last the new theatre is more or less finished and a hotshot director from out of town is taking over.

Hotshot's name is Stephen Fallow. He has ideas. And already he's talking to the *Advertiser* about them. About how he intends to shake things up at Khaos Theatre. About the new faces he intends to introduce. About the productions – groundbreaking and innovative – he has in mind to put on. I can't say too much at this early stage, he is quick to add. Then he lets slip that the first production under his stewardship is going to be a reprisal of a famous Tennessee Williams play from the 1940s – in honour of its seventieth anniversary. We're going all out on this one, he adds for good measure. We'll be inviting actors in to audition for the lead roles. And that's all he can say for now. Fine by me. Hotshot doesn't have to say another word. Already I think I know what the play is. Already I'm fairly certain of the part I have in mind to go for. Already I know that this is the chance I have been waiting for. There is no doubt about it: I am in the right place at the right time – just like the *Advertiser* says.

I am going to have to talk to Fleming about this. Fleming is my leading man, something I decided back when we first got together. He's no Brando, or, for that matter, Bogart, but when it comes to the theatre and movies Fleming is the only one around here who has something to say that I want to listen to. He has his own ideas too, mostly television stuff, and I try to tell him he needs to think bigger. But Laura, he says, widening his eyes, television is where it's at these days. Blah-blah-blah is what I say to that.

My phone chimes and here he is, I'm guessing, my man Fleming. He has probably seen the *Advertiser* too and wants to hook up. Mull over the play. Discuss how best to play the part with my name on it. I can practically hear him urge me on. Get this part, Laura. Get this part and you can kiss a long goodbye to all your worries. No more mother on your case about sorting out your life. No more talk of St Jude's. No more doctors and useless pills. Get this part, Laura, and your daddy will be so proud.

I've guessed wrong, though. It's not Fleming. It's mother, texting to let me know that my one and only darling sister has safely arrived.

Jennifer.

The I'm-going-to-singlehandedly-rescue-the-world member of our family.

# 3

I haven't spoken a single word to Jennifer since thanking her – via Skype – for the part she played in landing me inside St Jude's eighteen nearly nineteen months ago, and still reckon I would like to be presented with her head on a plate. I could see it on a silver platter in front of me. The long eyelashes. The perfect nose. Those exquisitely symmetrical lips. The oh-so-severed-neatly neck nesting in a bed of treacly blood and green-leaf garnish.

All of it good enough to eat.

And so she has finally arrived. The prodigal daughter. Returned home after all this time to be greeted on our doorstep as though she is the greatest thing since Cleopatra and mother has been waiting for this moment all her life. And with a brand-new family member in tow. Mother and me had heard all about him, seen a photo or two, watched his toothy antics over Skype, and now here he was in the flesh. Four years old, and counting, if my sums were right. Juan, he is called.

It was all of one week ago that mother had chosen to let me in on the secret that Jennifer was coming home in the first place. As though mother had woken up last Monday morning and decided that her current daughter was no longer sufficient and that the additional daughter, the one with the bit of pep in her stride, the one with good hair and all-round easy-on-the-eye features, was required, and urgently at that. And hey presto, here she is.

Jennifer. My I-really-can't-believe-I-am-almost-thirty go-everywhere save-everyone older sister. Offering a little bit back to the world, to quote a line from an early postcard she sent us from somewhere in the bowels of Bolivia. A picture of five fat women dressed in black ponchos, bowler hats atop their wrinkled noggins. 'Which one is Jennifer?' I asked mother at the time, and received a scowl that would have instantly curdled milk. I didn't care where she was or what she was doing. Never asked for any updates on the little bits she was offering back to the world, but any time a postcard came dropping through our letterbox mother was onto it like a starving wasp on jam. Feeding for the rest of the day, weeks and months to come, off the four or five itty-bit sentences Jennifer had scribbled. *Hello from the highest train station in the world. The air is so thin they have us chewing coca leaves. Greetings from the Atacama Desert. It hasn't rained here for four hundred years. Happy New Year from the floating island on Lake Titicaca. Patagonia says hi.* And of course the entire street had to be made quickly aware of Jennifer's current whereabouts, her latest intrepid adventure, the noble work she was doing in the slums of Brazil or the jungles of Paraguay. Every word on the postcard pouring out of mother as though she had spent the night before cramming for an exam and had to squeeze out every single utterance before she started to forget.

'How many postcards do you reckon Jennifer has sent?' I asked mother.

'Oh, I have no idea.'

'Take a guess.'

'I told you I don't know.'

'Six postcards. That's how many. Six postcards in as many years.'

'Don't be daft,' mother said, and straightaway started into the email she had received from Jennifer, announcing her imminent return.

Sometime over a week ago that email must have arrived. Along with a photograph – of Jennifer's ever-smiling self, seated with her boy at a table outside a clapped-out coffee shop, about to pull on the straw sticking out of the tall glass. A wiggly arrow was pointing to the glass, along with a bubble caption that said, Iced coffee! More fawning, then, as mother enlarged the photograph on the screen, placed the laptop on the kitchen table and sat staring at it for about half the morning. Then she was talking again. Asking me did I realize how long it was since Jennifer had last been home. Six years! Think of it, mother went on, as though it was a span of time impossible to fathom, an eternity. Then, her voice hushing, mother picked up the laptop and raised it high. As though Jennifer was someone to look up to, a beacon for people who had lost their way, a goddess from beyond the beyond lording over mortal earth. And all the time I was staring at the computer screen and thinking: a pity you didn't float away with that island on Lake Titicaca.

*

Be here when she arrives. Mother's words. She's been using them on me every day for the past week. 'What for?' I said this morning, warming up my best innocent face. 'You know perfectly well what for. To welcome her home,' mother said. 'What for?' I said again, going into full I-know-nothing mode, and mother gave me the frown she saved up for when I went one step too far. I smiled pleasantly and told mother I was a busy bee. 'What has you so busy?' she then wanted to know, accompanying her words with that little chuckle of hers I don't always care for, and then tried to make me promise to stick around. 'I can't,' I said. 'What do you mean you can't?' she gasped, and I muttered something about a doctor's appointment. I was tempted to make up an elaborate yarn about having to be at the theatre, a proposal that on account of what had happened a year and a half ago – the crisis, to use a word a couple of mother's friends seem to like – would have had mother tearing out clumps of her higgledy-piggledy hair.

'You're busy!' she blurted out again. 'Pull the other one, it plays Jingle Bells,' she said, offering me her leg. And I was thinking oh-so calmly: I'll show you. One of these days I'll surprise you. Then we will see whose turn it is for a mocking tune.

Tuesday came and went. Wednesday, Thursday, Friday and Saturday. But the expected arrival did not show up. 'Where is this phantom?' I demanded to know in my best couldn't-care-less voice while mother fretted at her phone.

At some point over the weekend – late on Friday night, I think – the phone sounded and mother ran to it and clutched it, nodding her flustered head. 'Tomorrow,' mother said, when she put the phone down. 'She'll be here tomorrow. Make sure to stick around tomorrow.' And like a top-of-the-class fool I did stick around, all the way into early Saturday evening, and I stood tap-tapping my foot off the floor while mother nodded her head through another late-night phone call communicating another no-show. 'Her flight has been delayed,' mother said. 'Weather problems.'

'What sort of weather problems?' I wanted to know.

Next day, Jennifer telephoned from the airport. 'She has landed,' mother said, lighting up like a flare. 'She is in the country.'

'Whoopideedoo,' I said, and stood there while mother nodded through what seemed to be a series of instructions which soon had her shuffling restlessly about the place, muttering to herself. 'Her bags haven't come through. And her VISA card isn't working. We have to get her a bus ticket.'

All this took so long that Jennifer missed the last bus over and she had to find a hotel room for the night. Which had mother calling out her VISA number again. Meantime, Jennifer's bags had ended up on another flight. And lo-and-behold, the following day, the bus she managed to catch broke down about halfway across the country. 'Why don't we send a limousine?' I suggested, mother scowled, and in her flustered state, hung up before Jennifer had a chance to say another word.

Then she decided the spare room needed another cleaning.

'What has gotten into you?' I said. 'You never want to clean anything.'

'I can't wait to see her,' was all mother had to say, when she finally tired of her sweeping brush and vacuum cleaner and had emptied a third or fourth toilet duck and had sat down at the kitchen table, a cup of tea resting beside the little bundle of taxi money she had ready for the imminent arrival.

'Remind me again who she is,' I said.

'It's Jennifer!' mother said, in her excitement not realizing I didn't require an answer to my question. 'Your sister, Jennifer!'

Then mother's phone went off again. 'Oh my God, you poor thing,' I heard her say. There was plenty more, but by then I had heard enough. I let myself out, crossed the road and perched myself on the flat-roofed boathouse from where I witnessed Jennifer's reception (arms, hugs, kisses, tears), and saw her and her boy tucked safely away inside our end-of-terrace house.

I am in no hurry rushing home to greet her. I have important things to do today and, sister or no sister finally arrived all the way from the other side of the world, I fully intend to do them.

First things first, then. Swing by the medical centre – aka the Goldmine. Check in with the Doc, collect my meds.

# 4

I message Fleming to meet me at the Goldmine, take a drag of my rollie and allow myself get distracted by a pair of terrorists. A man and wife pairing in yellow, who must have decided on their wedding day, or at some such vital point in their lives together, that from here out they were going to buy the exact same walking boots and wear the same colour raincoats and plant atop their noggins ridiculous and identical beanies. They mooch about on the quay, fiddle with a top-of-the-range camera, point into the harbour waters, remark to each other in their twang and drawl accents. A couple of full-sail Hookers catch their attention and click-click-click goes the camera. A flotilla of swans emerges and so excited is she that for a second I think the woman is going to dive into the water in order to get a close-up view of this all-white procession. Oh goodie, I think to myself, blowing a plume of smoke in their general direction. First we have Cleopatra announcing herself. And now the swans.

I take a last pull on my rollie, flick the butt in the direction of the teapots in raincoats, clamber down the back wall of the boathouse, duck around the side and join the terrorists on the pier.

I drift among the snap-happy legions as the harbour birds swoop, dive and soar away again. 'Watch out, be on guard,' I say to a cluster of camera-wielders as I jostle into them. 'Vultures everywhere,' I say, pointing skywards and fish with my fingers inside a coat pocket, grip and slide up my sleeve the third purse I have claimed this week. 'Vultures, vultures,' I call out as I step away.

Further on, a couple of swans have waddled out of the water and up the boat ramp, and are beaking the ground for stray crumbs and of course everyone is falling over themselves to get the perfect picture. 'Come on, swans,' I say, imploring them with outspread arms, 'smile for the camera.' One or two people look at me and I give them my full-beam smile and they smile uncertainly back and return their attention to the waddling swans.

I wander down the boat ramp, stand at the water's edge, look right and left, and fetch the purse from its temporary abode and shove it in the front pocket of my skirt. I take out my phone and am about to message my man Fleming when the lad in the yellow raincoat asks me to take a photograph of him and his darling wife.

'Do you know something I don't?' I say to him.

'What's that?' he drawls.

'Ach-so! You speaka ze English,' I say.

'Yeah,' he says, already taking a half-step back. 'I *am* American. As in, the United States.'

'Oh, Amerrrrrrica! Land of the free and all that jazz. Well, silly me,' I say, raising my hand and slapping my forehead good-oh. 'And there I was thinking all along you were a sauerkraut.'

'Pardon me?'

'Where in America are you from?' I ask. 'Wait. Don't tell me. Boston, Massachoooosetts.'

'No. We're from—'

'Wait. I'm guessing here. Chicago the Windy City?'

'Not Chicago.'

'Baltimore? We get a lot of people from Baltimore in our little city.'

'Not Baltimore either.'

'Just as well. Riddled with gangsters and no-goods, that place – so I hear. How about Miami? You've got great skin. Must get a lot of sun where you live.'

'We're not from Miami.'

'You're not from California, I hope. Please say you're not from California.'

'We're not from California.'

'That is such a relief. I hear in California they lock you up for thirty-five years just for stealing a vegetable.'

'Well, I don't know if I'd go that far.'

'How far would you go?'

'Come again?'

'Jail in California. You wouldn't go that far. So?'

'So what?'

'So how far would you go?'

'I'm not sure I follow.'

'Ah, I don't blame you. I'm a mystery, me. A mystery wrapped up in an enigma shrouded by a riddle, me. Now tell me more about this loofah-face tangerine thinking of moving into the White House. He seems to be infatuated with the word tremendous.'

'I beg your pardon?'

'You want a photo, right? With the white bird?'

Half-heartedly, he hands over the camera and joins his dressed-just-like-him missus who, from a safe distance, is in the process of making a series of strange-sounding squawks, peeps and coos at the unheeding swan. For the camera they pose as a love-dove couple wearing sunglasses. They stand wrapped around each other right at the water's edge while I pretend I am an expert camera operator. I should tell them that taking off their ridiculous raincoats will make the shot even more romantic. 'A little to the left,' I say instead, and they shuffle accordingly. 'A little to the right,' I say, and they shuffle back again. 'Excuse me, sir,' I say, 'could you take off your hat. Please, a couple of steps back,' I say to the woman. 'That's right. Just one more step, please.' And splash! She has stood into the water, a fact she makes known with one more bird-like squeak. 'Watch out,' I say. 'The tide is high this week. Wouldn't want to see you swept away. OK then,' I go on, raising the camera they have entrusted to me, 'on the count of three, everyone say Cryptosporidium. Five, four . . .' But they have had enough out of me. The man has already untangled himself from his love-bird, who is shaking her foot as though it has picked up something contagious after its brief contact with the tidal water. Meantime, her knight in shining armour stomps right up to me, all huff and puff as he reclaims his camera.

'What, no photo?' I say, shrugging my arms at him and putting on my best I-don't-understand face. Then I lean in close to him, hand shielding my mouth. 'What say you and me throw horse-face to the swans and get ourselves warmed up under the covers in your hotel?'

He cold-eyes me, rejoins his foot-soaked other half and the two of them walk quickly away.

'By the way, did you hear the news?' I call after them. 'They jailed a man for stealing anti-wrinkle cream. That's the bastard judge in this town for you. He'd do well in America, I'd say. Hey! You never told me where you're from.'

# 5

The crisis. Another reason for my stardom being delayed. I prefer the word mishap. Opening night at the Town Hall. Eighteen going on nineteen months ago and counting. I was playing the part of Honey in a Khaos production of *Who's Afraid of Virginia Woolf?* It was my first decent part. Mitchell the Imbecile was directing. I was so nervous, hadn't slept or eaten in the better part of a week, which I had convinced myself might be useful as my part required some histrionics. Just before my first scene I couldn't remember my lines. Not a single one of them. It's OK, Laura, I kept telling myself as I retched into the bucket while waiting in the wings. This happens to all the greats. As soon as you get out there you'll be fine. My cue arrived. On I walked. By now I was trembling. And all I could hear was the heart clapping away inside me. The other actors were looking my way. And then I couldn't breathe. It felt as though every organ inside me wanted out of my body at the same time, and now there was a logjam in my throat. I gulped. And gulped again. Had to bend over. Grabbed myself with both arms and tried to heave out of me whatever it was that was blocking my airways. I started to hyperventilate. I felt the strength go out of my legs. And down I went.

One thing I think I remember is the gasp from the audi-ence when I dropped to the floor. It's all right, I wanted to call out. It's something the character does. But any last-ditch energy had drained out of me, and then all I could see was a bunch of faces staring down at me. After that I just wanted to sleep.

I woke up in a bed in a room that for the few days I was in it took turns reeking of sour milk and gone-off goat's cheese. The people in St Jude's said I needed to rest up and for as long as it would take. A doctor came. He asked some questions, prescribed a course of meds for nervous anxiety, and by the end of the week suggested I think about a break. The theatre isn't going anywhere, he said. It will be waiting for me until I am ready to return. Mother nodded, and from her Skype laptop somewhere in the Amazon jungle, Jennifer wholeheartedly agreed. Eighteen months later and I have done precisely as I was told. I have taken a break. Rested up. Been by-and-large dutiful with my medication. As of right now, though, as of the very moment I read about this new production, I know the time has come for me to return to the stage.

Isn't that right, Laura?

Why, yes, Laura. Indeed it is.

*

I am barely halfway across Tone Bridge when my phone chimes. Pausing, I lean onto the bridge wall to check. *Where are you!* Mother again. No doubt she is filling home-at-last

Jennifer's head with all sorts of wonderful stuff about the pining sister who cannot wait to see her after all this time and hear all about her world-saving adventures. Ha! Ha! Like hell she is. And she needn't bother holding her breath for a reply from me. Instead I start tapping out another message to Fleming and allow my gaze drift to the rough-and-tumble river making its way into the harbour.

'Look who it is,' the Beggar Flynn's familiar voice snarls up at me from his sit-down back-to-the-wall perch.

'The one and only,' I say, without looking down.

'You make your first picture yet?'

'I didn't, Beggar. You make your first million yet?'

'I didn't. What's keeping you?'

'I'm biding my time, Beggar. Waiting for the right part to come along.'

'Let me guess. You want to play the good witch of the north?'

'Ah, Beggar, I don't think I have the sensibility for that role.'

'Fancy yourself as more of a killer queen, I suppose.'

'What other part is there? Anyway. It just so happens my agent was in touch. He has the perfect part for me. The lead in a forthcoming production and it is going to catapult me.'

'Catapulting, is it?'

'That's right. You have it from the witch's teat.'

Beggar grunts and I watch the surging water, grimy and petulant, roaring its troubled way into the harbour, the currents and everlasting wind generating waves, ragged and higgledy-piggledy – not unlike mother's hair – and with no clue as to the direction they should be taking.

'Hell hath no fury like this one, Beggar.'

'And you're an expert, I suppose? Tell me, can you see Dolores?'

'Would that be Dolores Taaffe from the Fair Green who reckons she can walk on water?'

'It would.'

'I can't see her, Beggar. When is she due?'

'About sixteen years ago. I'm not budging until she shows.'

'I can see Pisser Kelly under the Spanish Arch. Is he any good to you?'

'No.'

'I hear you, Beggar. Can't say I fancy Dolores' chances on these waves. I was listening to music on the street the other night and guess what the singer said in between his songs? Go on, guess.'

'I'm not guessing.'

'He said our river is the fastest-flowing river in Europe. There. What do you think of that?'

'I wish some of the skinflints using my bridge would jump into the fast river. That's what I think.'

'Things that bad?'

'Things are fine, thanks for asking. I just don't like certain people on my bridge.'

'You're a codder, Beggar. I so enjoy our little talks.'

And I fetch the purse from my skirt pocket and drop it into his cap.

\*

I'm almost at the Goldmine when her next message lands. *Don't forget to collect your meds.* Mother, mother. More and more I'm convinced she thinks my river doesn't run all the way to the sea. Especially since her new fancy man appeared on the scene and started putting notions in her head. I tend not to pay attention to her. Fleming aside, I tend not to listen to anyone. If you can't improve on silence, keep your trap shut. That's another one of the philosophies I've heard in my life to date, and one of the better ones at that. No doubt she is fretting as to how I will greet Jennifer, wants me on my best behaviour. All happy face and it's so good to see you, sister. That's OK, mother. I can be all that. I can switch on my charm and good manners smile. Now, if you'll excuse me, I need to talk with my doctor.

His name is Harper, but I just call him the Doc. The Doc is a good talker, has eyelashes worth fighting for, and when it comes to the Golden Age of Cinema, is sometimes willing to indulge every utterance that leaves my mouth. Every two weeks I'm supposed to swing by his den, where he greets me with a warm smile, some fresh and hearty chat, and a prescription upon which he scribbles what it is my shaky system requires. As far as my meds go mother keeps on my case. I suppose she's right, but of late I have been an obedient girl.

After the crisis I was put on a course of mirtazapine to quell my anxiety. Olanzapine to give me an appetite. Mogadon to send me to sleep, but I like the quiet hours of the night and so at times haven't gotten along so well with that one. Altogether then, the pills allow me participate in the world. Maintain my equilibrium. I suppose you could say that when it comes to the hurly-burly of life, they are my centre of gravity.

Usually, I make sure I have a nine o'clock appointment. It is the first available appointment and getting in first means I never have to spend time in the waiting room in the company of some old wheezebag suddenly turned yellow-green, or some precious mother with her non-stop cry-baby six-year-old, or some drama queen of a man whose life has come to a complete and irreversible standstill because he has a sore leg or runny nose or some other ailment a shoe up his asshole wouldn't cure. A nine o'clock appointment means I get in, get out and get balanced all in the space of a few minutes. Today I am running several hours late, but at least I know who I can blame. (That right, sis?)

'Look who it finally is,' Doc says, eyeing up his wall clock, when I land inside his surgery.

'Better late than dead,' I say back, sitting myself comfortably into the chair across from him and his doctor desk.

'Careful now,' Doc says, smiling at me, 'mocking is catching.'

'Doc, you've been saving my life for a year and a half now and I have to say I think you're doing a terrific job. So I have no fears on that score. If you ever need a reference you know where to come.'

'Coming from you, Laura, that is praise indeed.'

'Of course it is. And let me also say, this is one comfortable chair.'

'So. How've you been, Laura?'

'I've got a feeling I'm going to be busy, Doc.'

'Oh, yes?'

'There's a part coming up. It has my name written all over it.'

'Is that so?'

'In fact, as soon as we're done here I'm on my way to the theatre. A new director has taken over. I'm hearing only good things, Doc. Only good things.'

'Well, that all sounds very interesting, Laura. Do you feel you're ready to return?'

'As of precisely one hour ago and counting, yes I most certainly do.'

'I see . . . I was talking to your mother the other day. I hear there's a certain visitor due.'

'A certain visitor? Tell me more, Doc.'

'Your sister. She's due home for a visit. Has she arrived?'

'She might have,' I say, and Doc smiles.

'She's been away a while, hasn't she? I wonder would I recognize her.'

'If her photograph is anything to go by, she is now more or less perfect,' I say. 'I've set myself the task of finding one blemish on her. I'll let you know how I get on.'

'Oh, so you haven't actually spoken to her yet?'

'No.'

'But she's here? She has arrived?'

'She appeared on our road at precisely fifteen minutes past I-couldn't-care-less o'clock,' I say to that.

'You're a card, Laura. You really should think about finding a way to occupy that lively mind.'

'I know exactly what you mean, Doc. Every morning now it seems I wake up and ask myself the same question: appoint myself queen of the universe or annihilate the eastern side of town?'

'That's the side of town I live on.'

'Well, I'll make sure you're put on the to-be-spared list.'

'I'm glad I know you, Laura. You'd nearly have me convinced.'

'That's what my daddy used to say, Doc.'

'Are you not pleased your sister is home? And with a new member of the family to show off, I hear.'

'Well, to tell you the truth, Doc, I don't know how she ever made the time. According to the occasional bulletin we receive she is killed out saving the various places she's holed up in.'

'It certainly sounds like she's getting to see plenty of the world.'

'Not enough, if you ask me. A while back – during their annual all-night Skype get-together – she was telling mother a story about a lad in India with two heads. Born with them, he was. The two heads. If you ask me that's the place for Jennifer. Where lads with two heads are born.'

Doc shakes his head and smiles. 'Your topics of conversation never cease to amaze me, Laura.'

'Well, imagine if it started happening around here. You'd

have your work cut out for you then, Doc. We wouldn't
have so much time to talk.'

'No, we wouldn't, Laura,' he says, as he reaches for his
doctor pad and pen.

Doc is now busy scribbling out my two weeks' worth of
medication. Mid-sentence he puts down his pen and looks
at me, his eyes suddenly searching.

'Have you any good movies to recommend to me? I
haven't seen anything worthwhile in ages.'

'I wish I did. Television is where it's at these days, Doc.
That's what they're telling me. They keep trying to shove
boxsets at me. But if you ask me there's still nothing to beat
the silver screen.'

'The magic of the movies.'

'You said it, Doc. Speaking of the television, though,
have you seen a show called *House of Cards*?'

'Can't say I have.'

'It's on Netflix. Daft stuff altogether. The mother loves it.'

'I still haven't got Netflix, Laura.'

'Ah, you don't know what you're missing. This pair in
*House of Cards*. They are something else. A husband and
wife pair and they want to rule the world. Guess what they
have for breakfast? Apples and coffee.'

'Apples and coffee?'

'Yep.'

'I would never have guessed that.'

'That's why I told you.'

I ask Doc for a loan of his pen and scribble out for him
mother's Netflix login details. 'It's not everyone I would do

this for,' I say, as I pass the slip of paper his way and at the same time claim my prescription. 'But I suppose I have a soft spot for you, Doc.'

'You're a charmer, Laura.'

'I am, Doc. Charming as a helicopter slamming into Connemara bog, me. See you in a fortnight.'

\*

Doc writes up a fortnight's supply at a time. At first I paid no attention to the directions. Sometimes I had the pills all gone by Wednesday morning and the rest of the days could be tricky. Sometimes I forced myself not to take anything until later in the week, stockpiling my way through the days and then I got to have a bumper weekend. Sometimes I mixed and matched, applied my olanzapine dosage to my Mogadon and my Mogadon dosage to my mirtazapine and my mirtazapine dosage to, well, whatever I felt like. I tossed them back in one go. I lined them up on the kitchen table and then made colourful patterns and shapes. I tried to remember when a certain combination did not have the desired effect. And on that rare occasion when one of my little experiments did work out and the high bliss coursed through me, I made sure to stick to the drill until my system caught on to what I was at and no longer played ball. These days, however, I do precisely what the little plastic bottles say and drip feed everything properly into my tricksy system – until medication Monday comes around again.

Now that I have a theatre part to get ready for I am going to be on my very best behaviour.

Besides. When it comes to my meds, most of the time I haven't got a clue what they are at. Ignorance is bliss, Laura, I well remember one of my despairing schoolteachers telling me a long time ago. In that case I must be the happiest girl in the world.

One thing I know is that I am not going back to St Jude's. That place is for lost causes and I am not a lost cause.

Me?

I am going to be a star.

The West End. Broadway. The silver screen. That's where I belong.

Isn't it, Laura?

Yes, it is, Laura. Yes it most certainly is.

And so on to the Town Hall. Find out what this new director has in mind, check out the cut of his jib.

# 6

When I was little I used lie on the floor in my bedroom and write letters. *Dear Gloria Swanson, my name is Laura Cassidy and this is a letter to congratulate you on your wonderful movie career. I think* Sunset Boulevard *is one of the very best movies and I thought you were fantastic in it. So fantastic that at the end of a private screening Barbara Stanwyck knelt down and kissed the hem of your skirt. When I am older I hope to be a famous actress and take my place on the Hollywood Walk of Fame. My daddy says you get ten thousand fan letters a week. Well, this week you'll get ten thousand and one and I hope you get to read it before your eyes get tired. Thanks to you I am going to be a star. More than anything I want you to know that.* I would sign them from admiring little me and address them to the Walk of Fame in Hollywood. And, whenever I had a chance, I would take them as far as Barna Woods and drop them inside the hollowed-out oak tree I had discovered while out walking with daddy. It was my way of sending the letters out into the world and keeping them away from Jennifer's prying eyes, to be retrieved whenever I wanted to read over them. I kept a scrapbook in the hollowed-out oak too, I still do – inside regularly changed plastic bags. I even keep a knife, because you never know.

Into the scrapbook went clippings and photos and useful details about all my favourites. How they were discovered, memorable roles, the precise location of their star-name on the Hollywood Walk of Fame, what their real names were – reminders of happy times I like to peek through every now and then. And onto the front cover, in large curvy writing, I slapped the title of my scrapbook – a title I knew daddy would approve of:

LAURA CASSIDY'S WALK OF FAME

*

It's a hop, skip and a jump from the medical centre to the Town Hall. This is where Khaos Theatre are based until the new theatre opens. Up the concrete steps, through the double doors and I swing sharp right, avoiding reception and the fire-breathing dragon – aka Camilla the Hun – who doesn't appear to be on duty today anyway. Up the stairs, past the rehearsal studio and on into the coffee bar where I can already see the person who I assume is the new director at the window table – along with some of the new crew. Emily is behind the counter. She's the one I like. The dragon on reception seldom gives me so much as the time of day. Not so Emily. She has a nice smile. And empathy. Put her arms around the suffering world, Emily would. Quiet as a tinkering mouse, I slide up to the counter.

'Hi, Emily.'

'Laura! You gave me a fright.'

'Who? Little me? I wouldn't scare a ladybird, Emily. I wouldn't say boo to a tinkering mouse.'

I half-turn around so that I am facing the tables, all of them unoccupied, except for the one by the window.

'Hey, Emily. Is that him?'

'Yes, that's him.'

I take a good look in the direction of where he is seated.

'He's cute. A bit square in the shoulders. And he needs the tip of his nose lopped off. Cute, though.'

'If you say so.'

'I wonder has he a nice speaking voice. You look tired, Emily. Let me cover for you for an hour.'

'Laura, I don't think I can do that.'

'Poppycock, Emily. Go on. Take a break. Go and smoke a pack of cigarettes. Go and call your favourite boyfriend. Tell him you've no underwear on today.'

'You never lose it, Laura,' she says, laughing, and gets busy with the coffee machine. I return my gaze to the table she is preparing coffee for. There are five of them. The new director and his theatre crew – bunched around the one table. Sipping coffees. Talking theatre.

Behind the bar, Emily fills and sets up a fresh tray of coffees. I am all set to grab a hold of it and take it over to the crew, while running through my head how I will introduce myself, when he gets up and walks over to the counter.

'Hi,' I say.

'Hi,' he says back, all furrowed brow, broody and deep-voiced with it. Precisely how theatre directors of intent should be. 'I'll take those coffees.'

'You're in the thick of it over there, I see. You're the new director, aren't you? I'm Laura. I'm an actress.'

'An actress? That's great.'

'Yes, it is, isn't it?'

'Might I have seen you in anything?'

'Oh, you know. I haven't done much recently. But not for lack of wanting to. It's my health.'

'Your health?'

'It hasn't been the best of late. I won't bore you with the details.'

'Well, let me wish you a speedy recovery. Now, if you'll excuse me . . .'

'I hear you're planning a production.'

'Eh . . . yes. Yes, we are.'

'What's this it's called . . .? Oh, wait . . . it's a secret, isn't it?'

'Well, I suppose . . .'

'I understand. You can't reveal anything. It's OK. Don't tell me. I'll have fun working it out.'

'I see. Well, if you'll . . .'

'Would I be correct in saying the movie version starred Vivien Leigh?'

He smiles at that, but doesn't fully give it away.

'And next year is the seventieth anniversary.'

'Eh . . . yes.'

'That's a good reason to put it on.'

'We think so, yes.'

'The black-and-white movie version was made in 1951.'

'Actually, I didn't know that.'

'Did I tell you I'm an actress?'

'You did.'

'And my daddy. Around these parts he was a *very* well-known actor.'

'Good to know. Well, it was . . .'

'I suppose, when all is said and done, what I'm really trying to say is that I've been waiting for a suitable part to come along. You know. A part that has the ability to reach out and grab my heart and mind. I'm really interested in your new production. This could be the one I've been waiting for.'

'Well, eh, we're putting out a casting call, quite soon actually – here, you can read all about it in the paper. Why don't you come in and show us what you've got?'

'Oh, I will,' I say, placing my hand on the copy of the *Advertiser* he has indicated on the countertop. 'I will. And thank you. Thank you so much.'

'I better get back.'

'Of course you better. And don't let me stop you. And thanks again for this opportunity. You won't regret it. That I promise you.'

'Well, eh, you're welcome . . . Lorraine . . . but, you know, it's . . .'

'Laura.'

'I beg your pardon?'

'My name. It's Laura. L – A – U – R – A. Laura.'

'Eh . . . OK. I think I've got that.'

'Though I will probably change it – you know, when the time comes.'

'Well, that all sounds great . . . eh . . . Laura. I look forward to seeing you at the audition.'

'Me, too. And like I say, Stephen – it's OK if I call you Stephen? Thanks – like I say, thank you for the opportunity.'

Stephen rejoins the others. They turn collectively towards me, and I give them a friendly wave. Oh, I have a good feeling about this. As soon as I clapped eyes on him, I knew he was my kind of director. Not like the disaster we had before – with his big head and fake voice. Shiny teeth too. Never trust a lad with shiny teeth.

It won't be long now. Soon I will be part of their little gatherings, swapping theatre ideas, offering my suggestions to their eager ears.

It's going to be fun.

Isn't it, Laura?

Indeed it is, Laura. Indeed it is.

# 7

Mother has other ideas. She's not convinced the theatre is where I belong. Thinks it's a waste of time, bad for me, even. Especially after my opening-night mishap. Mother, I've said I don't know how many times, Mitchell the Imbecile had me so worked up I didn't know stage left from stage right, front from back, elbow from backside. Any wonder that by the time I had to go on I was a dithering wreck, could barely stand, let alone remember my lines. But mother is not all that convinced Mitchell was the cause. I worry about you, Laura. Her words for me when she detects I am in one of my not-going-to-entertain-a-thing-you-have-to-say moods. Feeling's mutual, mother, is what I say to that.

Because I do worry about her. Sometimes. She has barely set foot outside the house in two years – one expedition to the airport to welcome no-show Jennifer; one excursion to the theatre to see non-event me. She used to work in the library. Part time. Cutbacks meant she was one of the first to go. And she took it badly. One thing on top of another, she said, plonking herself in the sitting-room chair. She was no sooner laid off from the library than the big toe on her right foot decided it didn't like its present positioning and started to turn sideways. Pretty soon, it was more or less perpendicular to the rest of her foot. At first we joked about it. You'll have to get it sawn off. Maybe the entire foot – you know, to be sure. Hey, mother, it's time you toed the line. We need to break it and then reset it. That's what Doc Harper said. I asked to do the breaking part. Some other lucky fellow got the gig. It was while she was laid up she discovered boxset TV. Skype became popular too. Then our neighbour, Yoohoo Lucy Garavan (crackpot), mentioned some dating sites to her. It might even have been Jennifer. Then enter (in the flesh) Peter Porter. And his life's mission to haul mother out of the country for a long weekend. Good luck with that, Peter.

I can still hear her pleading voice from when I was laid up in St Jude's. *What did I tell you? What did I tell you? I told you something was going to happen if you didn't let up. I told you. Promise me, you'll take it easy. Promise me . . .*

Have a think about finding yourself a job. That's what she would say in months to come. Something that isn't too taxing. Something straightforward. It might be a good way to set your mind in other directions.

Other directions! Something straightforward! What precisely had she in mind, I wondered? Brain surgeon, missile inventor or apocalyptic physicist? She rolled her eyes when I started putting these possibilities to her.

To a certain extent, however, I was willing to agree with mother. While waiting for their big breakthrough, most of my favourite stars tried their hands at a variety of scrape-the-barrel occupations. Gloria Swanson worked as a sales clerk in a department store. Lana Turner took typing classes. Lauren Bacall worked as an usher in a theatre. And Barbara Stanwyck had two jobs – a dancer and a typist. If it's good enough for them, it's good enough for me. That's what I decided and so not long after my discharge from St Jude's I applied for a job as an office slave. To secure this job I had an interview to get through, and of course, in the lead-up to the interview the anxiety kicked in, and I was fretting over the questions I would be asked and what I would say in reply. Just say you're hardworking, I kept telling myself. They have certain words they listen out for at interviews and when you say them you get a little tick beside your name. That way they know who to choose when all the interviews are over. Sure enough, at the interview the question was asked. How would you describe yourself? Hardworking, I said, without batting an eyelid, at which point the interviewer put down his pen, looked from me to the second interviewer and said, 'I don't think I've ever heard an answer to that question that did not contain the word hardworking.' 'I'm also flatulent and laborious,' I said next. 'And I can have five orgasms in quick succession. How many times have you heard that?' From memory, if the look on their faces was anything to go by, neither interviewer had ever heard that answer. Didn't get me the job, though.

All was not lost. A short while after that I spotted on the library noticeboard the ad asking for tour guides. It was walking-tour guides they were looking for, to haul groups of terrorists about the place and spin yarns about our fabulous little city. Why not, I thought. It will keep my vocal cords ticking over, provide some badly needed pocket

out of the toolbelt tied about his waist, a beef and brawn stew heading my way.

He helps me to my feet. His strong arm. His gentle-firm touch. I have a good mind to collapse again. But I don't want him thinking I am a drama queen, putty in his hands.

'Nice pickup,' I say, doing my best to remain limp in his arms after he stands me up on my dainty feet. 'A girl could really fall for you.'

'Is that so?' he says, smiling, his gentle-giant voice so easy on my ears.

'Tell me, big boy, how long until opening night?'

He takes a hammer out of the toolbelt and taps it off the hard hat he is wearing.

'We're getting there, I think.'

'I don't mind waiting a little longer if it means getting a gander at you every day.'

'You're a charmer, aren't you,' he says, putting on a big smirk.

'And I like your hat,' I say, and he starts to laugh. 'Are you fitting double seats? Play your cards right and I'll let you take me along on opening night. We might even take a private box. Know what I'm saying?' I raise my eyebrows for effect.

'Go on and let me finish here or the thing will never get done.'

'That's what you said this time last year.'

I do as he says, though. Treat them mean, keep them keen. 'I'm sure it will all be worth the wait – just like you,' I tell him, blowing him a little kiss as my phone buzz-buzzes with what I can only by now assume is an alert of Fleming's imminent appearance. But I am wrong. It's mother again, her sweet words putting the kibosh on my happy vibe. *Where on planet earth are you? Your sister is asking for you.*

Where on planet earth are you? Jennifer is the one she needs if she's looking for an answer to that particular question. And I can imagine the stuff Jennifer might have by way of reply. *Oh, mother, earlier I was in Kandahar, Afghanistan, saving a woman from a bunch of madmen about to bury her up to her neck and fling rocks. Then I went to Somalia to prevent all the babies from starving to death. After that I rescued a couple of villages from annihilation somewhere in the Amazon jungle.* There is no doubt about it, she's a hero, our Jennifer. A shining light righting all the wrongs in the world. As for yours truly? Right now, as of this very moment, I am up a do-not-disturb camel's backside chewing a bunch of freshest daisies. I have a little chuckle and my phone buzz-buzzes again.

*See you in fifteen. Usual place.* This time it's Fleming. Wanting to meet up in Barna Woods. I am about to reply and let him know he will see me precisely when he sees me when my phone buzz-buzzes a third time. *Be at the house very, very soon or else.* Or else what, I'm wondering, and hot on its heels arrives the next message. *On your way get something from Brady's. Something nice. And don't forget your meds.*

Mothers. As far as I'm concerned there are two kinds: irksome and I forget the other.

# 8

I've known Fleming for almost a year and a half. He's a few years older than me. Five. Maybe fifteen. Who knows? For a time after we first got together I wasn't even sure that Fleming was his first name or second name. He is six feet tall and looks like Paul Newman in *Cool Hand Luke*. I wish. He's a spaghetti string of a man with caved-in cheeks and a backside that reminds me of a peanut. Though he does have a decent speaking voice, and sometimes the light even picks up the baby blue of his eyes.

We first crossed paths down town, by the entrance to Buttermilk Lane. A film unit was shooting a scene and I had stopped for a gander. Onlookers, please put your fingers in your ears, someone from the crew yelled out, this is going to be loud. Then came the command, Action! and a string-vest skinhead brandishing a machine gun emerged from a side door, pointed his weapon my way and began to ratta-tat-tat. I hadn't heeded the close-your-ears warning and the shock alone had me clutching my chest as I was sent reeling backwards. I ended up on the seat of my skirt. For a moment everyone looked at me, bystanders and film crew alike, we-told-you-so written all over their faces. Best performance we've had all day, hollered the crew member who had issued the initial warning, and he started to clap. Everyone laughed and joined in the applause, and it was while all this was going on that the helping hand reached down and assisted me back on my feet. Hang on, he said, as soon as he saw that I was OK, and he spun around, sought out the loudmouth filmmaker and popped him right on the kisser. Let's go, he said, hurrying the pair of us away from there. I thought it was romantic.

For the rest of the day we sat together outside Little Mary's. I thanked him for being my knight in shining armour. He smiled and told me it was what he was born to do. I smiled and told him my name. He smiled again and told me when he was eight, under cover of dark, his father hotwired their neighbour's car and drove it like a bat of out hell out of town and was never seen again. He told me his mother was a zombie who gets by on cheap vodka and daytime TV. He told me he shared a house with his five brothers who drink Aldi beer all day and knock each other senseless all night. He said he liked spending as much time as he could away from the house. He told me one day he would like to have a son. He asked me was there anything I wanted more than anything and I shared my movie-star dream with him. He told me the worst thing about dreams is waking up. Besides, he said, television is the place to be. Then he told me he had it within him to go places – if he was bothered. He could be leader of the country if he wanted to. Fly a fighter jet. Figure out cures for cancer and megalomania. Prevent war. If I wanted to I could be a spaceman, he told me. I told him I'm pretty sure he's one already.

More drinks arrived. Hours flittered by. Some day I might do something that lands me in prison, he said. Like what? I asked him, but he didn't offer anything. I'll cook for you – some day, he said instead. Some day? I asked. When my brothers leave town or die, whichever comes first. Just don't hold your breath. I asked him why his brothers had to leave town or die in order for him to cook. He shrugged and said because they are territorial and self-involved. Tell you what, I would later say, and after I had discovered that his brothers considered Fleming fair game for their we-are-tough-men antics, let me cook for *you*.

He asked me what I liked, where is my favourite place, who do I want to be. I didn't bother answering the first two questions. I told him Lana Turner's father had been bludgeoned to death after winning big at a travelling craps game. I told him Veronica Lake's father died in an industrial explosion when she was twelve. I told him Barbara Stanwyck had been orphaned at the age of four. So you want to be the famous daughter of a long-dead father, he said to me. Already halfway there, I replied.

He claimed to know the names of every American president – from the very first to the present day. He could list them in order too. Ask me to do it anytime you feel like it, he said. So far I haven't asked.

He told me he had a job looking after a rich man's house. Clipping hedges. Weeding. Mowing the lawn. Walking the shit-a-lot dog. Gathering up all the turds that came out of shit-a-lot. He told me he had a nickname for the rich man. Frogface Two. He told me he had been fired from the job that very day. Why? I asked, and he told me he had flung dogshit at Frogface Two. Why? I asked, and he told me Frogface Two had called him a loser. I am not a loser, he then said, looking intensely at me. I just don't want to win. I told him I didn't like the way those people back there had laughed at me. And one day a few months later, when I was feeling lowly, he told me if I jumped into the abyss he would jump right in after me. I thought that was romantic too.

Those first few hours zipped by. People came and went. The evening cooled.

'I have to go now,' I said.

'Go where?' he asked.

'To my doctor.'

'Really?' he said. 'Can I walk you?'

I thought that was most romantic of all.

*

And here I am. Barna Woods. I like it in here. There is nobody to answer to and I can come and go whenever I feel like it. The trees are my friends. They swish and sway and lean my way for some chummy chat and glimmers of light flit through the resilient leaves. There's this craggy, dead-limbed thing that I climb from time to time – when I am in a lofty kind of mood. And of course there's the hollowed-out oak.

I hear Fleming before I see him, scratching his way, grunting and tut-tutting, and as usual saving his best curse words for the innocent brambles nicking him here, there and everywhere.

'I think we need to have a think about our meeting place,' he says when he appears and then stands over me, shaking leaves and twigs out of his messed-up hair.

'Nice to see you too,' I say, as I clamber to my feet.

We go right in, to where the trees are thickest and the roots are pushing up through the ground, and where I hug the tree trunk best suited to my wraparound arms while Fleming gets up close and personal. 'Wait,' I say, pausing him briefly and hitch my skirt fully up and make him whip me with a tree branch. Ha! Ha! I do no such thing. I coo and titter at his sudden need to declare me some kind of woman, and even permit myself a wheeze of genuine contentment. 'Thanks, big boy, you can get ready to finish up now,' I say over my shoulder, and a few shuddering moments later he is in a crumpled heap.

'I was thinking,' I tell Fleming, once we're sitting back to back upon a sturdy stump, smoking the after-sex rollies I've made for us. 'When I become a world-famous star I am going to buy all this.'

'All what?' Fleming says, as though there is nothing except fresh air around us.

'These trees. All the leaves and roots and bramble bushes will belong to me.'

'Oh, and precisely when is that going to happen?'

'Sooner than you think.'

'That's a line I have heard before.'

'Keep talking like that and I won't tell you about the opportunity I have.'

'Opportunity? What sort of opportunity?'

'What do you mean what sort of opportunity? A *theatre* opportunity. I am going to have an audition.'

'I thought you gave up those things after what happened last time.'

'I have put that particular experience behind me, Fleming. And I don't expect to hear you mention it again.'

Fleming shrugs and it's then I notice the swelling on the side of his head. I'm tempted to ask him about it, but can guess the answer. One of the perks of living with five volatile brothers.

'I almost forgot,' he says, cutting into the silence. 'Did your sister show up?' I wince at the question.

'Maybe. Then again, maybe not.'

'When do I get to meet her?' he goes on, sounding a little bit too interested, and I jab his kidney with my elbow.

A moment of blissful silence passes.

'She came all the way from Mexico, didn't she?' he says next. 'That's the other side of the world.'

'Thanks for the geography lesson, but, yes, I do know where Mexico is.'

'Is she going to stay around for a while?'

'Hello? Last time I checked my name wasn't Nostradamus. I'm thinking of killing her.'

'Is that before or after you kill yourself?'

'Hey!'

'How does she look?'

'Couldn't say.'

'What do you mean you couldn't say?'

'I only saw her from a distance.'

'And so desperate were you to see me, you couldn't stick around to say hello to her.'

'Don't flatter yourself, Fleming. You're not *that* good.'

'Admit it. You couldn't wait to feel me inside you this afternoon.'

'Keep talking, Fleming. And you will see what you will be feeling inside *you*.'

'Promises, promises. I watched one of those Lana Turner movies you recommended. *The Postman Always Rings Twice*.'

'And what is your verdict?'

'Two enthusiastic thumbs up. Those pencil-mark eyebrows and that skin. Wow. I mean wow. I think I could go for Lana.'

'I planned on having one husband and seven children but it turned out the other way around.'

'Huh?'

'Just something she once said.'

'I'm going to hunt down some more of her movies. Does your sister take after your mother or father?'

'What?'

'Who is your sister like? Your mother or your father?'

'That is none of your concern.'

'Is it your father?'

'Why are you so interested in this?'

'I'm just making conversation.'

I take another drag of my rollie. I wanted to see Fleming

in order to share my theatre news. I thought he might be impressed, might even have an encouraging word or two, and all he can do is lie on his backside and talk about that other one. I wish I hadn't said a word about Jennifer coming home. Listen to him. Here he goes again.

'Wonder what it's like in Mexico.'

'Couldn't say. I've never been.'

'Play your cards right and your sister might invite you.'

'That is one thing I am certain won't be happening.'

'She's one of those aid workers, isn't she?'

'Fleming, please stop saying things I have no interest in.'

'I'd say you're more interested than you let on.'

'Well, I wonder who died and made you Sigmund Freud.'

'No need to get snippy with me.'

'Fleming, I came here today to tell you about this part I am up for.'

'Tell away. I'm not stopping you.'

'It's a reprisal of a famous play from the 1940s. To mark its seventieth anniversary. Which one do you suppose it could be?'

'I'm surprised you don't know,' Fleming says. 'With all your knowledge.'

'Oh, Fleming, of course I know. I just want to see if *you* know.'

'Oh.'

'Well?'

'Well, what?'

'Do you know?'

'Tell you what. Why don't you just tell me.'

'Sometimes you are no fun, Fleming. No fun whatso-
ever.'

'Come on then. Out with it. Tell me what it is.'

'I don't think I want to now.'

'I'll take you for another roll in the mulch if you do.'

'You can roll by yourself.'

'Are you sure you're ready? You know, to return to the
theatre.'

'Exactly what are you trying to say now, Fleming?'

'Television. That's where it's all happening these days.'

Here we go again. According to Fleming television is the
place to be. It's a Golden Age. Anybody who is anybody is
to be found doing something on television. Fleming has his
own ideas for TV shows. Concepts, he calls them. I try my
best not to listen when he starts in on his latest one.

'*A Streetcar Named Desire.*'

'Come again.'

'The name of the play.'

'Oh, yeah. I've heard of it. Good title. Brando is in it.'

'He's in the stage version *and* the film version. Vivien
Leigh is in the film version. In the role of Blanche DuBois.
That's my part – in case you're not sure.'

'You know, being flippant doesn't suit you. Not one bit.'

'For my audition I'm thinking of doing the I-have-
always-depended-on-the-kindness-of-strangers scene.'

'Suppose they want you to do something else?'

'Then I'll do that as well. That way they will be doubly
sure they have who they are looking for.'

'You sound very sure of yourself.'

'*Now* what are you trying to say?'

'I just hope you are not setting yourself up for a disappointment. That's all.'

'Fleming, right now all you have to do is listen to my lines. Don't speak. Just listen. Think you can manage that?'

'I think we should go for another roll in the mulch instead.'

'Oh, boy.'

'Or tell me more about the sister. I'm curious.'

'I'm bored now, Fleming. I'm going to gather some mushrooms.'

'I have one more question.'

'Spare me.'

'How are you going to kill her?'

Fleming. He's always teasing me. I suppose it's one of the things about him that keeps a girl coming back for more. We're together, Fleming and me, through muck and mirth. Sickness and health. Better and worse. More worse than better, but hey, you can't always have the fairy tale.

# 9

Mother is on the case again. *Be here inside the next twenty minutes or else.* Or else what, mother? I do so wish she'd complete some of these text messages now and then. It might prevent the occasional misunderstanding between us. I fully accept our existence together. She with her new man, boxset television and tricksy foot. Me with my fondness for dark-of-night soups, devotion to the silver screen and recently stalled career. At times either one of us a crutch for the other – like we have been since Jennifer took off. She gets so annoyed with me, though, and who can blame her? Especially in the kitchen. I am constantly boiling the kettle. Thirty-seven times in one day she clocked me at. The tin of teabags needs regular replenishing. Sugar has become a precious commodity. What can I do? Drinking tea is one of the things I now do best. Heating up cans of spaghetti. Making Chef brown sauce sandwiches. Night soup.

Mother connects my unconventional food habits with what happened at the theatre, and who am I to say she is wrong? The early hours in the kitchen have provided the setting for some of my finest moments. And also some of mother's. (It's three o'clock in the morning, Laura! What are you at?) And yet no matter how reasonably I put it, my alive-and-well theatre ambition doesn't seem to register.

Sometimes I think I should become something more vigorous. Like fire. And I'm not talking about a fluttery flame or two, easily doused with a splash of water or quickly smothered by a sturdy boot. I am talking about proper fire. The blazing Bette Davis fasten-your-safety-belts kind. The kind that will burn high and far and wide. Flames that roam and make you dizzy. A conflagration. That is the word I am looking for. In this, Fleming might be of some use. When the time is right I can persuade him to strike the match. Here, I'll tell him as I produce the blowtorch I have liberated for my purposes. How is it the saying goes? Build a man a fire, keep him warm for a day. Set a man on fire, keep him warm for the rest of his life. And here is mother again. *Pick up some quinoa in Brady's. Chocolate Emeralds. And get an apple tart.* Quinoa. What is that when it's at home?

*

'Ah, look who it is,' Glick Nolan says when I saunter into Alice Brady's shop.

'Who is it?' I say back.

'How's the patient?' Alice asks from behind the counter.

'Which patient would that be, Alice?'

'Your mother! How is her foot since the operation?'

'Let's just say she has very quickly figured out how to rest up.'

'Anything strange yourself, Laura?' Glick says, opening the newspaper he is holding.

'Oh, I'm a busy bee, Glick. Flat out, I am.'

'Is that so?'

'Got to get my act together for a very important part.'

'A part, is it?'

'That's all I can say for now. They've sworn me to secrecy. Don't want the press sniffing around. Not to mention the paparazzi.'

'Ah, the paparazzi,' Alice says, offering Glick a sideways look.

'Listen to this,' Glick says, peering into his *Advertiser*. 'Man jailed for stealing anti-wrinkle cream. That's a strange one, isn't it?'

'Why, not three hours ago I was telling a nice couple on Nimmo's Pier all about that, Glick.'

'The defendant claims he wanted the cream for his girlfriend. He better pray he gets locked up after an admission like that.'

'What can I get you, Laura?' Alice asks me.

I ask for a naggin of brandy and watch Alice stand it on the counter. Grab four or five bags of Chocolate Emeralds (I like them as well as mother). Then the shelves of wine catch my eye. Mother doesn't like me having wine, or any other kind of booze. She is right not to but any time I see wine my happy hormones lick their lips and say guzzle guzzle. In for a penny, in for a pound. That's what I say. You may as well be hung for a sheep as a lamb. By the look in her eye sometimes, mother will gladly volunteer a sturdy noose.

'I didn't know you drank brandy, Laura,' Alice says.

'I don't. I need some wine too.'

'Don't we all,' Alice replies with her ridiculous laugh. She gives me a long minute or two to join in, and I stand there drumming the counter with my fingers until she gives up.

'Well! What sort of a wine would you like?'

'Red,' I say, and she puts three or four bottles on the counter beside the brandy.

I pick up the first one. *A bright crimson red whose plum and raspberry aromas mingle elegantly with vanilla notes after six months aged in French oak barrels. Well balanced, with sweet tannins and a velvety finish.*

'Your mother doesn't drink it either,' Alice says. 'Brandy, I mean.'

'No.'

'So you've just decided to buy some anyway?'

'Listen to this, Alice,' I say, picking up the second bottle. 'A deep black-cherry colour, an intense bouquet with scents of vanilla, French toast and coffee, entwined with notes of red berry fruit and dry plums. On the palate it is silky smooth, structured and complex with well-integrated oak, and a remarkable finish.'

'It's for the returning sister. The brandy,' Glick says, delighted to be able to offer something significant to the conversation.

'Ah, that's right,' Alice says, her twitchy nose settling down now that the mystery has been resolved. 'I almost forgot. It's your sister, isn't it? And how is Joanna?'

'Jennifer,' I say, with gritted teeth.

'Jennifer, Jennifer. That's the one. And how is Jennifer?'

'I hear she's doing powerful work in poor countries.' Glick again.

'This one is a cabernet sauvignon,' I say, holding up the third bottle and trying to picture Glick after I have bumped the bottle down on top of his head. 'Medium-bodied with rich aromas of berries, clove and vanilla. On the palate, it delivers fine concentration with flavours of ripe black fruit and earthy undertones.'

'I heard drinking one glass of wine a day is the same thing as doing an hour's exercise,' Glick says next.

'You must be the fittest lad in the world so, Glick,' I say, paying, and I grab the booze and sweets, and without further ado I trudge out of there.

*

En route to the house, I conjure what will be said when mother is fussing over our reunion. Oh, look who it is, Laura. She has come such a long way. You are to be polite and friendly and welcoming. You are to make her feel at home. Do you think you could manage this, Laura? Do you?

Polite and friendly and welcoming. Why certainly, mother, I can do that. I can be all that and more. Little me? As well as being a troubled genius I am a natural-born charmer.

And, tell me, mother, what would you like me to say to my oh-so-perfect sibling? What version of my complicated self should I present?

Should I try a semblance of the truth:

*Why hello, Jennifer. It is I, your little sister, Laura Cassidy. I am now all of twenty-five years old, though I have been told I would pass for seventeen. I am four feet eleven and a half inches tall, and proud to have made it this far. I like making soup, belching at terrorists and sitting up in the quiet hours of the night. As well as belch, I can spit, curse, glare, hop, skip, climb, jump, barf, lick, gibber and bite. I have been known to make shadows leap.* Though when I want to, I can drift with the ease of the clouds and the tides.

I cross the road, narrowly avoiding a manically honking motorist. A perfect candidate for the tides – the high and all-devouring kind.

Perhaps I could offer Jennifer some of my Femme Fatale technique:

*Hey, sister. What say you and me blow this joint once and for all? With knives in our nylons, pistols in our furs, we can rescue ourselves from the quicksand shadows of this dirty town.*

Then again, I'm not so sure I want Jennifer as my accomplice.

Maybe I could announce myself with something startling. Something short and succinct, and that instantly catches the attention:

*Why hello, Jennifer, did you know there is a devil in charge of me? That's what mother reckons, and I take it as a compliment.*

Maybe I should hint at the dark places I have thoughts about visiting. Secret affairs with ledges of tall buildings. Flings with high-up open windows. Brief encounters with railway bridges. Wait and see, sister. I am only getting started.

I pass the swan sanctuary and the boathouse, the path curves and I find myself slowing down as I approach the house.

Maybe I should just tell her precisely what the genius in St Jude's said to me. Paralysed by fear I am. Ah! That caught your interest. He's also the one that said I could pass for seventeen. Something to do with my sluggish emotional development. And an inability to function properly in the world. But, you know, I'm not so sure I see things this way myself. I am stuck. Those words do not belong to the genius. Once again, they are mother's words and so do not count.

Hmmm.

That doesn't sound right. It's sending out the wrong impression. It's not a good way to say hi to someone I haven't seen in six years. It's not a good way to go about renewing my acquaintance with my wonderful save-the-world sister.

I've reached the house and I linger at the gate.

Maybe I should just reveal all:

*Oh, and did I tell you, Jennifer? I'm going places, set to be a mover and shaker. Any day now worldwide fame beckons for me. Not for me this leaky old waterfront street with its perfectly attired terrorists, bobbing boats and crazed seabirds. No. I am going to be a star. Something that was decided a long time ago. Daddy, actually, remember him? He's the one who first gave me the idea. It's just a matter of time before someone spots me. Plucks me out of the horde and hauls me off to Tinseltown. You'll see. A signed napkin from me will be worth thousands. Touch me anywhere and you'll never wash your hands again.*

But of course, she already knows all of this.

And so, right now, if it's all the same with you, *sister*, I don't have time for you. I have to meet my fans. Sign some autographs. Mollycoddle a reporter from the weekend editions. *In your own words, Laura, tell us what inspired this latest role . . .*

Isn't that right, Laura?

Yes it is, Laura. Yes, indeed, that's right.

## 10

'Where on earth have you been?'

'I had things to do.'

'Your sister is here. She's been here all day. And Juan is so tired we had to put him to bed. Where on earth have you been?'

'Oh sister, my sister. How could I possibly have forgotten my precious sister?'

'Hush, will you?'

Fine by me, I am about to say, but there is no time. Jennifer has appeared, and is now standing in front of me. That recent photograph of her was not lying. Time away has transformed her. The sparkly hair. The long, slender legs. Violet eyes, if you don't mind. But the first thing I notice are her arms. They are perfect. Brown, blemish-free and oh-so lean. I cannot stop looking at them. And am gripped with an urge to touch them. And so I reach out my own arm to do just that. Except that Jennifer thinks I am offering my hand and she takes it in both her own, pulls me to her and wraps her arms fully around me.

'Laura!' she says, once she has squeezed the last drop of air out of my mangled lungs.

'That's me,' I say back, my voice little more than a wheeze.

'It's so wonderful to be here,' she says. 'I can't wait for us to have a good catch-up. Mam has been telling me plenty already. It's going to be wonderful. I just know it is.'

She takes another hold of my hand and keeps going. Throughout all this it's-going-to-be-wonderful talk, mother gives me her suspicious eye. What does she think I am going to do? Pluck Jennifer's nose off? Yank out the woman's waggy tongue? Those violet eyes?

Then she stops talking. Obviously, it is now my turn to come out with some of this you're-wonderful goop, and when I don't oblige, the pair of us stand opposite each other without a word being said.

'Well, aren't you going to say something?' mother says, anxious to break into the silence.

'You have beautiful arms,' I say, and let go her hand and look from my own to her perfect arms. Then she laughs, while mother rolls her eyes and ushers us into the kitchen.

Don't ask what made me blurt that out about her arms. Don't want her laughing either. Am ready to clear out of there again, slam the kitchen door on them, get upstairs. Too late. Mother is pulling out chairs, gesturing for Jennifer to sit, bopping around her like someone made of spring, here and there grabbing Jennifer and hugging her all over again.

'Oh, look,' mother squeals, when she has finally released Jennifer. 'My two daughters. Together again.'

She clears tears away from her eyes. I grip the fork I could use to help her. Jennifer sits there and puts on an amazing smile. As though she has just popped by for a cup of tea and a ham sandwich. Her tears at a halt, mother is talking again.

'What can I get you, Jennifer? Look at you. There's not a pick on you. And you must be hungry again. Did you get something nice in Brady's, Laura? Did you get the quinoa?'

Mother doesn't wait for an answer. Another brown loaf she had baked earlier is set down. Some packaged meat. A bowl full of green leaves, sprinkled seeds and chopped tomato that has seen better days. Cups, plates, knives, forks and spoons. A little jug of dressing to go with the salad, for crying out loud. Another check-in with Jennifer to make sure the jet lag isn't at her. The Cleopatra treatment in full throttle.

'You're very quiet, Laura. Have you got nothing to say to your sister?'

I don't. For now, though, I do as I've been told. I sit down at the table, across from Jennifer. I can feel mother's eyes like hot irons on my face. Jennifer is only too happy to jab into the silence.

'You look good, Laura. What are you up to these days?'

Listen to her. Two minutes inside our house and thinks she gets to know everything about me. I shrug my shoulders, have no intention of answering. Mother has other ideas.

'Your sister has asked you a question, Laura.'

For a little effect, mother clicks her fingers. I have just grabbed the salt cellar and in my eagerness I twist the cap right off and empty a small mountain of salt onto my plate of food. At once, Jennifer rescues my plate and begins to clear away the salt, salvage what food she can. Mother is fast to join in, and now I am thinking: high time I was out of here. 'Help yourselves to my share,' I say and grab a bag of Chipsticks from the fruit bowl, stand out of my chair and go up to my room.

\*

I lie on my bed and stare up at the faces on the walls. Gloria in her pomp. Barbara, sultry and poised. Coy Veronica. And Lana – all pout and platinum blonde. When I first saw *The Postman Always Rings Twice* I tried to persuade mother and then Jennifer to dye my hair the same colour as hers. Had a go at removing my eyebrows so I could paint them back in the way she did. I thought she had the best frown – so bold, so daring, so not-going-to-take-any-guff-from-anyone. She wasn't even ten years old when her father's beaten-to-death body was discovered on a San Francisco street – little wonder she had to toughen up. Right now, she's looking at me with a look in her eyes that says, *What's keeping you, girl? You know we're waiting for you. You know we all think you've got what it takes. There is a star on this Walk of Fame just waiting to be lit up with the letters that spell your name. But it's not going to be here forever. So then, Laura, chop chop.* Barbara and Gloria nod their heads in agreement. Veronica smiles her coy smile. They know precisely what Lana is talking about. They've all had to make it the hard way, and something tells me they know that is how it's going to be for me too.

\*

I reach for my phone and message Fleming. Nothing back from him, but someone I haven't heard from in quite a while has been in touch; someone I hadn't really expected to hear from once she flew the coop; someone I'm surprised has time to write. *Hello Laura! It's been quite a while . . . but here I am, writing to you from afar. I wanted to get in touch to ask how my favourite understudy has been and share a little of my own adventures . . .* It's quite a lengthy email and so I go on my laptop to read it.

*So, yes, I've been in London for a while now, it's where I was discovered, caught my big break. Happened well over a year ago, actually, at about a quarter past ten on a wet Tuesday night after a local production of Shakespeare's* King Lear. *I was playing Cordelia, the most loved daughter of them all. A well-known theatre director was in the audience, and after the show he came backstage and there and then offered me the lead in his next production.*

*Well. Less than two months later I was seated in front of my dressing-room mirror in the Apollo Theatre, as ready as I could be for my West End debut as purring and snarling Maggie the Cat. Every theatre critic in the land was present. Actors from stage and screen. One or two movie producers. The who is who and the crème de la crème. Oh, Laura! Cast and crew alike were bigging*

*me up no end. I had no idea how I was going to
get through the next couple of hours. I really didn't.*

*We took a thirty-minute curtain call. And fifteen
minutes of that was for me and me alone. The rest
of the cast stood back, and then disappeared
altogether, as I stepped tentatively forward to
accept the standing ovation. Brava! Brava! There
was camera flash. Blown kisses. Flung roses, if you
don't mind! I waved and bowed and gathered up
the red flowers and left the stage to an ear-
shattering crescendo.*

*You should have seen the morning editions. A
wonder to behold! declared both the* Telegraph *and*
The Times. *Luminous! So ran the one-word verdict
in the* Guardian. Total Theatre *agreed. An actress
already touched by greatness. More please and
soon! In no time it seemed every theatre critic was
gushing to the gills so enraptured were they all. The
consensus: A star is born.*

*And this is how it has been. All the parts you
and me spent countless hours with. Lady Macbeth.
Ophelia. Turns with Chekhov's* Three Sisters. *I've
even alternated in the roles of Martha and Honey
for a sell-out run of* Who's Afraid of Virginia
Woolf? *Henry Balsam-Cumberfeld, the well-known
super-agent, flew across the world to see me
perform this daring stunt, and in my dressing room
after the final performance he offered me the sun,
moon and stars. Of course, I hmmmmed and*

*aaahed, and the most powerful agent in show business went down on bended knees and implored me to join his stable of talent. Since then it's all been a bit of a whirlwind.*

*But enough about the theatre! I'm through with all of that. From here out it's the movies for me. Did you see my debut? (Title =* Shirley Temple Killer Queen.) *I play the better-looking and much cleverer half of a twin-sister assassination squad. We've just taken out a high-profile politician with past dealings with the terrorist organization responsible for the death of our parents. So now we're on the run. Gun crazy we are! And we have a motto: Shoot first, and then shoot again. It caused quite the stir in this London town, my own contribution being singled out. My next one is already in the can too. (Title =* Unhitched.) *It's really, really good. I mean they are really bigging up this one. Can't say too much at the moment (Sir Henry – that's what I call him – has me sworn to secrecy), but already there's talk of awards. Silver Bear. Palme d'Or. The Golden Tiger or whatever that thing is they give out in Venice. There is even talk of – I hardly dare say the word – Oscar. And there I go putting the hex on everything. We're off to Venice tomorrow, actually. Me and Henry, the cast and crew.* Unhitched *has been selected for screening in competition. Apparently we will arrive at the red carpet by gondola! I'll let you know how* *we fare out. Oh, and the London premiere is in a couple of weeks. And we're set for a US release before the year end – you know, so it will be eligible for the \*Oscars\*. Imagine. Yours truly at the biggest night of the year in Tinseltown. I'll send you tickets to the London premiere. I think I still have your address. (Do you still live by the little harbour?) Oh, bother! They are screaming for me here. They want me wearing the latest haute couture on the Venice gondola, I must dash for a fitting. Write back and let me know all your news. And I mean all. Kiss, kiss. Bang, bang. You're dead! Mel. x*

Mel. Imelda. Imelda Ebbing. Imelda J Ebbing. My acting buddy from way back (don't know why she's referring to me as her understudy). We were at drama school together. Hit it off from the get-go. Liked the same plays, the same movies, the same stars. We used to have so much fun playing off each other. Some of the others, though. They used to rag her all the time. About her 'overbearing' technique. About her 'high' ambition. About her name even – especially once she insisted on sticking in that middle initial. Imelda didn't care. When the time comes I won't need to change it. That's what she would say. Looks like she was right about that. Funny thing her getting in touch just as my own opportunity turns up.

I'm about to click on the link at the end of her note – something about this imminent London premiere – when

Jennifer comes knocking on my bedroom door. I am fully prepared to ignore her, but she keeps it up, and when at last she clocks that I have no intention of budging, the doorknob turns and in she walks.

'May I come in?' she says, already comfortable in the soft chair by the window, legs crossed one over the other.

Let me guess, I say to myself, not looking at her. You have been dispatched by mother to check up on me. Are taking it upon yourself, even, to unlock the door that leads inside me. Have a good goo around. Find out a secret or three. Get to the bottom of me.

'Mam said I should check in on you. We've been talking away and suddenly we realized we were forgetting all about you.'

'That's OK,' I say.

'No it is not OK. Sisters don't treat each other like that.'

'If you say so.'

'Laura, I want us to be *friends*. I want us to be able to talk to each other. Tell each other things. And I want you to know that you can tell me anything. And I mean *anything*.'

I must have flinched when she said that last bit, putting her dramatic emphasis on the word anything. And I can tell that she has spotted my reaction, and now she is sitting back comfortably in the window chair, and I wait for a new expression to take over her face, smug and superior. Aha, it will say. You are not at all the firecracker you've been made out to be. Look at you, with your knotty hair and patchy skirt. The spindly arms on you. The scratched legs. Wait 'til you see. By the end of the week I'll have you eating out of my hands.

'So why are you here?'

'Sorry?'

'It's a simple question.'

'You know why I'm here. To spend time with you and mam. Introduce you to Juan. Let him get to know you both.'

'Why now?'

'What? I don't know what you mean. It's been on my mind for some time. I didn't want to leave it until . . .'

'Until what?'

'Mam said you've been doing OK recently.'

'Mam, is it?'

'What would you like me to call her?'

'Oh, I can think of some names.'

'What has mam done to you?'

I decide against any more answering. Don't want this one thinking she is getting the upper hand.

We stare silently at each other. Deciding to call a halt to this early skirmish, she throws her gaze about the room.

'Look at all these posters.'

'I do that sometimes, yes.'

'Who is that?'

'Gloria.'

'Gloria?'

'Swanson. Gloria Swanson.'

'And that one?'

'Stanwyck.'

'What do all the black crosses mean?'

'They're dead.'

'Oh, and there's *All About Eve*. I've seen that one.'

'You and the whole world.'

'The Lana Turner has seen better days. She wouldn't be very impressed with all those smudges.'

I don't say a word to that. Just watch her eye up my posters, certain she is going to ask more about them. But no. It is back to the oh-so-polite questions.

'Do you think you'll be able to show me around the harbour tomorrow? I hear it's come on since I was last here. All those cafes and bars and shops. What do you do for fun? Is there someone special I should know about? You can talk to me, you know. Anything at all. I'm a good listener.'

Hear that. Now she thinks she gets to know all about my love life. Next thing she'll be asking for an introduction to Fleming. Picture his salivating face at that. And I can tell she is about to make a lunge for me, envelop me in those arms.

'How long are you staying?' I quickly ask, but she doesn't answer. She is out of the chair, heading my way and before I have a chance to roll out of the way she is on the bed beside me and has wrapped me up and is clutching me to her chest. I get a scent of something peachy. Strands of her hair tickle my neck. She squeezes that little bit tighter, and I don't resist her embrace the way I ought to.

# Part II

## *ALL RIGHT, MR DEMILLE, I'M READY FOR MY CLOSE-UP*

# VERONICA LAKE

November 14, 1922 – July 7, 1973
aka The Peekaboo Girl

**Inducted:** February 8, 1960
**Star address:** 6918, Hollywood Blvd
Father died in industrial explosion when she was twelve
Troubled childhood. Expelled from boarding school
According to her mother, diagnosed as schizophrenic
Made seven films with Alan Ladd
**Real name:** Constance Frances Marie Ockelman

(*note to self:* she was dead right to change her name)

## 11

Jennifer's arrival home means lots of visitors. Any combination of Fiona French, Yoohoo Lucy Garavan, Odd Doris and Dolores Taaffe. Already this morning, three of them have commandeered the kitchen table. Forlornly, Fiona French flosses the piercings in her ears, picks her nose and, in the hope of finding something worthwhile, gropes at every piece of food mother puts out on the table. Dolores Taaffe is in her trademark combo of red perm, zealously rouged lips and green dress. When I was little she used to tell me she was a queen and could walk on water. Do it so, I'd say to her, pointing to the harbour, and she'd look at me and say only the king could ask that of her. Odd Doris has been that way ever since the roof of her house caved in on her fifteen years ago. Sometime after that she bought our banger of a car and forgot to collect it despite handing over to mother a thousand buckaroos in cash money. Doris, mother would say over the phone, when are you going to collect your new car? Yoohoo Lucy isn't with them. She lives just a few doors down and has hightailed it to Spain for a couple of autumn weeks to get away from the west wind. I am easily penetrated. Her words, not mine.

Jennifer is entertaining everyone with her delay-at-the-airport story and how she ended up sitting beside a-famous-who in the waiting lounge. They cocked up her booking and so they upgraded her to first class. And she got to hang out in the VIP lounge. 'And you will never guess who sat down beside me. Go on, guess,' she says. Fiona and Doris start to guess. 'Bono!' Jennifer squeals before they get very far. 'Bono turned up.' 'Did you say anything to him?' mother asks. 'For a minute I didn't say a thing. How could I? I was in shock. Then he looked at me, dipped his shades and smiled. Yes, he said, it's really me. I've had enough and am running away from it all. Then he laughed and told me he was only joking. The band was about to embark on the South American leg of the tour and Bono wanted to do some humanitarian work, so his people had made it happen.' 'In the VIP lounge?' I say, and mother glares at me. 'He asked me what I was up to in this part of the world,' Jennifer goes on. 'You should have seen his face when I told him. He quizzed me for the next I don't know how long. You know, he said, leaning into me and lowering his voice, the world doesn't see its best people. Then he said he would mention me during his concert in La Paz. And would dedicate a song to me. Then he actually began to sing. By now, others had realized who it was and had gathered around. He wasn't in the least bit fazed, just kept on singing. And then he reached out and held my hand. I nearly passed out. Then he took Little Juan's hand and invited us to sing along with him. So we tried. Then others joined in. By the end of it all the entire VIP lounge was singing.'

Mother laughs. Odd Doris and Dolores laugh. Fiona French thinks it's the best story she's heard in ages. Then the four of them start grilling Jennifer about what else she is up to. And that is how it is. Five minutes home and already popular everywhere. In our house. Along our road. At the harbour she talks to the terrorists, takes their picture, points out a nice view of a boat on the water, tips them off to places not mentioned in the guidebooks, places pointed out to her by her array of new friends. In Brady's shop she is already Alice's favourite customer, with her requests for apricots and lentils and chia seeds and mung beans and the other strange-sounding tat that comprises her and Little Juan's diet. A couple of days ago I saw her staring at the nearly completed theatre and one of the buildermen – *my* builderman – spotted her, the entire length of her, and nibble me down to my wishbone if he didn't stop what he was doing and make it his business to be all about her. A minute or two later the pair of them were laughing together and, of course, not wanting to miss out on this miracle apparition landed amidst the rubble, all the other builders had to put down their chisels and get in on this laughing act. At last, her precious time with this ever-increasing band of admirers came to a conclusion, and she continued on her untroubled way, moving lithely about the place, taking in the neighbourhood and the harbour and the nearby streets, presenting herself to every corner, as though every step she took had the power to bring her immediate surroundings into existence. She was almost too good to be true. Made me want to burrow a way inside her and let loose a barbaric bug.

She has cast a voodoo spell on mother. For the first couple of jet-lag mornings it was tea and toast in bed, and aside from keeping an eye on Juan for an hour or two here and there while mother fusses all over her returned daughter, I have had little to do with Jennifer. Which suits me fine as I need to think about the theatre part I am up for without any distraction. I spot Little Juan sitting out by himself in the front garden and have just set down a bowl of Chipsticks in front of him when this week's *Advertiser* arrives. Straightaway, I relieve the delivery boy and scour the entertainment section. And, yes, my hunch is correct.

The call for auditions has been announced.

'Listen to this,' I tell Little Juan, sitting into the deckchair beside him while holding up for his benefit the open pages of the *Advertiser*.

*Khaos Theatre Company invites actors to audition*
*for its forthcoming production*
A STREETCAR NAMED DESIRE
*Town Hall. Friday, September 23rd, 10 am.*

I knew it was going to be *Streetcar*. Good. Now I can completely focus on the scenes I need to get ready for audition day.

'Did you get any of that, little man?' I say, looking over at my companion while nodding to the open newspaper. 'The key words are theatre, actors, audition and forthcoming production. That's me they're asking for. I'm going to be on the stage again. And not before time. Stick around and you'll get to see me. Play your cards right and I might even score front-row tickets for you. Mark my words. It will be worth the wait.'

He looks at me, shrugs his shoulders and slumps into the deckchair. I should really start calling the little fellow by his proper name. Since his arrival we have taken to bumping into each other very early in the morning. At first he hardly said a word, then it was in a lingo I don't understand. *No hablo la lingua*, I said to him, and he flashed a toothy grin my way. After that, though, he started using bits of English, and when he wants to, has little difficulty making complete sentences. But mostly he just shuffles silently about the place, looking for something to amuse himself with, his black, overgrown curls moving in several directions at once. Every time I see him it's like I am looking at a mop.

I read over the newspaper bit again. Trace my fingers along the title of the play. He certainly enjoys a bit of intrigue, our new theatre director. I wonder what other grandstand announcements he has up his sleeve.

'What do you think, Juan?' I ask the little fellow, nodding at the *Advertiser*.

Juan doesn't say anything. He just slumps further forward in the chair, chin in his hands.

'Why the long face?' I ask.

He shrugs again. I offer him the bowl of Chipsticks. He shakes his head, though I can tell he wants to.

'Let me guess. You prefer mammy's very special guacamole mung bean salad. Your loss,' I say, tucking in. And I return my attention to the newspaper.

For the next few minutes we sit like that. I skim the

paper and munch Chipsticks. Little Juan sits there, not saying a word. Presently, I peek out at him from the paper.

'Tell me, have you ever made a movie?'

No answer.

'Because, I have this great amazing idea for a movie and need some help getting it off the ground.'

He half-turns his head towards me.

'You heard me. I'm talking about a co-production here. The debut feature from the Juan and Laura Studio of Movie Excellence. As well as being directors, scriptwriters, dolly grips, clapper loaders and executives in charge of production, guess what else we are going to be? We are going to be the stars. What do you say to that?'

He says nothing to that.

'*Bueno.* I can tell you are in total agreement. Listen carefully now. I'm going to give you two star names and you have to pick one. *Comprende?*'

A brief shrug of the shoulders.

'Good boy. Are you ready? Brando or Bogart?'

'Bogart,' he murmurs, after an uncertain moment or two.

'Excellent choice. Bogart is the man. You're good at this. In fact you're so good I'm going to let you pick my name too. OK? This time I'm going to say three names. Lana or Gloria or Barbara?'

'Lana.'

'Ah, so you like the platinum blondes. Another excellent choice. Are you sure you haven't been in the movies before?'

Another shrug.

'OK. Bogart and Lana are the stars of our movie. This is

a first, let me tell you, never been done before. So Lana is not a happy camper. She's fed up at home. There's nothing much happening in the town she lives in. She needs a little excitement in her life. OK. So what is she going to do? Hmm? What happens when women need a little excitement?'

He looks crossways at me.

'Bogart happens! OK? So Bogart appears and guess what he and Lana are going to do. Go on. Guess.'

'Get married,' he says, looking my way and not batting an eyelid.

'They most certainly are not getting married,' I say a little too dramatically. 'They shoot up the bank, empty the safe, steal a fast car and hightail it out of town like there is no tomorrow. Guess how much they find in the safe?'

Another shrug.

'Only about *un millón de dólares*. That enough for you? Good. So Bogart and Lana have robbed the bank. And now the cops are gunning for them. Especially the chief of police who just happens to be Lana's sister. She also likes Bogart, so she's doubly mad because he skedaddled with Lana and not her. Luckily, she's useless at her job and not as foxy as Lana. But she's not going to give up the chase. Now all we need is a name for her. Any ideas? Her name is . . . Lydia . . . Perfect. Her name is Lydia and she is not going to stop until she finds Bogart, locks up Lana inside a prison cell and throws away the key. Any questions?'

He looks at me, uncertain. Then says, 'What happens next?'

'I'll tell you in a few days. OK? We're partners in crime now, you and me. *Comprende?* Good. *Alto cinco*, partner.'

I raise my hand and he high-fives me, and this time accepts the proffered Chipsticks – just as Jennifer appears, shimmering and daisy fresh.

'Look at you two,' she says when she joins us, already eyeballing the fist of Chipsticks Juan is clutching.

'We're the best of friends, me and Juan,' I say, patting his curls.

Jennifer approaches, takes the Chipsticks out of Juan's hand and halts her boy as he makes to grab another handful out of the bowl. Juan gets out of his chair and wraps his arms around his mother's waist, and gestures to the snacks she has taken from him. Jennifer shakes her head, sorry, no can do. Juan frowns the frown of someone who has been denied the only thing that matters.

'They won't kill him,' I say.

'Listen to the expert.'

Again, Jennifer turns to her boy. Behind her back I stick out my tongue and fan my hands.

'I have to go as far as the bank,' Jennifer announces.

'Off you go. Myself and the little fellow will hold the fort.'

'I won't be long. Tell mam, will you.'

Without waiting for an answer she leaves us be, one more time warning Juan away from the Chipsticks. And giving her hair an elaborate flick as she opens the gate, off she goes.

'I just thought of something,' I say to Juan, watching

Jennifer walk off towards town. 'About Lydia. The chief of police. She can fairly go on once she starts. Like one of those wind-up toys. Or a demented turkey.'

I stand out of the deckchair and do an imitation turkey-walk about the garden, while at the same time emitting out of me an ever-escalating litany of gobble-gobbles.

Juan regards me as though I really am a turkey.

'OK, little man. Because you are such a good listener and your mother has abandoned you, I think a little reward is the order of day. And so I am going to put the pan on, cook up one of my very special breakfasts. Now, tell me. What would you like? Beans and black pudding? That is another excellent choice. Come on then, and here, you can read the paper. Before too long you'll be reading all about me.'

I leave him in the sitting room, in front of the TV, and for the next few minutes I join mother and her friends in the kitchen. Mother half looks at what I am frying up. 'It's all for me,' I say, chopping up the pudding.

A few minutes later I am in the sitting room and have slapped a plate of beans and black pudding down in front of Little Juan. He looks at the plate. Then he picks up a piece of pudding as though he has never before seen anything like it. Then he looks at me.

'Ah, you're going to try the pudding. Made from the blood of swine. Around these parts it's considered a delicacy. Get it into you. It's full of blood. And swine.'

He takes a nibble. Then decides he likes it. So much so that I end up giving him my share. He has shoved the twelfth or thirteenth piece inside his gob by the time mother gets involved and a look on her face that says *Good grief, what are you trying to do to him?* She whips the plate away from Juan, muttering something about toast and butter as she returns to the kitchen.

Home from the bank and Jennifer's VISA card still isn't working. None of her cards are. There has been a hitch at the Spanish-speaking end – apparently she should have told someone in the bank she was travelling abroad – and now she must wait for some bank located in some impossible-to-get-a-hold-of corner of Mexico to transfer some money. 'I badly need to get some things. I need to get some things for Juan,' she announces dramatically, throwing out her arms for added effect. Again she looks at her no-good cards. Again she wonders what is wrong with the faraway bank, shakes her head as though it is a travesty of epic proportions, and, uh-oh, I'm thinking, here come the water-works. But before they do, mother has said the magic words. 'Let me help.' And let me help too, I want to scream. Let me march straight out the door and all the way out to sea as far as my offshore account. Here you go, Jennifer. It's all for you.

I do no such thing. I haven't stirred from the kitchen. And now Jennifer is on about her luggage. It still hasn't turned up and she is running out of clothes. She has some summer things, loose-fitting linens, singlets to show off those lovely arms, a light skirt or two. But nothing that is any match for an afternoon of the west wind. Today she is wearing one of mother's woolly jumpers. It's a loose fit, completely shapeless, not at all what she has in mind, I'm sure, when presenting herself to the outside world.

'I don't know what is keeping my things,' I hear her say, doing my best to slide towards the front door and out of the house without being seen. Besides. What does she want from me? An Ave Maria? Too late. Mother has spotted me and is waving me into the sitting room and talking up how Jennifer and Little Juan are going to stay with us for a little while and would it be too much trouble for me to be more sisterly.

'They've already been here *a little while*,' I say.

'Well, they're going to be here *another* little while,' mother says.

'How will the suffering world survive without her?' I say to that, and mother gives me one of her long looks.

'Jennifer is having a bad time of it, Laura,' she says next. 'Try to be more understanding.'

'I understand she's well able to flick her hair at buildermen.'

'Have you anything better she could wear?'

'Like what?' I say.

'What do you mean, like what? Your sister's luggage has been delayed. Until it arrives she needs some clothes. If it is not too much to ask, could you find something.'

I am about to point out the complete and utter futility of this, any fool could take a look at luscious Jennifer and spindly me and see that we are a mismatch, but I can tell anything I have to say will travel straight through mother's head.

'No, I can't,' I settle for, heading for the door.

'What does that mean, no I can't?'

It means I would like a sturdy boatman to row you and Jennifer far away out to sea. This is what I want to say. 'It means I have to go to work. Goodbye, see you later,' I say instead, and I am out of there.

## 12

For the past few months my hiatus from the theatre has provided ample time for my stint as a guide offering walking tours to the lorryloads of terrorists who, without fail, rock up every summer and seem to forget to go home again. The group I have to meet right now I am reliably informed is to be a mixed bag of nationalities. As per usual, our meeting point is by the fountain at the top of the Square.

Fleming is already there. Since making him aware of my temporary career he tags along as a pretend terrorist. At some point, upon receipt of our prearranged signal, he will start into a combination of daft, interesting and provocative questions, the idea being that my elaborate and thorough responses will supplement my meagre wage in the form of above-the-going-rate gratuities from our impressed assemblage. These spoils are shared. Some for me. Some for Fleming. Though Fleming's share always seems to have an unhappy knack of finding its way into his brothers' pockets.

So far this season Fleming has been an overly zealous Ruud from the Netherlands wanting to know in great detail about all the efforts to keep tidal water out of Flood Street. His impersonation of a sailor from Lithuania nearly landed everyone in hot water when he suggested a side-trip down to the docks and invited us aboard the gunboat he assiduously assured us he was assigned to. His attempt at a drunken Australian copper miner was foiled by a member of the tour group called McGelligot who, from Adelaide himself, was taking an enforced sabbatical from the mines of his homeland and had decided to visit the old country. And I had to summon layers of diplomacy I had no idea existed inside me when, in the guise of a Mexican boxer, he a little too convincingly took offence at the pair of Texans who made the mistake of referring in glowing terms to a certain wall a certain presidential candidate has been banging on about. I can't believe they thought you were Mexican, I would later say to Fleming while divvying up the extra cash dollars. He nodded his head and said he couldn't believe they thought he was a boxer.

Of course his own personal favourite was the occasion he pretended he was a television producer from Berlin scouting locations along the Wild Atlantic Way for a television mini-series involving a teenage assassination squad. For that particular walking tour he shaved his head and introduced himself to everyone as Fritz Schmelling. Pity for Fritz that we had Dieter from Düsseldorf and Heinrich from Hamburg along for the ride that particular afternoon – they knew more about the Wild Atlantic Way than myself and Fleming and everyone else put together.

Today we have agreed that Fleming is to be a visiting professor from some eminent British university with a healthy yet thorny interest in all things historical and Irish. He has an accent he is dying to try out on his unsuspecting targets, and he has been practising by constantly repeating aloud to himself the line To Hell or to Connacht. Now, standing at the top of the Square in the moments before to-day's group turns up, he keeps massaging with his thumb and index finger the ends of an imaginary handlebar moustache.

The group arrives in twos and threes. As promised, an eclectic bunch, and I get quick introductions from Bjorn from Sweden. Abelardo and Mercedes from Spain. Lisa from Canada. A minuscule woman from Minnesota whose name I don't catch. A cigar-chewing colossus from Boston. A trio of Nikon-wielding youngsters from Shanghai. And a doddery-looking fellow from Brooklyn in corduroy shorts and unbuckled sandals who prefers to give his profession – painter – rather than his name. Following the painter's example, Fleming steps forward and in his best accent intro-duces himself as Professor Emeritus out of Oxford.

'Oh? You don't look old enough to be retired,' the paint-er says and Fleming twiddles the end of that imaginary moustache.

I begin with my usual guff about where we are and tell them about the speech JFK made in this very spot. 'If you look that way on a clear day you can see all the way to Bos-ton,' I declare, pointing off vaguely. 'Right,' guffaws the cigar chewer. 'Hey,' I say, holding up my hands. 'It was Ken-nedy who said it, take it up with him.' And I beckon them to follow me.

'So,' I tell them when we pause at the Browne Doorway, 'we are just outside the old city walls. And on this very spot they used to carry out public executions.'

'What?' asks the cigar chewer, summoning a surprising level of incredulity.

'How did they do it?' asks Lisa from Canada.

'How do you think they did it?' snaps the minuscule woman from Minnesota. 'They strung them up and chopped their heads off. Isn't that right, miss?'

She looks to me for affirmation.

'Yes, it is,' I say, happy to corroborate. 'They had a wonderful gallows. Could drop eight people in one go. Top-quality rope too. Back in the day, this town was considered one of *the* places if it was a good hanging you were after. And,' I go on, mostly for the benefit of those eager for some added gore, 'there was a huge cauldron they used for parboiling heads.'

'When did they stop the public executions?' Abelardo from Spain wants to know.

'At approximately six pm next Tuesday,' I say and nearly everybody laughs.

From there I take them the short walk to the recently installed statues of the two Wildes – Oscar and Eduard – and because I haven't been bothered finding out anything about the other fellow concentrate at length on the sad story of Oscar and his tragic demise. I pause at Lynch's Castle and tell them the story about what Judge Lynch did to his son. I show them the King's Head bar and tell them how it got its name.

'There sure is a lot of death on this tour,' observes the cigar chewer.

'Don't you worry,' I say, injecting a little levity into my

voice and giving him my sincerest smile. 'I have a feeling you will live to tell all the tales to your buddies back in the Big Apple.'

'I'm from Boston,' he says to that, rolling his eyes in Fleming's direction. Fleming nods and twiddles some more.

We move on to the Spanish Arch, where I let them wander about the open spaces of the harbour, and it is while I am waxing lyrical about the Armada and the awful things that happened to the shipwrecked Spaniards that Fleming comes into his own.

'This arch is not Spanish,' he intones crisply, getting busy with his fingers. 'In fact, I'm not sure it even qualifies as an arch.'

'Architecturally, it is not Spanish,' I say, taking my cue. 'It is in fact an extension of the medieval city walls built by the Normans. Because of its Western European location, this little city of ours has always had a close trading relationship with Spain and Portugal. Back in the day lots of Spaniards took up residence here. And so the arch was named in honour of our Spanish brethren.'

Abelardo and Mercedes are thrilled with this piece of news. 'I'm pretty sure I have some Spanish blood in me,' the cigar chewer adds for good measure. I can see Fleming reckoning his share of the tip coming our way.

'Does anyone else have a question?' I say before hauling them to the tour's next venue.

'What do you do when you're not doing this?' asks the woman from Minnesota.

'I'm an actress,' I say. 'Like my daddy before me.'

'Goddamn, I knew it,' harks the cigar chewer. 'Do something for us.'

Just at that moment it starts raining and from somewhere I hear what I assume is someone's attempt at a Michael Caine impersonation.

'The rain in Spain falls mainly in the plain.'

I am vaguely disturbed upon discovering that the someone is in fact Fleming, whose handlebar moustache, along with his Oxford accent, has suddenly disappeared.

'Hey, that's pretty good,' says Bjorn from Sweden.

'Thank you, my good fellow,' Fleming says, his accent – to my relief – back in situ.

'Hugh Grant, yes?'

Bjorn turns my way to supply the confirmation that Fleming has withheld. But I myself have been diverted. I have spotted Stephen Fallow. My director. He's walking slowly along the quay with a young woman, with whom he appears to be in deep conversation.

'This way, ladies and gentlemen,' I announce, and to the bemusement of Fleming, for one, I lead my group in the direction Stephen and the woman are taking.

The rain decides to hold off and Stephen and his lady-friend continue along the river as far as O'Brien's Bridge, where they veer off in the direction of the Town Hall via Market Street. They cut down by Bowling Green – precisely the route I would eventually have taken my group along, as it so happens, and, ensuring that I have Stephen in my sights, I signal for people to pause outside the row of terraced dwellings – where Stephen and his ladyfriend have also paused.

'Good heavens,' Fleming declaims, his accent becoming ever more clipped. 'What class of wretched sod has to endure living conditions such as these?'

'So this is where Nora Barnacle lived,' I say, shaking an admonishing finger at Fleming and then pointing to the plaque on one of the lesser-kept dwellings. 'Before, that is, she became muse and inspiration for the great monologue at the end of a book called *Ulysses.*'

'We would certainly like to hear an excerpt from this monologue,' Fleming says, looking around at everyone. 'Wouldn't we, people?'

'Oh, yes!' says the woman from Minnesota, clasping together her minuscule hands.

'Well said!' Fleming intones. 'Come on then, give us a flavour.'

At which point Fleming twiddles the end of his moustache and, noticing that Stephen has lingered, Yes I will so, I tell my expectant audience and off I go into the sorry saga of many's the suitor to have walked me along the nearby river path set me down on the grassy bank plied me with a litre of fortified wine said i was his north south east west his sun moon stars entire universe plied me some more said he was going to take me to a special place oh what's the rush i said ply me some more he plied implored beseeched said i was his best dream his favourite place his only wish i set his heart racing his head spinning his blood charging at which point he lunged so desperate was he his jaw collided with the bottle is your head spinning now i asked him there was no reply he was out cold

which puts me mind of the cherub-face looker who asked me for thirty seconds of my time hopped from leg to leg he did like a lad badly in need of release was awfully disappointed upon discovering i wasn't going to be the one to facilitate this inevitability said i was crushing his heart his will to live still he stood there hopping for his cause which when all is said and done was lost on me so i walked leaving him hopping there by himself for all i know that's what he's still at hopping out his days

the days come in the days go out that's what the next lad said a contemplative type with a penchant for wham bars and go-fast cars come for a spin with me he said roger that i said and it was pedal to the metal along the straight and narrow round the short corner and slam! head-on into the wall he swore on his ruptured spleen had not been there last time he took someone joyriding that's ok i purred stroking his scratched face with a broken nail all the go-fast excitement had gotten me in a hot and bothered kind of mood i had already helped him free himself rolling down the seats we were just as the engine caught fire a police siren sounded and he was out the back door of the car going gone vanished into nearby trees

and the trees remind me of the time i was with a trunk of a lad from Bohola fidgeting with his buttons keep going he said keep going you beauty i bet you say that to all the maidens i said i do indeed he said but your hands are something else altogether your hands are extra special there should be an award going for your hands of course i was flattered curious and knowing full well it would send him up the walls i stopped fidgeting with his buttons to take a gander yes i said i do believe you are right my hands are splendid they are splendid he said put them back where they were instead i rolled him over helped him wriggle out of his stressed jeans leaned over myself to feast upon his buttocks like basketballs they were cantaloupes even cantering cantaloupes a good name for a band but better name for these miracle shapes i now beheld touched tickled all over poor lad beside himself he was couldn't contain himself like that other one he was going gone vanished

what is it with these lads i asked myself next time i am not going to touch any part i am going to lie back and discover what the brouhaha is all about yes i will do precisely that i said it to the lad i ended up backstage with after an am-dram production of *macbeth* sssh don't call it by its name it's bad luck now come here to me you beauty he said urging himself against me there is no going back now no going back! out out damn fool of a man i howled at the beefburger be gone with you

and oh my yes just when i thought it was all a lost cause there appeared along the riverwalk what can only be described as an apparition my very own adonis oh a proper prince i'm talking the full bit arms feet shoulders legs and everything in between oh my his tasty lips and edible ears his blond curls his temple bones eyelash to toe he was dazzling opened his mouth and spoilt it all every girl i know wants a piece of me he said some pieces more than others he said all donkey-guffaw and beating-chest proud i'm vulnerable too he said i can be sensitive like fish and birds swim away i told him find the deep end of the ocean fly away i told him vanish into the oblivious sky

and then just as i was most definitely on the point of forever calling it a day my man fleming turned up slid down alongside me hi baby he said that was all it took i was so hot and eager ready for him i wanted to scream i wanted him so so bad wanted him to put his mouth on every part of me wanted to watch his intent face as he kissed me clean do anything you want to me fleming and be quick about it yes I will he said oh when i think of his touch yes turn me over oh yes caress me caress me oh yes take me now big boy take me with tragedy and restraint oh yes let my howls drive you further and further oh yes faster and faster oh yes until i am beyond myself spinning spinning oh yes take me don't stop go on go on oh yes oh yes oh yes further deeper fill me up oh yes make me beg for more more more oh yes please do anything you want anything so long as i live to tell the tale oh yes ecstatic i am throbbing and quivering oh yes gush all over me oh yes on fire i am my hands my heart my lips oh yes fleming oh yes oh yes oh yes . . .

I am a few more orgiastic lines into my Molly Bloom tribute, have noticed that a few passers-by have stopped for a gander, to my delight Stephen Fallow and his ladyfriend have stuck around, and so for the finale I splay myself against the door of Nora's house and slide up and down while slapping the walls either side of me for some extra dramatic effect, indeed so effectively that a couple of locals have opened their bedroom windows in order to listen in and another passer-by has actually stopped to enquire am I in need of medical attention. 'Of course she is all right,' whoops the minuscule woman from Minnesota. 'She is having an orgasm!' And she bids me to continue. And so instead of pausing mid-passion and with a little further encouragement I do as requested, with gathering enthusiasm it must be said and at greater length than is probably necessary. Everyone in the group hears me out, waits until I have given everything and, when at last I expel one final last-ditch Yes! and crumple in a theatrical heap at the foot of Nora Barnacle's door, there is a spontaneous round of applause.

'Hot damn,' calls out the cigar chewer from Boston. 'I want to meet this Fleming guy. I want to shake his hand.'

'I want to do more than that,' says the minuscule woman from Minnesota.

At which point I gather myself, bow, curtsy, dust myself off and politely enquire if anyone has questions they would like to ask.

At once I hear Fleming pipe up in his best academic voice.

'Was that really from the monologue?'

'Well, it certainly wasn't from the latest Mills and Boon,' quips my woman from Minnesota, and I enquire if anyone has read the letters.

'What letters would those be?' she asks.

'The love letters from James Joyce to Nora Barnacle,' I say, raising an eyebrow when there are no takers. 'It just so happens I have a printout of one of them right here. Would people like to hear a sample?'

A loud whoop lets me know the answer, and I warm up my best butter-wouldn't-melt voice. I am about to start in on Joyce's earthy description of Nora and her effective hands and what she seemed capable of doing with them, when I notice that Stephen and his ladyfriend have started to move off.

'Change of plan, everyone. The professor would like to take over.' I shove the letter in Fleming's hands. He splays himself across the door of the house, by and large everybody has a good chuckle, the Minnesotan cheers loudest. 'Yes, goddamn it!' she cackles, the others offer more applause and, between the letter and my lusty performance, mentally I congratulate myself for the large tip that will usher my way in the not-so-far-off future. At which point I make my excuses and scoot after Stephen.

## 13

Having marked the important September date, I need to find out more about the audition. Give Stephen Fallow a feel for the sort of roles I can do. Let him see that the part of Blanche DuBois has my name written all over it, that he need look no further for his leading lady.

The young woman with him hangs off his arm and every word he utters. At a suitable distance I follow. They cross the Salmon Weir bridge, and walk as far as the canal, where they pause for a moment of happy-talk together before parting ways. The young woman continues straight ahead. My director strikes out along the canal and I am not far behind. He turns into the first side street, stops at the end house. He has keyed open the door and is about to disappear inside when I announce myself.

'Hello,' I say. 'It's me again.'

'Hel . . . lo,' he says, turning around.

'You probably remember me. From the Town Hall. You know, when the press release went out about your new production. I think you paused for my little performance back there – with the terror . . . tourists. I'm Laura. The actress.'

'Laura?'

'I know, I know. I really ought to change it. I saw the

notice in the paper about the auditions. This is going to be huge.'

'You're very kind.'

'And you are so modest. It's a very attractive quality. This town has been crying out for a decent production for ages and it is obvious you are the right man for the job.'

'That's very nice of you to say so. Now, if you . . .'

'No need to thank me. Thank that remarkable CV of yours. The West End. The Royal Court. Broadway. Sydney Opera House, for God's sake. I bet you've got some stories to tell. Have you? Some good stories to tell?'

'Well, I don't know about that.'

'And I think someone is being modest again. Hmmm. *A Streetcar Named Desire*. I can't believe you're doing this one. It's one of my favourites. I'd give anything to have seen the original on Broadway. The movie version is good too. My daddy played Stanley Kowalski. He was with the Claddagh Players. Perhaps you heard of them? Famous theatre group from these parts.'

'No . . . no. Can't say that I have.'

'They disbanded several years ago. Oh, well. The star that burns twice as brightly and all of that. Would you like to see my Gloria Swanson or Barbara Stanwyck routines? I do a very good femme fatale. And a tomboy. An out-and-out thug even. My woman on the verge is pretty good too. I can do pretty much anything except a damsel in distress. I draw the line at those. I can do something now if you like.'

'Well, I'm a little busy at the moment.' Half-turning away from me, he pushes open his door.

'Of course you are. The *Advertiser* said you are on the list of people to look out for. Well, I'm on the lookout. Be in no doubt about that. Are you sure I can't do my woman on the verge for you? It won't take a minute.'

'Maybe next time.' The door suitably ajar, he takes a step inside.

'Something else, then?' I say, taking a step after him. 'Go on, just say it. Anything you want. Quiet. Loud. Listening. I can do a great listener. Someone who is just waiting for the other person to shut up so I can start. I can convey plenty with my eyes. If I'm in the mood I can have an entire world going on behind them. You know, like Garbo.'

'Now is probably not the best time.'

'A quick accent, perhaps? Not a problem. A southern belle? The way Vivien Leigh does it?'

'I better go inside,' he says, stepping fully into the house.

'Before you do, can you tell me a scene you have a particular fondness for? Something with Blanche and Stella? Or Blanche and Stanley? All three together, perhaps? Like I say, I can do it all. Oh, I'm so glad we have you. You're what our town has been crying out for. A breath of fresh air.'

'Well. Goodbye now.'

'Oh, yes. You have a masterpiece to put together. See you at the audition. You sure you can't give me any tips?'

'Just give your name in at the Town Hall.' He closes his door on me. I understand. He's a busy bee. Needs to be by himself, serve himself some creative time. I step up to the front window of his house, give him a friendly wave when he appears inside his sitting room. He looks like he has seen a ghost, and for the next minute or two he makes a great fuss of looking for something. He locates his phone and starts calling someone. But there is no need to stick around to find out who it might be. I've gotten to say my few words. Make an impression.

It's going to be fun.

Isn't is, Laura?

Yes, it is, Laura. Indeed it most certainly is.

# 14

I don't believe it. Imelda has been in touch again.

*Dearest Laura, rather thought I might have heard back from you. That's OK. If you're anywhere near as busy as I am right now I completely pardon you. Where do I start? I mean where do I start? What am I saying, I know exactly where to start. Venice. Where else!* Unhitched *won the Golden Lion (how the Italians laughed when I called it a tiger, thought it adorable). And – wait for it – guess who won the Volpi Cup for best actress? That's right. Can you believe it? Jennifer L was the hot favourite – the shoo-in – and needless to say she wasn't best pleased when my name came out of the envelope. Everybody else, though. They were thrilled for me, gave me a standing ovation. Oh, Laura! It was all so surreal. I can't even remember what I said in my victory speech, who I thanked, where I ended up that night. I've attached a pic. And, yes, that is a Donatella Versace number I am squeezed into. But enough about clothes. I was a huge hit in Venice. And I think I've fallen in love – with Venice, I mean. The canals. The bridges. The coffee. The wine. And maybe one or two men. Ha ha!*

*I got back to London late last night. Oh, Laura! It is not even Monday afternoon and already this week I have given three phone interviews, done copious face time with the latest gaggle of vloggers, ignored I've lost count of how many calls from Sir Henry wanting me to sit down with myriad moneybag producers. Time and time again I've had to put off meeting with some perfume company that wants to give me a million dollars for salivating at some putrid new fragrance a rabid skunk would most likely skedaddle from. Oh, and wait for this. My publicist has presented me with an agenda which decrees I be in not one not two not even three but four places at identical times on Wednesday afternoon. How are we going to work this, I said to Falstaff (my publicist, and I know what you're thinking, but yes, that is his real name). Work what, Melly? (That's what Falstaff calls me.) And I had to point out the flawed schedule to him, the schedule he himself had drawn up. He didn't even realize! And here. Just as I write this, along comes yet another request to go on morning television. Hello and goodbye! Don't they realize I like my beauty sleep? And the offers! They are rolling in. (Today alone: some kitchen-sink nonsense about a self-harming woman and her kleptomaniac little boy. A magical-realist fable involving some*

*kind of forest-woman certain in her belief that no
one ever dies. A voice-over in something called* The
Marzipan Hippo. *Oh, and a television adaptation of
the play that made my name.) Television, Laura!
Can you believe that? Utter insanity. Oh, and I have
a stalker. A hack from some gutter press. He's been
trailing me for I don't know how long. We had a
showdown at the airport, actually. I still don't know
who let him into the VIP lounge. Anyway, Ennio
(yummy! – more about him anon, I hope) came to
my rescue. OK. They are actually screaming for me
now. Get in touch, please – I want to hear from my
favourite understudy. Kiss, kiss. Bang, bang. You're
dead! Mel. x*

*PS Don't forget the premiere. Leicester Square
on the Thursday!*

*PPS There's some footage of me almost falling
out of the gondola – look it up!*

Vloggers. Premieres. Television talk shows. My, my. Isn't it
well for some? Not to mention all the offers she seems to
feel are clogging up her days – anyone would think her a
little ungrateful the way she is going on. And what is this
understudy nonsense she keeps banging on about? Venice
gondolas! Look it up, she says. Afraid I don't have time at
the moment, Imelda – or should I say *Melly* – sort of busy
myself, so if it's OK with you I'll take a rain check.

\*

It's Friday. A day I use to set aside a couple of hours for my weekly trip to the cemetery. I am going out the door when mother hijacks me. At once, as I knew she would, she starts in at me about making more of an effort with Jennifer. She cares about you. She wants the two of you to be friends. And there is a mini-sermon about how tough a time Jennifer has been having. 'You didn't mention Alonso, did you?' I hear her say when I tune in again. 'I did last night, and she became very upset.' And I have to stand there and listen to another saga. Something to do with Jennifer and her man, Alonso, deciding to return to Mexico recently. The plan being that Alonso would travel on ahead, find a place, get settled, then send for Jennifer and Little Juan. They said goodbye to each other at the airport and that's the last Jennifer has seen or heard of him. 'I think she's given him most of her money,' mother whispers at the conclusion of her story. 'Don't say a thing to her.'

'Mum's the word,' I say, continuing towards the door, but mother hasn't quite finished yet.

'Invite her somewhere. Do something together.'

'OK, OK,' I say, wanting it to stop, and go take a look for her.

To my great relief Jennifer is busy chasing her luggage, her Mexican bank account, and organizing some forms for her next work contract. I am loath to interrupt such important goings on. Assuring mother I will check in with her again, I leave her to it. And carry on out of there.

*

Stepping through the rusty cemetery gates, I make my way as far as the grave I have come to visit.

'Hello, daddy,' I say, when I reach the headstone. 'The bother of the house is back.' I set down the brandy I've brought and perch myself on the gravesite's granite edging, adjusting my bony posterior to ensure the best possible position.

So, daddy. Today I have three pieces of news for you. Two important pieces and one not-so important. The important news has to do with the theatre here in town. That's right, Khaos Theatre. And before you say anything, yes, I know this is the same theatre company that put on that nonsense version of *Virginia Woolf*. And yes, it is the same theatre company with a certain director who wondered was I the right fit for his theatrical vision. But listen to me. That imbecile has hightailed it to another outfit unlucky enough to secure his services after his vision flopped like a weeping willow. And now this very same company is suddenly all talk of a different approach and the first thing they have done is hire a brand-new hotshot director.

I've already met with him a couple of times – he reminds me a little of you, actually, except his nose isn't as manly as yours, and his hands are smaller. He has some great ideas, daddy. He says he's going to shake up the theatre in this town. And listen to this, his first idea is none other than a Tennessee Williams classic from the 1940s. That's right. *Streetcar*. Can you believe it?

His name is Stephen Fallow. I like that name. It oozes respect and admiration. Just the right amount of authority.

It has an aura. And I am certain that, as we become better acquainted, it will be clear to Stephen that he and I were born to work together. I tell you, daddy, he is cut from a very different jib than the washout he has replaced. He has oodles of experience, has done important work in London and spent time in New York and parts of Europe, and – wait for it – has been a fan of old movies since he was a boy. I really get the feeling he thinks I have what he is looking for. He was even good enough to hear me out while I ran a couple of my own ideas past him. This is it, daddy, this is the chance I have been waiting for.

I was so excited I stayed up last night and watched *Sunset Blvd* three times. Oh, daddy! I do so enjoy Gloria Swanson. No one plays a former star looking to make a comeback quite the way she does. *Have they forgotten what a star looks like? I'll be up there again, so help me!* That's a line that could have been written for me. They don't make them like they used to. That's what Doc Harper says during our talks and I am not inclined to disagree. Which brings me to my second piece of important news. Imelda has been in touch. Remember her, daddy? Imelda Ebbing. She's been treading the boards in London. And gone down a storm if her reports are anything to go by. I'll say this for her – she's well able to big herself up. A little too able, if you know what I mean. Memory loss seems to be a problem for her too – she has it inside that noggin of hers that I was once her understudy. Understudy! Now she's making movies. She even mentioned something about me coming over to the premiere of her new one. I was just about to send my reply to that . . . *thank you so, so much for the invitation, dearest Imelda, but sadly I will be unable to attend the premiere, you see, I have an acting career of my own to be getting on with* . . . when mother turned up. At first I thought she had gotten up and come downstairs to let me know my night-time mooching about was interrupting everybody's beauty sleep, and that I would have to cut short my time with Norma Desmond. But no. She just sat into the sofa alongside me and for a few minutes watched the movie with me. Then she rubbed my arm, said something about it being great that Jennifer is home and isn't it great to finally meet her little boy. Which brings me to the not-so-important piece of news – I almost forgot to mention it. Your other daughter has appeared. All the way from Mexico she has come – little boy in tow. Mother – and pretty much everyone else for that matter – is falling over themselves to get close to her. You should see her. Lean arms, shining hair, brown as a slab of Dairy Milk chocolate. Actually, I have a photograph I can show you. Ah, here she is. I suppose she has a great face – a face for the big screen, as you would say. According to mother she's home for a while. Won't that be grand? Right, mother. With her listen-to-me jibber and I-am-saving-the-world swagger. Mother, along with everyone else, seems to think she has Glinda the Good Witch staying with her, but I am on to her little act.

Anyway, home she may be after all this time, most likely I am not going to have much time for her – now that I have the role of a lifetime to get ready for. I've already got half an idea for my audition. It's going to blow everyone away.

I just know it is. Watch this space, daddy, you are going to be so proud.

I am still holding the phone in front of me, am about to delete the photograph and pretend-feed it to the worms poking out of the ground when I hear her.

'Hello.'

'What are you doing here?'

'Same thing as you.'

'Well, this is my time. Go find your own.'

'Well, I'm here now. Is it OK if I stay for a little while?'

I say nothing to that. Swing around. She can talk to my back if she wants.

'I heard you talking.'

'God bless your ears.'

'I wasn't listening. I just thought it a nice thing.'

She moves closer to the headstone. Rights a vase of wilting flowers that has overturned. Replaces the flowers with some tulips she has brought. Picks up and looks at one of the black-and-white movie postcards set down against the gravestone.

'Remember the two of you used to watch those old movies together.'

'Hmmm.'

'If you have time to spare, maybe we could see one together. A movie, I mean. Something at the multiplex.'

'I don't go to multiplexes. Anyway, I'm busy.'

'Oh. And what has you so busy?'

'You're not the only person in the world with things to do.'

'OK. Another time, then.'

For a couple of minutes she stands graveside without uttering a word, then turns as though to leave again. Then she pauses and looks my way. 'He was my father too, you know.'

I bet she wishes she was here by herself. I'm sure she'd have plenty to say to daddy. All that wonderful-me-saving-the-world stuff. Tell him all about her little boy. I feel the blood stir inside me. Jennifer is speaking again.

'What has you so busy that you can't come to the cinema?'

My blood is galloping now. She lingers for a moment, slow-turning around. I try not to, but she is giving me too much time. And there. I've done it.

'If you must know I have an audition to get ready for.'

'What?'

'That's what you heard. I'm practising.'

'Practising?'

'My lines. For the part I'm going for.'

'In the theatre?'

'It's a fairly big part.'

'Really?'

'That's why I came out here. You know, try to get inside my character's head.'

'OK . . . does mam know?'

'No and I don't think I want to tell her just yet. I want it to be a surprise.'

'OK . . . but . . .'

'So would you mind keeping it to yourself? For now, anyway. It can be our little secret.'

'OK . . . but do you think that's a good idea?'

'Dance first, think later. That's my philosophy.'

She doesn't say anything to that. Have nothing else I want to say either. Instead, spin myself around so that I am no longer looking her way. Picking up on my attitude, she isn't long gathering herself. My eyes follow her as she starts to move away. Keep going, I hiss, keep going until you reach the end of the world. And then step right off.

And there! 'Do you want to go for a drink?' I hear myself call after her. She stops and turns around.

# 15

When her time came along Jennifer did a course in community support. Or was it How To Rescue the World in Five Easy Steps? Whatever it was called, she had no sooner graduated than she was anointing herself saviour of the developing world and had informed mother of her intentions to hightail it to the bowels of Somalia in order to feed a starving village. Once she had fed the initial village, she moved around the rest of the country. According to her own report, word soon spread of her good work and her services were in big demand. People in the remote jungles of Paraguay wanted her. The slums of Brazil. And the Mexicans. The Mexicans were lighting candles that she would show up. She didn't need a second invitation and was soon making plans to travel to Latin America.

Her plan was to start in Cuba, finish in Buenos Aires and rescue everywhere in between. A few weeks after she left we got the phone call about drama number one. His name was Felipe and he lived with his mother and pregnant sister. She bumped into Felipe on the streets of Havana. He had just lost his job and his pregnant sister was struggling. Jennifer tagged along with him to a cafe in a ramshackle neighbourhood so that she could meet the sister and hear the sad story in detail while she plied the unfortunate Felipe with cigars and mojitos. Presently, some more sad-luck couples joined the conversation and shared their tales of woe, and time and time again Jennifer was reaching into her money belt and fishing out note after note of the special high-value currency foreigners had to use. Naturally she was instantly popular and invited to take a little tour of the neighbourhood, and in each humble abode she was brought inside she was fed some rice and beans, and she in turn felt obliged to offer something by way of a gesture, and the people poured her glasses of local moonshine and she was the toast of the neighbourhood and the long and the short of it was that she woke up in her hotel room the following day with a splitting headache and an empty money belt. Mother didn't need to hear another word. She went straight to the bank and waited until she was assured over and over that, yes, the money transfer was on its way into Jennifer's account. As soon as she received it, Jennifer was on the next flight out of Havana.

In Mexico she met a freedom fighter or revolutionary, some sort of activist who also wrote poetry and had been in a Mexican film Jennifer was surprised we hadn't heard of, and he had been a champion boxer, and had a bag of degrees in business and marketing, and he had even thought long and hard about becoming a philosopher and a monk, but instead had started several businesses that had him travelling here, there and everywhere, and Jesus Mary, I was thinking, when this report arrived, with all this going on how on earth did he have time for wu-wu with Jennifer. Maybe with all that becoming-a-monk stuff going on he was somehow going to manage an immaculate conception. I said as much to mother when Jennifer Skyped to share the amazing news that she was going to be a mammy. Immaculate conception or not, mother was delighted with Jennifer's news, and when I had nothing worthwhile to contribute to the happy occasion, she scowled at me and suggested I have a long think about changing my attitude.

Of course mother had plenty to contribute, didn't need to be asked once let alone twice, was only too happy to toddle off to the bank and ensure another transfer was safely on its merry way into Jennifer's account.

The baba arrived, we met Juan over Skype, and mother wondered aloud when everyone would get to see each other in the flesh. The timing wasn't good, however. Jennifer and Alonso had decided to move further south. Alonso had some important things going on, first in Ecuador and then in Bolivia and then maybe in one or two other places – it was all very vague.

A couple of years later she was due home for Christmas. We – mother and me – bussed it up to the airport to welcome her home. So as to quickly spot her elder daughter appear with her luggage, mother had positioned herself in front of the arrival gates. That way, upon spotting Jennifer, she could let out a big whoop, rush through the waiting crowd and throw her arms around the homecomer. 'I want to hear everything,' mother practised asking Jennifer on the bus to the airport. If she didn't say it once she said it a hundred times. Jennifer never made it that Christmas. We waited four hours at the airport, maybe seven. Turned out she'd had to change her plans. 'A last-minute crisis,' Jennifer told mother a couple of days later, among other things, when the call explaining her no-show had finally come through. She couldn't make it the following Christmas either. Or the one after that – last Christmas. By then, she was busy helping forest clearers and seed planters in central Paraguay. That's what she said when that call came through. Ask her is there anything she needs? mother said to me when I accidentally answered the phone to her. What for? I said. We'll get a Christmas box ready for her, mother said. What is this *we* business? I said, not that it made any difference. And into the Christmas box went two night-lights, a bandwidth transistor and a pair of adjustable walking boots, as well as various pills to help ease constipation and diarrhoea, which essentially meant tossing extra boxes into the trolley when out shopping for mother that anxious Christmas week. Mother briefly contemplated sending out a batch of axe handles when Jennifer happened to mention how tough the work was and how poor the tools. Why don't we just show up and clear the forest for her, I said back to mother, and received another of her milk-curdling looks.

*

We're in Little Mary's now, tucked away together inside the smaller of the two snugs. I've just set down a pair of drinks, two pints of not-quite-settled Guinness over which Jennifer is emphatically enthusing.

'Oh, this was a good idea,' she says, reaching for her drink. 'Much better than going to the cinema.'

'To much better ideas,' I say, raising my glass.

'Cheers,' she says, taking a mouthful of the stout. 'Oh, that is so good. Do you know, I can't remember the last time I had a Guinness.'

She lifts the glass and takes another gulp.

'So tell me,' she says, wiping the froth from her top lip. 'What's the audition for this time?' Already, I'm sorry I mentioned it.

'*Streetcar*,' I say.

'*Streetcar*? What sort of a name . . .? Oh wait, you mean *A Streetcar Named Desire*? Oklahoma Williams, right?'

'Tennessee,' I say, gritting my teeth.

'Tennessee. That's what I meant. I think I've seen the film. It's about two sisters, right? And Marlon Brando. Yum-mee. Except he ends up not being very nice in it. Am I right?'

'Maybe.'

'Which of the sisters are you hoping to play? Wait! Let me guess. There's Stella. She's with Brando. And what's this the other one is called? The one who arrives on the streetcar at the beginning. It's a French-sounding name.'

'Blanche.'

'Blanche! That's it. Blanche DuBois! What a great name for a character. She's the scheming one, isn't she? The one who isn't what she appears to be.'

'It's more complicated than that.'

'Oh, then I'd say that's the part for you.'

She reaches for her glass again, doesn't seem to see me glaring at her, or if she does, is paying no heed. This time she finishes the drink, reaches for her wallet and stands up.

'Do you know what this Guinness tastes like?' she says.

'I think so,' I reply.

'It tastes like MORE. Tell you what. Let's have another drink and you can tell me all about what you've been up to since . . .'

'Since what?' I say, but she is already on her feet, making her way to the bar. At once I get busy with a message to Fleming. *In Little Mary's. Help!*

Moments later, she is back with two fresh glasses.

'Here we are,' she says, setting down the glasses and reclaiming her spot across from me. 'They say the first one is medicine. After that, who cares?' With either hand she flicks back her hair and angles her head so that she has a better view of the barroom.

'This place hasn't changed a bit, has it?' she says. 'One or two familiar faces up there, too. Billy Gibbons is there. What's this he's called?'

'Billy the Lush.'

'That's the one. It was really good of mam to look after Juan for the afternoon. Give us a chance to catch up like this.'

'How long are you staying?' I ask.

'You know, I haven't decided. Right now, I want Juan to get to know his granny and auntie.'

'Ah. So that's why you've been visiting non-stop since he was born.'

'Listen to you! You couldn't care less if you never see me.'

'Think what you like.'

'Thanks.'

'Don't mention it.'

'Oh, Laura, I don't want to fight with you. I want us to be friends. I want to root for you with this audition. I want things to be . . . Hey! Who is this fellow mother is seeing? He was there earlier, just before I left. Peter something or other, I didn't catch his second name.'

'Porter.'

'Porter. Really? What an appropriate name. Well, then. Here's to Peter Porter.' And she raises her glass and holds it aloft until I have raised my own. We have just clinked when I hear the resounding greeting.

'Hello!'

Fleming. It never takes him long to reach the bar when he is summoned. But this must go down as some kind of record. I wonder what could have enticed him to get here so quickly. And here he is. All arms and legs, clambering in on top of us.

'Don't tell me,' he says, elaborately wagging a finger in front of her. 'You must be Jennifer. I've been hearing quite a lot about you.'

'All good, I hope.'

'Like I say, I'm hearing plenty.'

Jennifer smiles and Fleming smiles, and space is made in the snug for the new arrival. Briefly, I wonder what would happen to those smiles if I were to grab each of them and mash their noggins together.

'Aren't you going to offer your friend a drink, Laura?'

'Please. Call me Fleming. Do what your sister says, Laura. Get Fleming a drink.'

'And I'll have a refill, Laura. Thank you.'

I leave them to it and make my way to the bar. I'm tempted to keep going, clear out of there altogether, but can't stomach the thoughts of them having a good time in my absence.

The barroom is filling up. I spy a woman in the other snug reading *The Memoirs of Sherlock Holmes*. A merry-looking fellow has taken centre stage in the main bar area. 'I feel like a bubble in the neck of a bottle of champagne,' he says, over and over again. Spellman, the journo from the *Advertiser*, is in, a limpid, wiry thing with a ridiculous quiff. Hawkins from the *Tribune*, camera dangling from his chubby neck. A lad with a fiddle walks in. 'I'm Goodtime Ray,' he announces, plants himself in the corner by the window and begins to draw his bow. His woe-is-me lyrics quickly bring Fizzy Bubble's jig to an end. Spellman and Hawkins move to the counter. 'I wouldn't like to hear Bad-time Ray,' growls a lad with a boiled head and beetroot neck.

'Same again, Laura?' Gerry the barman calls out when he spots me. I include the addition to the order, and while I'm at it nod to Billy's near-empty glass and he silently consents.

A familiar-looking couple enter the bar – the tourist couple from the pier, this time with identical baseball caps emblazoned with the words Virginia Beach. They sit themselves at the low table nearest the woe-is-me fiddle player. I am about to hail them when someone else clamps a hand onto my shoulder.

'Hello!' It's the minuscule woman from Minnesota. 'I never got to congratulate you on that performance during the walking tour,' she says, and presses a fifty into my hand. 'Keep it up,' she continues, making for the door.

'You have an admirer there,' Gerry says, leaving down the Guinness to settle.

Mr Virginia Beach stands up and has reached the bar before he turns around to his missus and in a heavy drawl wonders what she might like to drink. Without looking up from the selfie she is about to take, she mumbles something about soda water.

'Howdy,' he says when he has turned towards the bar again. He has no idea who I am.

'Howdy,' I reply.

'So what's hot in this town?' he asks me while trying to catch Gerry's attention.

'I am,' I say, and he starts laughing.

'That's funny. I'm going to remember that one.'

He grabs his drinks and returns to his wife. Gerry slaps my change onto the counter.

'You bothering my customers again?'

'I'm the only customer you need to worry about, Gerry.'

'I wonder what planet beamed that notion into your noodle.'

'Keep talking like that and I won't let you keep the change.'

'I'm just happy if you pay for the occasional drink.'

He tosses a couple of bags of crisps at me and turns to serve someone else. I pocket my change and am about to pick up the drinks when I feel the tap on my shoulder.

'Where did you go for those?'

Before I have a chance to claim them, Fleming has grabbed two glasses, marched them swiftly to the snug. I grab my own drink, the crisps and, by the time I have rejoined the boozers, Fleming and Jennifer are the best of friends.

'And I hear you do good work in the poor countries,' he says.

'Oh, I try to make a small difference here and there,' she replies.

'Here and there!' Fleming says, almost spilling his drink. 'I'd hardly call the places you've been to here and there. And how dare you say small difference? People like you are in short supply, let me tell you. People like you make *all* the difference. Laura, we are in the presence of a modern-day miracle worker.'

Listen to him. Miracle worker! And look at her. Lapping it all up. Every ridiculous bit of it.

'And I hear you have a little boy.'

'Yes. Five years old next birthday.'

'Wow,' Fleming says to that. 'I'd love to meet him.'

'Here, I have a picture.'

Jennifer sets down her glass, reaches for her purse and plucks out a photo which she passes over to Fleming.

'There's a good-looking fellow. Takes after his mother.'

'Not to mention his father,' I add.

'Of course,' Fleming says, still looking at the photo. 'Laura mentioned him. What's this you said his name was, Laura?'

'His name? Oh, I can't think. Help us out here, Jennifer.'

'Alonso,' she says, quietly. Very quietly.

'Sorry, can't hear you,' I say, shielding my ear.

'Alonso,' she says again, some of the wind gone from her sails.

'Alonso! That's the one.'

Fleming is beaming. He grabs the drink in front of him and takes a hearty gulp. 'You know, this is great,' he says, setting down the glass. 'We should make a plan to do something together. The three of us. There's lots of stuff happening. Hey! We could do something with Juan. I'd love to meet him.'

'You said that already,' I say, giving Fleming my best glare.

'I think he'd like that,' Jennifer says, warming again to Fleming's enthusiasm.

'So tell us, Jennifer,' he says next, giving all his attention to my sister. 'What's Alonso up to these days?'

Jennifer freezes, her glass poised at her lips. She takes a sip, and without watching what she is doing, she sets down the glass on a bag of crisps. The glass topples over and the stout spills everywhere.

She's on her feet again, steering clear of the spillage. Fleming hurries off to get a cloth. And a refill. 'No need,' she says, eyeing me. 'I have to go now.' By the time he gets back she is ready to leave.

'I hope you're not leaving on account of a spilt drink,' Fleming says.

'No . . . no. I . . . I need to get to the bank,' she says, and hurries out of there.

Fleming sets down his own drink, spreads out his arms and looks to me as though to say, What just happened?

## 16

Quay Street is packed. Terrorists are tucking in at outside tables beneath the restaurant awnings. The madman of Druid Lane leaps out of doorways, calls out randomly and clamps his ears to cracks in walls. The woman in black zig-zags her mongrel dogs towards the harbour. Goodtime Ray has pitched himself and his fiddle at the bottom end of the street, near the bridge. Seabirds squawk over the Claddagh.

'I wish you'd said something, Laura,' Fleming is saying. 'About Alonso. Hang on. You didn't do that on purpose, did you?'

'No harm done,' I say.

'No harm done? Your sister was practically in tears. I think you should call her.'

'That I will not be doing.'

'Well, if you're not going to, I am.'

Before I have a chance to ward him off, Fleming has snatched the phone out of my hand, is scrolling for the number. Half-heartedly, I make an effort to retrieve my phone. But he manages to keep me at arm's length.

'She's not answering,' he says, giving up and handing over the phone. 'Not that I blame her.'

'She'll be fine,' I say. 'She always is.'

Fleming looks at me and shakes his head. By now we

have reached the bottom of the street, where it opens out into the harbour.

'I want you to apologize to her,' Fleming says again. 'Apologize to her from me. Promise me you will.'

I shrug.

'Laura. Come on. That wasn't nice back there.'

'OK. OK. I'll apologize.'

'You better.'

'Jesus, what is this? I said I would.'

'What did you do that for anyway? It can't be easy for her, Laura. Especially if she's been left to bring up a little fellow all by herself.'

'Well, aren't you the shining knight all of a sudden.'

'I'm just pointing out the obvious.'

'Well, point somewhere else. I've had enough for one day.'

I check my pockets for more cash, feel for the fifty recently pressed upon me. I turn around and start back in the direction we have come from, reaching Little Mary's just in time to greet the terrorist from Virginia Beach.

'Howdy,' I call out.

'Howdy,' he says back, taking a good gander at the outside tables.

'Looking for something?'

'Yeah. My wife.'

'Lost her, eh. That tends to happen to wives in this place.'

Back inside I go.

*

A few hours and several drinks later, I have retraced my steps back to the harbour and am crossing Tone Bridge.

I pause halfway across, greet the Beggar Flynn and look out into the harbour. The sun is dipping, shadows drift across the Claddagh, and the city seems suspended between the hustle and bustle of daytime and its panoply of after-dark allure. For once the west wind has called it a day, the swans are out and the harbour water appears as a sheet of glass reflecting the colours of the Claddagh and the Long Walk.

A calm before the storm.

'Isn't that right, Beggar?' I say, without averting my gaze.

'Isn't what right?'

'Storms, Beggar. I'm talking about storms.'

I turn away from the water just in time to see him hiss after a pair of suited men who take turns stepping over the cap placed in the middle of the footpath. The first of the men then tosses an empty cigarette box over the bridge wall, and I follow its progress as it lands and then settles on the surface water before the current carries it away.

'Did I ever tell you what happened to my daddy, Beggar?'

'Did I ever ask you to stop calling me Beggar?'

'Ah, Beggar, when have you and I ever done what we are asked?'

If Beggar has anything to say to that he is keeping it to himself. I tip the remains of the fifty into his cap, continue across the bridge, turn left and stroll towards Nimmo's Pier, not stopping until I reach the raised wall along the wind-ward side of the pier-end.

I loved coming out here with daddy when I was little. Especially in the autumn and winter months. The days were shorter and colder and wetter, there were fewer people around, at times we had the pier and the west wind all to ourselves. Whatever the weather we always walked to the very end and then stood side by side, wordlessly taking in whatever we could see. Swans. Fishing boats. The occasional Hooker, ever graceful on the water. The wind did its best to blow us hither and thither, and eventually daddy would motion for us to head back. Sometimes he might gather me up and haul me, kicking and squealing with delight, until he put me down again. My favourite moment was when the pier lights came on, whereupon daddy would hunker down beside me, wrap one arm around me and with the other point to the blurry lights. *Look, Laura. Can you see it? The Walk of Fame.*

It was during autumn and winter that the Claddagh Players would put their shows together. I can see them all, gathering for an evening of rehearsals in the hall they used. Cajoling each other. Arguing over who should play what part. The names I heard them call each other. The faces I saw. Greece McLoughlin. Kilala Joyce. Billy the Lush. Chopper Fallon. Jinx Fahy. These were the ones I remember most. The stalwarts. The ones that insisted the show must go on and, for a while anyway, made sure it did. There was a flaming Rita Hayworth-style redhead that turned everybody's head whenever she chose to turn up. Her name was Josephine Blake. All Josephine had to do was hint that she'd like to be involved and there would be a part for her.

After rehearsals everyone would sit around and talk plays and scripts, big up all the shows they were going to put on, all the theatre adventures they were going to have. National tours. Festivals. And after that – who knew? At some point daddy would drag everyone back to the house and they would settle in the kitchen for a long night of drink and song and banter. The longer they sat up the larger the adventures became. They would take turns telling stories, sing songs and fill their glasses with wine and beer and whiskey, and on and on into the little hours of the night they would go. Sometimes, if it was clear, they would take the party outside, into the front garden, guitars and drinks and song and dance going until first light. Sometimes, I joined them. Other times, I was content to watch them from my bedroom window. Always, I wanted to be a proper part of their troupe, and time and time again I swore to myself when my time came I would be just like them.

Every autumn they chose a play. They talked about the best way to stage it, they built their own sets, cobbled together old clothes, learned how to rig up the lights. They rehearsed until they knew their parts back to front.

Best of all was opening night of their chosen show. Didn't matter what it was. *Juno and the Paycock. The Playboy of the Western World. Philadelphia, Here I Come! A Streetcar Named Desire. Death of a Salesman.* The hall was packed. The place buzzing with anticipation. Along with Josephine Blake, daddy played the lead role in *Streetcar*. Stanley Kowalski. On stage he looked like he had been dipped in a barrel of grease. I was riveted to every minute

kicked in and she tries to convince everyone that a rich and dashing admirer has just been in touch to invite her on a cruise of the Caribbean. And the deliberate cruelty bit – after Stanley confronts her with all he has found out about her. That might work. Then there is the ending itself. The doc and matron have arrived to cart her away to the funny farm and so deluded is Blanche that she thinks it really is the dashing admirer with his pockets on come to whisk her off on his yacht. *I have always depended on the kindness of strangers.* That always goes down a treat. Then again, maybe not. Everybody else going for the part will have thought along those lines. I even go back to the very beginning, where Blanche arrives at her sister's place in New Orleans, just so as I can say all those stations along the tramline. *They told me to take a streetcar named Desire, and then transfer to one called Cemeteries and ride six blocks and get off at – Elysian Fields.* Then I read over the scene where Blanche goes on a date with Stanley's best friend, Mitch, especially the part when they return to the empty apartment and Blanche gets to telling Mitch of her early love and what happened to him and why, and something mysterious happens, something fragile, that seems to reveal itself in the dark-of-night moment Blanche and Mitch share together. It reminds me of what daddy said to me all that time ago: life is just a few moments when it all comes down to it. And, yes, I think. This scene might be the one.

Happy with what I am resolved to do, I message Fleming to let him know, ask can we hook up so as I can try out my scene, but all he is interested in knowing is have I apologized to Jennifer. *Tomorrow,* I message back, and that is the end of the conversation.

I'm about to toss my phone when I notice the message from Imelda. It's a friendly link to *Stage & Screen,* and of course I cannot resist clicking on it, and when I do it loads up the glossy cover image and lo-and-behold I am face to face with my acting buddy of yore. It's a flattering image, photoshopped good-oh (way too much gloss, *Melly dearest,* way too much) and there is an extract from the interview she has done for the illustrious arts magazine. Her answers are far too lengthy and so I just read the questions, a medley of gushing invitations to explain her appeal, list the parts she was born to play, her advice for budding starlets, current state of mind, finest accomplishment to date. *Imelda, everything seems effortless to you. What is the secret?* Yes, Imelda, do share with us the secret of your success. Raw talent? Incessant toil? A special diet only you are privy too? *And lastly, Imelda, in your own words, how would you like to be remembered?* Blah, blah, blah, blah, blah.

The women on the wall are not going to let me leave it at that, however. *What are you at, woman? You're every bit as talented as Imelda Ebbing (what sort of a name is that!). If she can do it, you can too. Come on, now. Snap out of it.* Then, as though suddenly seized by some momentous thought, Gloria stirs herself, angles her face in my direction, unfurls a braceleted arm, and with a curling index finger motions me towards her. *Closer, Laura. Closer. The cameras are turning. They're waiting for the star. Are you ready? This is your life. It always will be. There's nothing else. Just you and the camera. And all those wonderful people out there in the dark.*

That comment, though – the one about everything being so effortless – reminds me of something I remember hearing Billy the Lush say to daddy all that time ago. You make it look so easy, Frank, Billy had said, still shaking his head hours after an opening-night performance of *Streetcar* that had brought the audience to its feet. And I remember daddy freezing to the spot where he was standing, and then staring intensely at something only he could see. Being on stage is easy, he finally said. It's the real world, getting through the days hours minutes, that's the difficult part.

I hear you, daddy. I really do.

## 18

Peter Porter is in the kitchen the following morning. He and mother met on a dating site – after, it must be said, she had considered and in her own way auditioned several non-starters. For a time I had even chipped in my tuppence worth – when asked, of course. Amongst those most vivid in my memory include Damien the archivist, Manus the dentist and Steve the insurance broker. Mother liked that Damien was involved with printed matter. I wasn't gone on his height (six feet six), his looks (think Freddy Kruger meets pretty much any of the Munchkins in *The Wizard of Oz*) nor his keenness for arching his eyebrows in surprise every time mother said something (boo! I said, and he didn't even blink). Oh, look, mother said upon perusing Manus the dentist's profile, he's offering free check-ups. Mother, I said, backing away from the garishly real tooth on the screen before us, allow that man inside your mouth and I will set your hair on fire. Then came (and quickly went) Steve the insurance broker (drooling mouth, noisy nose, goodbye Steve); Bruce the estate agent (Bruce, mother, Bruce!); Brian the auctioneer (going once, going twice, and keep, keep going until well out of sight, Brian) and Paul 'To be honest after all this time I'm still not sure what it is I'd like to do with my life but right now I'm really into bees – it's time we all started thinking about the bees, right?' If you say so, Paul, now please – buzz off. Early promise was shown by primary school teacher and father-of-four Brendan (soft spoken, kind eyes, wife killed in a car crash). Then we met the four (little Hitlers) and I told mother that I would never speak to her again if she did not at once take out an irreversible restraining order. Jerome the plumber looked good – so long as the looking was confined to his online pic. In the flesh he was a bit of a let-down. Actually, he reminded me of the American presidential candidate – orange on the outside, hollow on the inside, get rid before anything has a chance to happen.

For a while I thought it was fun being on the side that gets to choose who gets to set foot inside our door. Plus, I liked it that mother sounded me out, it was something we were in together, a conspiracy. That is until she started to realize that my opinions had a tendency to veer somewhere between oh my God please say you are *not* going out with him (Damien, Manus, Steve and Bruce) and bring that man inside this house and I will not be held responsible for what happens (Brian, Paul and Brendan). There were one or two I will admit to being vaguely curious about. But by then it scarcely mattered because mother had started – via Skype of course – to involve Jennifer in her deliberations.

And, la-di-dah, enter Peter Porter.

To look at him you would not think his name is Peter Porter. He is tall, and angular, with large inquisitive eyes, and he seems to propel himself forward via the use of his knees – as opposed to his feet. Though he has little hair, he likes to use a comb. According to his profile he used to play table tennis and had a walloping forehand. These days, he works in a camera shop on Shop Street and likes showing mother the latest 'photograph of the week', whether it is a photograph he or someone else has taken he doesn't say. To me, he is more Philip than Peter. More Phibbs than Porter. And leaving and entering rooms do have a tendency to present him with difficulties. Last time he was here, he went upstairs to use our bathroom and, moments after he had excused himself, mother and me could hear this persistent rattling sound. He then reappeared, holding in his hand the handle of our bathroom door, and enquiring as to the existence of a second toilet. Still. He and mother get along well together – at least they have for the four or five months they have known each other. He calls by on his days off. Once or twice I have bumped into him tiptoeing out our front door late into the night. This is the first time we have crossed paths at breakfast. And recently he has ramped up his mission to haul mother out of the country. Whisk her away from it all. What I should do is get him to take some profile shots of me. I'm going to need them where I'm headed.

Isn't that right, Laura?

Yes, it is, girl. Yes, it most certainly is.


'So what is going down, Laura?' he says to me when I show up in the kitchen. For some reason he likes addressing me as though he is an edgy rock 'n' roll promoter, and I am his protégé all set to conquer the world. To be fair to him, he is not a million miles away.

'You tell me, Peter,' I reply. 'You look as though you are ahead of the day.'

Peter smiles. I smile. He combs over some rogue strands of hair. I drum the table with my middle and index finger. Peter reaches for the cutting knife.

'Would you like a slice of cheese?'

'No,' I say.

'Why not?' he says, a look immense disappointment suddenly taking over his face.

'Don't eat cheese,' I say. 'It complicates my dreams.'

He cuts a slice for himself. I am about to leave when he clears his throat.

'Laura, can you help me with something?'

'Me?' I even sound surprised to myself.

'Mary – your mother – has never been outside the country.'

'OK.'

'If she was to go somewhere – outside the country – where do you suppose she might choose?'

'Paraguay,' I say, without blinking an eye.

'Paraguay!' Peter Porter did not expect that answer.

'Oh, yes,' I say, summoning as much earnestness as I can. 'She dreams about the jungles of Paraguay all the time. Has she not said anything?'

'No. No, she hasn't.'

'We're such a secretive family. Meet us in an elevator and we won't tell you if we're going up or down,' I say, and leave him to his uncertain pondering.

## 19

I do what Fleming has told me to do and square things with Jennifer. He'll stay on my case if I don't and no doubt mother will get wind too. I'm sorry for bringing up Alonso like that, I say when I seek her out. Steering the conversation that way was cruel and childish, and I suppose I was a little jealous of all the attention Fleming was giving you and wanted to get at you somehow. I shouldn't have done it and I am really, really sorry. She looks at me, wary, suspicious even, for a few seconds I honestly can't say which way she is going to fall, will she accept my humble words or throw them back in my face? Then she makes a beeline for me, tells me it's all right, let's put it behind us, from here out we are going to be the best of friends, and once again I find myself wrapped up in those arms.

To further extend the olive branch I offer to cook a meal for everyone. Myself and Jennifer and Little Juan. Mother and Peter Porter. Jennifer thinks it a great idea and of course feels it ought to be a joint effort and so offers some suggestions. No, no, no, I insist, I have it all under control. Then I message Fleming to get himself over here. And bring something nice to cook, I tell him, it's time to deliver on a promise made the very first time we met.

*

Later that same day Fleming turns up with a purple eye, a shopping bag of ingredients, and announces he is taking over cooking duties. He is holding aloft a tin of tomatoes and a packet of spaghetti, and what happened this time I am about to ask, trying not to look at his eye, when Jennifer reaches around me and drags Fleming inside. Purple eye or not, she is delighted to see him, and now she, too, wants in on the cooking, is already examining what Fleming has arrived with. Then Little Juan appears, and Fleming makes a huge spectacle out of their first meeting. Well, well, well. Who have we here? No, let me guess. And he proceeds into listing out an increasingly ludicrous-sounding batch of boys' names that aren't boys' names or girls' names or any kind of names for that matter. Is your name Snickers? Is it Scallion? Sun-dried Tomato? Wait. I think it's Bean Sprout. Yes, that's it. Come along, Bean Sprout. After an initial bout of shyness that has Little Juan cling to his mother's skirt, it is only a matter of time before Fleming has the little fellow in stitches. 'Oh, and did you hear about the magic tractor? It turned into a field.'

As soon as he has stacked up the ingredients, he enlists Little Juan into the cause. 'I am Big Chef,' Fleming says. 'And you are Little Chef.' He even produces two paper hats, one for each of them. And the little fellow is only too happy to muck in. 'First things first,' Fleming declares. 'A pair of cocktails for the chefs.' And he produces some fruit juice and sparkling water and gets busy pouring and shaking and spilling stuff everywhere. Little Juan giggles and covers his face with his hands. Jennifer squeezes her boy and points at Fleming. 'Who is that silly man making a big mess? Who is that man calling you Bean Sprout?' I can think of a few answers I'd like to offer, but now a food fight has commenced and already I have been zapped in the face by a clump of Branston pickle, banana peel and wedge of bitter lemon.

Fleming and Juan and Jennifer chop and peel and cut. Mother and Peter Porter appear and insist on joining in. Something gets bunged in the oven. Peter Porter pours the wine he has managed to magic up. An hour or so later the six of us are gathered around the kitchen table. Mother and Fleming are already talking television.

'Have you seen *The Wire*?' she asks him.

'Of course,' Fleming replies. 'What's your favourite season?'

'I like the one where they go into the schools.'

'Yep. It's a class act. I follow David Simon on Twitter.'

'Who is David Simon?'

'The writer. The creative genius behind *The Wire*.'

'Oh.'

'Fleming thinks TV is where it's at, mother,' I say. 'He has his own ideas for shows.'

'Oh, really? Have you seen *House of Cards*, Fleming?'

'Nonsense,' Fleming says. 'Every bit of it. You need to see *The West Wing* if that's the sort of thing you're after. The Aaron Sorkin ones.'

'Who is Aaron Sorkin?'

'He's another creative genius,' I say. 'Isn't that right, Fleming?'

'I have the entire boxset. One hundred and fifty-six episodes. I'll bring it around.'

Mother is thrilled and, suitably encouraged, Fleming segues into a lengthy sermon on the merits of *The West Wing* over *House of Cards*. Bored now, I turn to the others.

Peter Porter is grilling Jennifer as to what her stomping grounds have to offer the intrepid traveller. 'What about Venezuela?' Peter asks. 'I'd love to see the Angel Falls. Or the Salt Flats in Bolivia. Or Buenos Aires. I hear that's well worth a visit.'

'And don't forget my suggestion, Peter,' I say, with an elbow-and-wink.

'And what was that?' Jennifer wants to know.

'Oh, I'm afraid it's top secret,' I go on. ' A surprise. That right, Peter?'

Peter smiles. 'What about Mexico?' he asks.

'Don't get her going on Mexico,' I say, and from mother receive a please-don't-start look. But Jennifer's already had enough out of me. She gets up from the table and switches on the kitchen television. Flicks through the channels.

'Leave that on a minute,' Fleming says when something about the upcoming US presidential election pops up.

'Who do you think will win?' Peter Porter asks of no one in particular, and at once and in unison Jennifer, Fleming and mother pile in with their opinions.

'Who do *you* think will win?' I say, turning to Little Juan. And the two of us proceed to make faces at each other, at the others, and with the others, especially Jennifer, distracted by the television, we polish off the last of the Curly Wurlys and Stinger bars Fleming has brought for dessert.

A short time later everyone has eaten their fill. I'm not sure exactly what it is we have eaten – I doubt anybody is – if the empty plates and bowls are anything to go by, Big Chef and Little Chef have done a good job. Bean Sprout, I say to Fleming after the little fellow has been put to bed. You think that's good, he is fast to say, we decided to call you Chipsticks.

Later again, after Fleming has elaborated on what happened to his eye (brothers, fists, yet again) and, courtesy of the Mogadon he was suddenly curious about, has fallen asleep on my bed, and Peter Porter has done likewise in the sitting room (without Mogadon), I notice mother and Jennifer talking quietly together in the kitchen. It's more Jennifer than mother and I move closer to the half-open door in order to catch what is being said. To my amazement she begins with an apology, and I am just in time to hear Jennifer tell mother how sorry she is for not making it home more often. Summertime. Christmas. The occasional birthday. She is so sorry. Sorry is the last word mother wants to hear out of Jennifer's mouth. 'You're here now, and that is all that matters,' mother says, squeezing her older daughter's shoulder. 'My life is a mess,' Jennifer says next. 'What are you talking about?' mother says. 'Look at what you have done. Look at all the good work you are doing. Look at Juan. And speaking of birthdays,' mother is fast to add, 'a certain someone has a big day coming up. A certain significant birthday. And we should do something to mark it. Something special.'

Big day or not, Jennifer sounds like she is going to need more persuading. Her faraway bank now maintains that Jennifer Cassidy does not exist. And her luggage is proving impossible to trace. Jennifer shakes her head and berates the pair of fools she has earlier spent an hour talking to. Soon the entire Mexican nation is getting it from her, whatever its unfortunate involvement in this ever-deteriorating situation. Nor has she been able to get through to her boss. She needs to sort out a start date for her new contract, and every time she tries to get hold of Ultan (Jesus!) she either gets a leave-a-message, which she proceeds to do in her best phone-call accent but doesn't hear back, or a strange-sounding dial tone, which has her suspect that either the service provider is playing games with its customers or the phone itself is damaged. To cap it all there has been no word from Alonso. Throughout all of this, mother sits opposite Jennifer, listening intently to every detail. Presently the waterworks are turned on, their arrival immaculately timed and in beautiful harmony with the dramatic preamble. All in all it is a re-markable performance, deserving, I for one feel, of a round of ecstatic applause. *Brava! Brava!* Mother, though. She doesn't see things this way. She has grasped one of Jennifer's hands, while the other offers a hankie that Jennifer uses to dab her sniffling nose. And more and more I am thinking: this one is good. Really, really good.

And cue mother pulling out all the stops to cheer up Jennifer. And this is when I make the startling discovery that this imminent birthday mother has earlier alluded to, this so-called significant special big day she wants to put together, is not for Little Juan after all. It is Jennifer she has in mind. It is Jennifer's birthday that is just around the corner. Her thirtieth birthday.

How remiss of me to allow it slip my mind.

When I half-tune in again, all I can hear is talk of the great evening in store. With plates of this and platters of that and I'll get Peter to bring his guitar, mother says. And Yoohoo Lucy Garavan might help with the food. Fleming too. We can invite some of the crew from the neighbour-hood. And we'll take a spin around the shops for something nice to wear. Laura might come with us. It'll be fun, Jennifer. Little Juan will have fun too.

If mother will be looking to me for this plan to grow some feathers and fly-me-to-the-moon wings, she can think again. And quick as a match I skedaddle to my room.

## 20

I narrow down to two the scenes I want to do (Blanche tells Mitch of her first love and of how she betrayed him; Blanche, knowing she now has nothing to lose, reveals her sordid past to Mitch) and in my room take turns practising both of them. Mother and Peter Porter sit in the kitchen and over tea, wine, and other assorted treats, the one painstakingly tries to alight on a mutually agreeable place to visit and the other heatedly throws her arms into the air and repeats the words no, no and no! Jennifer commandeers the sitting room and spends her time on the phone alternately trying to locate Alonso, get through to her boss, describe the contents of her luggage, and let the Mexicans have it for the great job they've done denying she exists. Meanwhile, Little Juan passes his time trotting from room to room with varying combinations of amusement and perplexity as he witnesses the women he is related to in varying states of emotional disorder.

When it gets too much I make myself scarce. I stride around the harbour. Along the river. The canal. Waterside. The quieter parts of town, at less busy times of day. On a couple of occasions I haul myself as far as Barna Woods. I check in with the trees, perform my best lines for them. Eventually, I take a break and reach deep inside the hollowed-out oak and flick through the scrapbook, pausing here and there when something of interest catches my eye.

On the bridge, I chat with the Beggar about storms that come and go, and storms that outstay their welcome.

I swing by the Goldmine and collect my meds.

I do an extra shift or two of tour-guide duty. I take a busload of Americans through the Saturday market, spin yarns about potatoes (potatoes from Kerry are the most expensive. Longford, Leitrim and Roscommon potatoes are going for a song. Potatoes from Dublin are given away). I bring a bunch of unusually impressed Germans inside St Nick's and share all my info about the ancient church. I show a collection of curious Asians the Cathedral and delight in their over-the-top enthusiasm for my graphic descriptions of all things squalid that happened inside the women's prison that stood on this very site. So pleased am I that I haul them to the Town Hall on the off chance I'll get to perform one of my chosen scenes for Stephen's benefit.

I pick my spot outside the building and have the tour group gather round. I explain to them that I am to be the lead in a forthcoming production and that I like surprising my director with impromptu teasers from the part I am playing. Then I produce my *Streetcar* paperback, flick it open, and have hit my stride, declaiming poetically about long, rainy afternoons in New Orleans as I summon my young prince out of the Arabian Nights to move willingly closer, when the doors of the Town Hall swing open.

Alas, it is not a prince who presents himself, willing or otherwise. Camilla the Hun appears on the steps and wants to know in no uncertain terms precisely what I think I am at. The sour head on her. The officious hands. In her spare time she probably strangles kittens. 'Ah, go chase some apes in hell,' I spew at her and usher my faithful troupe well out of harm's way.

*

Home again and mother is taking tea with Fiona French, Odd Doris, Dolores Taaffe and home from Spain Yoohoo Lucy. Jennifer has joined them too. But it is Lucy who is holding court. Laying it all on about her recent trip to Alicante, and the eating habits of the Spaniards. How, apart from a couple of hours shut-eye in the afternoon, they eat all the time. Except they don't make sows of themselves like we do around here. No. What they do is nibble. A bowl of olives here. A plate of sardines there. Perhaps a saucer of pigs' tongues. The most divine stuffed mushrooms. The sweetest cherries. The juiciest oranges. And as for the ham . . . three words, ladies, three words. *To die for.*

'Hello, Laura, and how are you today?' she takes time out to say as I pass through, while at the same time giving me her head-to-toe once-over so as that she will later have something to offer on one of her pet subjects – how I have been doing since my little incident on opening night – and how recovery from something like what I went through takes time, especially when the cause is probably a little more deep-rooted than mere performance anxiety. Yoohoo

Lucy has the knack of always sounding like an expert. I will say that for her. 'Hello to you, Lucy,' I reply without stopping. 'I hear you flashed the nipples in Alicante.'

I have already exited the kitchen and am about to continue up the stairs when Jennifer starts in on our little rendezvous at the cemetery, and instantly I am listening for her to tell about the audition. Instead – ha! – she relays how she overheard me talking to daddy. And this acts as a signal for mother to share some more of her concerns. My spells in bed. Sometimes for days. With the curtains pulled. 'She wanders through the house at night when she thinks I am asleep,' mother says. 'She doesn't stop boiling the kettle. She doesn't stop smoking in the sitting room. She goes through phases of not eating. Then she binges. In her room a mountain of dirty clothes. Sometimes I think it never ends. One night I heard her downstairs in the kitchen. And I got out of bed and went down to see. The kitchen door was ajar and I looked around and there she was. Sitting in the chair by the window. Sobbing quietly to herself. I've lost count of how many nights she has spent like that. And not being able to do anything. Not knowing what to do.' And mother reminds Jennifer about my time in St Jude's. And how good the doctors had been or tried to be, and how uninterested I had been in anything they tried to say or do, until it got to the point where they had no choice but to send me on my way, there were other patients in need, others more appreciative of the resources. And not a word out of mother about why I hadn't quite seen eye-to-eye with one of the doctors there, especially after it emerged he would not be happy until he started multiplying the number of things wrong with me and had them all rolled up and packed tightly inside little me so that he really didn't know where to start. She continues on about how I've been for the past couple of years and she talks about my appearance and how do you think she looks, I hear her ask Jennifer. And Jennifer is straightaway into talk about my pallor and my skin, and the importance of a good diet, and she yammers on about those mung beans and chia seeds, and cultured vegetables and activated almonds, and I cannot tell what mother makes of this yak, but she tells Jennifer a story of my finicky eating habits, my phase of avoiding eggs because I got it inside my head that they were bad news. And there is a little chuckling at that. And mother mentions the theatre again, and how she knows how important it is to me, but that at the same time how she wishes I could move on with my life. She seems stuck, Jennifer, I hear her say. And I wait for Jennifer to tell mother about the audition. Go on, I dare you. But she doesn't say a word about it. 'Does she still keep the scrapbooks?' I hear Jennifer ask. 'Scrapbooks?' mother says. 'What sort of scrapbooks?' 'Oh,' Jennifer says. 'They were full of stuff about movies and actresses. Stuff dad used to tell her. Stuff she would find out for herself. You know, where they were born and how they were discovered and what they got up to in their spare time. And she had pasted in photographs. And newspaper clippings. What's this she had written across the cover? Laura Cassidy's World of Movies. Something like that. She wouldn't let anyone see it. But she didn't hide it very well. And the

That was a month after Frank died, I hear mother say.
Sometimes I think she's been up on that rooftop ever since.
Well, mother.
I'm not so sure I am in total agreement with you there.
And not for the first time.

*

*Dearest Laura,*

*I am miffed at you. There was a certain premiere
I was hoping to see you at and I am guessing you
didn't turn up – unless you managed to evade my
eagle eye, which I suppose is not beyond the
bounds of possibility given my necessity to spread
myself amongst so many on the night in question.*

*I have to say, you missed quite the evening.
Armani provided my ensemble on this occasion.
The teal suited my complexion. The crowd seemed
to agree. As soon as I stepped out of the limousine
they cheered and applauded and called out my
name. Imelda! Imelda! The photographers couldn't
get enough of me either. Turn this way. Turn that
way. Over here. No, there. Eventually I had to
summon Falstaff (initiative clearly not a word in his
dictionary) and have him usher me further along
the red carpet. Time was pressing and some people
wanted to talk to me. About the movie. About my
dress. About anything really, so long as I was
standing next to a talking head with a microphone*

*and offering my adorable self to the camera
pointing straight at me.*

*And just when I thought things couldn't get any
more surreal, who turned up: only a certain director
you and me used to wax lyrical about for hours on
end – I'll let you guess who – and as soon as he
clapped eyes on me he made a beeline for the mic I
was poised in front of, pushed his face alongside
mine (eyebrows! oh my God) and, for the benefit of
the watching world, into the camera in that fast-
talking New York accent he declared me the finest
acting talent to arrive in over half a century. Of
course I blushed (who wouldn't?), pointed to myself
and playfully dismissed his comments ('Are you
talking to me?') while at the same time stammering
something to the effect that you're not half bad
yourself, Mr Scorsese. Please, he said, holding up his
hands. Call me Marty. We'll talk, he said, wiggling
those eyebrows, and then disappeared into the
auditorium.*

*After the screening (oh! joyous), there were more
interviews and photographs with cast and crew, and
other hangers-on who insisted on being in a photo-
shoot alongside me. It all became a tad tedious to
tell the truth, and naturally no sign of Falstaff to
whisk me away. Then there were parties to attend –
Dorothy Somebody and Prada affairs – and more
interviews to give and more photographs to pose
for, and I was approached to be an ambassador for*

*another rancid perfume, and a famous hair product
wanted to offer me another million dollars for
saying a totally inane catchphrase. And there was a
completely annoying little pixie from* Film
Magazine *wanting to do an exposé (so draining,
Laura. It really is). And of course there were movie
men, schlepping and schmoozing and climbing
through each other in their efforts to get to me.
Three words, Laura. Three words: hello and
goodbye! And that pest of a stalker rocked up.
Thankfully, Ennio was near at hand. Ennio Tesara.
Have you heard of him? He's an opera singer
(swoon – what a voice!). We were introduced in
Venice. This is the second time you've come to my
rescue, I said to him on this occasion. Well. He
puckered those opera lips, leaned in to me, and in
that Italian accent whispered in my ear the words,
'I was born to rescue you.' Oh, I can manage – for
now. That's what I said back. Then I winked at
him, turned on my heels and threw myself into the
party.*

*I couldn't get over all the famous faces. It was
supposed to be a small affair, but the place was
packed. Look at all these people, I said to no one in
particular. There is only one reason these people are
here, came the swift reply. It was Marty again. Oh,
and what reason might that be, I said, knowing full
well the answer but wanting to hear him say it
anyway. He didn't say a word either. Merely pointed*

*his finger at me, and at once I threw my arms
incredulously to the sky.*

*Now, Laura, I want to tell you something, but
you must swear not to breathe a word of it. He
wants me in his next movie. Marty, I mean. Now
guess what his next movie is about? It is to be a
biopic of – wait for it – Gloria Swanson. Can you
believe it? Apparently he's been trying to get it
made for years, but between one thing and another
(idiot moneymen with no vision or backbone, other
projects getting in the way, a never-ending search
for the actress with the all-encompassing qualities
the part requires) he hasn't been able to do it. Until
now, that is. And now that he has seen yours truly
in action, he has realized that this project can no
longer remain on ice. At long last the missing
piece – the most important piece – has finally
presented itself. Oh, Laura! I was so excited I
grabbed his head with both hands and planted a
smacker right on his lips.*

*We had a pow-wow that lasted more or less the
rest of the night. He loves Gloria almost as much as
I do. And he was thrilled, ecstatic even, at my
enthusiasm for his vision. You should have seen
him. Like a little boy, he was. Skipping about the
room when I did my ready-for-my-close-up routine.
Remember you and me used to take turns do it?
Such fun! Not a word to anyone. It's hush-hush, off
the record for now. Oh, my. I have Ennio in my ear*

*again. (That voice . . . It dissolves me, Laura, it*
*really does . . . ) Gotta fly. For heaven's sake, write*
*to me. Kiss, kiss. Bang, bang. You're dead! Mel. x*

That night I can't sleep. And once I know nobody else is still up, I get out of bed and go downstairs and occupy myself in the kitchen, then take what I make to eat into the sitting room where I manage to get through all of *Nightmare Alley*, *Kiss Me Deadly*, *Detour* and as far as the scene in *The Big Heat* where Lee Marvin hurls a pot of boiling coffee into Gloria Grahame's face, at which point I hear the others rousing themselves upstairs and make myself scarce.

## 21

Day before my audition and I've arranged to meet Fleming in Barna Woods. I want to go over my scene one last time. Not for the first time he is keeping me waiting. Even after I send forth a little giddy-up *come and get me big boy* enticement.

I lie down among the trees. Reach out my arms, caress windblown leaves either side of me without them getting the wrong idea. Pretend-scream at the laughing branches. Share a gory secret with the nearby stump. Listen to me, stump, I begin, I am only going to say this once. Aha! I have its attention now.

Maybe I should stay like this forever, close my eyes and let time fritter silently along. Maybe I will one day. Maybe I will fall into a deep sleep. Maybe I won't wake up for a hundred years. Maybe when I do, everything will be different. I won't look the way I used to. I will have acquired a reputation for being a remarkable person. All manner of people will crave time in my company. In their eagerness they will bump, jostle, knock, clamber over each other to get to me. And I will confer with my loyal sycamores and decide who among the clamouring hordes is deserving of this special time.

And still no sign of my leading man. Who does he think he is? And more to the point what part of his brain has him thinking I have nothing else to do with my time other than wait for him to show up? Once again, I reach for my phone. *Last chance, big boy.*

I've gobbled down a half-bag of Chocolate Emeralds and am about to share one of my best secrets with the stump I am developing a soft spot for when I hear him. All huff and puff and completely over-the-top swearwords for the tree root that never fails to trip him up.

'We really need to find another spot,' he says, removing with a flamboyant sweep of his hand a stray bramble from his fleecy hair. He's not averse to a little theatre, is Fleming. Aids-and-abets his lofty notion of himself, I suppose.

This time we go further in, where the trees are thickest, the roots visible. We wrap ourselves around each other within the remains of a makeshift campground others have left after them. I kick off my boots and pull down my jeans and we grind and heave for the two or three minutes we are good for. 'That was profound and unforgettable, Fleming,' I say. 'You have missed your calling.' I wouldn't mind but he actually looks like he believes what I am saying.

I yank back up my jeans and tie on my boots. Moments later, we are sitting back to back on the tree stump, smoking rollies.

'That was great,' he says.

'What was?'

'The meal we rustled up the other evening. With Jennifer and your crew. How is she? Jennifer, I mean.'

'Still over the ground,' I say.

'And the kid. Juan. What a character. Did I ever tell you I love kids?'

'Fleming, are you trying to wind me up?'

'No.'

'I've told you before. Wind me up at your peril.'

'I'm just taking an interest, Laura.'

'Well, take an interest in something else. In case you've forgotten, I have an audition tomorrow morning. I thought you might like to hear me out while I run my scene past you.'

'I am interested.'

'You sound so convincing.'

'Laura. Please. Now, I'm all ears. Let me hear what you've got.'

'I've decided to do bits from Blanche's hot date with Mitch. Especially when Blanche and Mitch return to Stella's place. Stella and Stanley are still out, and Mitch thinks he's landed on his feet when Blanche invites him inside. But of course all Blanche wants to do is talk and she ends up telling Mitch all about the young boy she was once in love with and how she let him down. It's quite a long speech for Blanche. Lots of emotion, and a killer punchline to finish.'

'Sounds great.'

'You ready to listen, then?'

'Give it to me, baby.'

By now I am on my feet and moving among the leaves. And I deliver the lines I have been going over in my head, in my room, along the pier, pausing where it matters, reaching for the high point. By the time I have manhandled

Fleming up beside me for the smooching bit I am almost sorry it isn't the real thing.

'You were right about the emotion,' Fleming says, as soon as I have released him. 'That's really sad. I like that bit at the end about the searchlight going out. You were very strong there.'

'Why, thank you. I've been working hard on those very lines. I'm so pleased you noticed.'

'The boy in that scene. What happened to him?'

'He put a gun in his mouth and blew out the back of his head.'

'She really let him down.'

'Yep.'

'You can do it again if you want. And this time spend a little longer on the lusty bit. Rough me up a little more, too. I liked it when you did that.'

'I have to go now, Fleming.'

'Hey!' I hear him call after me as I skip restlessly out of there. 'Good luck, Laura. I'm rooting for you.'

*

That night, I swallow my last remaining mirtazapine and make a note to swing by the Doc first thing. I run through my lines. I look at another scene or two. I watch the movie version on my laptop. I get up and go down to the kitchen and pull out the ingredients for the soup I decide to make. In the kitchen I run through my lines again, moving around as I go, here and there switching emphasis, occasionally adding a gesture to the beginning of an important line, a suitable reaction at the end. Upstairs again, I try to get to sleep running favourite movie scenes past my mind's eye. Later, wide awake in bed, I think about the time daddy played Stanley. It gets me more antsy, and I stand out of bed and without turning on the light pace the room for the next hour or so. At some point, mother pokes her head inside the bedroom door, wants to know what I am at, hushes me, disappears again. For the next while I sit by the window. The west wind whistles and mist-rain swirls its way into nooks it hasn't been in before. I look towards the pier, the lights are blurry, faintly visible. Still and all. They are there. I know they are.

I open my laptop to discover that the rumours have started – *Imelda Ebbing to play the lead in Martin Scorsese Gloria Swanson biopic*. And not averse to this golden opportunity to fan the flames, Imelda seems more than willing to corroborate. *It's the role of a lifetime. I cannot think of a part I'd rather play. I am so chuffed to be associated with such an amazing project and to be working with such an esteemed director. A dream come true. It really is.* Lest there be any remaining doubt she adds that she is already researching the famous star of Hollywood's Golden Age. Her early roles in silent cinema. Her fading popularity with the emergence of sound. On the wall, Lana rolls her eyes and wonders what has me so obsessed with Imelda's progress. Veronica scoffs and Gloria herself beckons me to her with that curling finger. *Words. Chitter-chat.*

*Gobbledegook. Nonsense. We don't need dialogue, Laura, we have faces!*

Later again, I'm in the sitting room, flicking through the DVDs and am about to play *Laura* when I spot another I haven't watched in a while. *Whatever Happened to Baby Jane?* I slip it in the player, watch it as far as the scene where Baby Jane serves up a dead rat to her wheelchair sister, and then go back into the kitchen to check on the soup I have left simmering.

I'm stirring the saucepan when I hear the door open and in he pads. Barefoot. In a Spiderman T-shirt that is too small for him and shorts he has to hold up.

'Well, hello to you. I suppose you caught a whiff of my delicious soup. Want to try some? My very own recipe.'

I dip the ladle and hold it aloft for him to see.

'Lunatic soup,' I call it. 'Please don't ask me what's in it.'

I bring the ladle to my mouth and make a great show of slurping down a couple of mouthfuls and then wincing immaculately.

'Hmmm,' I say and throw in a couple more mushrooms. 'What's that I hear you say? You certainly like your mushrooms, Laura. Yes, I do. Must be all that pathos.'

I grab the bowl of mushrooms and hand it to him.

'Be my guest,' I say, and motion what he must do. Quickly he empties the rest of the mushrooms into my seething pot. I dip and taste again. Juan looks on with gathering amusement.

'What time is it?' I ask him.

'Four o'clock,' he says, pointing to the clock on the wall.

'Four o'clock in the morning. Perfect. It always tastes better after midnight,' I say, already ladling into two bowls.

While waiting for the soup to cool I grab a marker and batch of yellow Post-it notes. 'This is something I used to do when I was little,' I say, and invite Juan to copy me scribble numbers onto the Post-its and then slap them to various parts of myself. Wrists, calves, thighs and restless feet. My flimsy chest and pasty cheeks. The shallows of my ribcage and the hollows behind my knees. I don't let him stop until every part of me gets a value. Then I do the tot and say it loud how much I am worth.

'Let me hear you say it,' I tell him.

'*Un millón de dólares,*' he says, flashing his teeth.

'*Correcto,*' I say, checking the temperature of the soup. 'And you know what that means? It means I get to take my place along the Walk of Fame.'

We sit with our soup for the next few moments. Then, and to my great surprise, Little Juan is the one to break the silence.

'Where is my daddy?' he asks me, his voice quiet and deliberate, wanting a response.

'That,' I say, smiling his way, 'is a question I used to ask myself every day.' And I allow my arm to rest around his slender shoulders and draw him closer to me.

'You know what? I want to show you something. But you're going to have to promise that this is going to be our secret. Deal? I need to hear you say it.'

'Deal.'

'*OK, compadre. Alto cinco.*'

We high-five, I take his hand and gently open the front door. We cross the road. Stiff breeze and not-so-half-hearted rain. At the boathouse I point Little Juan towards the pier. 'Come on,' I say. 'This is the way.'

We continue onto the pier. The breeze is stronger. I hunker down, grip a hold of Juan and point.

'Can you see?' I ask him.

'*Qué?*'

'Out there. The starry light. The Walk of Fame. Can you see?'

He shakes his head, looks disappointed, worried even.

'Sometimes it's hard to see. That's OK. There's something else I want to show you. Over here,' I say, guiding us to the pier wall. 'Here,' I say, using the light of my phone to find the carving daddy made all that time ago. 'I've never shown this to anyone. Here. The words in the wall. Can you see?'

Again, he shakes his head. It's blowing hard now. The rain comes on fuller. One more time I run the phone along the wall so as he has a chance to see. *Nada*.

'OK. Wait here for a moment.'

I climb onto the wall. I look around me. I look down at the little fellow, at his expectant little face.

'OK. Come on.' I reach down my arm and haul him onto the wall beside me. I hunker down and point.

'Now can you see?'

He shrugs. Brings his hands to his face to ward off the rain. The wind is taking his hair every which way.

'Tell you what. We'll try something else.'

I lift him down from the wall and haul the pair of us back as far as the boat ramp, and the partial shelter the quay wall now provides. 'Come on,' I say, taking Juan's hand and leading us down the ramp to the water's edge. 'OK. Now we wait.' And just as I say it, a swan rounds the bend and allows the current take its elegant form towards us. A second swan appears. A third and fourth. Moments later the entire flotilla has appeared. '*Mira!*' Juan gasps, pointing with his finger. He stares at the all-white procession, his face a picture of wonder. I hunker down beside him and for I don't know how long the two of us stay like that together, watching the swans glide over the surface water.

\*

Someone is shaking me. *Laura! Laura! Wake up!* I open my eyes. Rub them. Open them fully. Look around. There is no one in the room except me.

It's bright out, sunlight on the window. I realize I am lying on the bedcover. Must have drifted off.

What time is it?

Jesus!

I jump to my feet. Glance in the mirror. Hmm. I will have to do. There is no time. I hurry out of the room, and bound downstairs and out the front door.

Ten minutes. I have ten minutes to get to the Town Hall.

No time to sort my eyebrows. Do my hair.

No time to swill a cuppa.

No time to chow with my man, Juan.

No time to tell Jennifer to cut the sore throat she tells me she has acquired overnight.

No time to raise my eyebrows at Peter Porter when I see him trying to slink downstairs upon letting himself out of mother's bedroom.

No time to swing by the Doc to collect my meds. Doesn't matter. There is no time to get nervous.

Don't even have time to call by the cemetery for a pep talk with daddy.

Just get to the Town Hall, Laura. Just get to the Town Hall and get the goddamn part.

I'm out of breath by the time I reach the Town Hall. Camilla the Hun is on reception. She points upwards with her raised pen. Where else would I go? I push through the double doors and take the stairs in twos and threes.

The bar is full. Quickly I size up everybody. A glow-in-the-dark redhead is taking turns biting her nails and scratching her elbows. A bobbed brunette in mismatched clogs is standing up and sitting down while throwing out her arms as though it is otherwise impossible for her speak. She should save her energy for something else. Operating a washing machine. Stacking shelves. Gardening. Another one is wearing a figure-hugging mini-dress and spray-on false-tan. Perhaps her audition is going to involve offering Stephen a lap dance. She has thin lips. Close-together eyebrows. Socks on her arms. Socks! A one-hundred-per-cent please-please-love-me-do if ever I saw one, probably Mr

Sheens her breasts every morning. Beside love-me-do, a man or woman – it's difficult to tell – is running hands through dreadlocked hair, muttering lines. Another one – all glitterlips and pissed-on-green eye-shadow – is yakking away into her phone as though she owns the place. Who died and made her la belle dame sans merci?

I have no sooner sat down than someone is calling my name. Laura Cassidy. LAURA CASSIDY! 'Yes, that's me. Here I am.'

Standing up again, that dizziness riffles through me and I feel a sturdy arm grip my elbow. 'Are you all right?'

Yes, yes. I'm fine. The door to the studio is held open for me.

All right, Mr DeMille, I'm ready for my close-up. And I plunge into the darkness.

# Part III

## *IMMORTALITY BECKONS*

# LANA TURNER

February 8, 1921 – June 29, 1995
aka The Nightclub Queen

**Inducted:** February 8, 1960
**Star address:** 6241, Hollywood Blvd
Father murdered after an all-night craps game
Discovered aged sixteen sipping a Coke at
the Top Hat Cafe on Sunset Boulevard
Owned 698 pairs of shoes
**Real name:** Julia Jean Mildred Frances Turner

*'I planned on having one husband and seven children
but it turned out the other way around.'*

## 22

Hello, daddy, I say, taking my usual perch graveside. I suppose you want to know how my audition went. I wish I knew the answer to that myself. It's been ten days and still no word from Khaos. Every time I phone the Town Hall I am put straight through to the answer machine. There are no replies to my emails. They'll get in touch when they have some news, Fleming says every time I bring it up, which is quite often. They – Khaos – are also getting ready to move into their new home. That's right, daddy, any day now it looks like the Story House will at long last be ready.

On audition day itself I showed up and did my scene – naturally I had a last-minute change of heart upon walking on and looking out only to see Stephen Fallow sitting in the front row all cosy-cosy with his ladyfriend. Giving Stephen all my attention, and before realizing what I was at, I had started into the scene with Blanche's lovely observations about the rainy New Orleans afternoons as she bids the youngster come inside and then tells him he is like a prince and that I *want to kiss you – just once – softly and sweetly on your mouth*. By which point I was moving stage right, and I walked down the steps and proceeded over to Stephen in the front row. He was so surprised when I leaned into him, took his face in my hands and kissed his mouth. I got the idea from Imelda, actually. Something she said she did at some gala event she was invited to. I closed my eyes for the kiss, allowed my lips linger, and by the time I had straightened myself up, reopened my eyes and took a look around to try and get a sense of how it had gone, Stephen Fallow was no longer in his seat. In fact, he had almost reached the door of the rehearsal studio. Where is he going? I called out. My director? But if the silence that greeted my query was anything to go by, no one seemed any the wiser. One of his assistants looked my way, someone I had never seen before. Thanks for coming in, we'll let you know, she said, and busied herself with a couple of others seated in the same row.

Outside the studio I had a good goo about the place, but there was no sign of him. Just a few wannabes still waiting their turn. Strange, I thought. I was about to go back inside and check if I had somehow missed him when I saw his ladyfriend. I was on my way over to her when her phone went off and she scarpered out of there faster than she had any right to considering the heels she had on. I wanted to return back inside the studio, but auditions were still in progress. I waited in the lobby until long after auditions were finished, until Billy the Lush wanted to lock up for the evening, at which point he told me Stephen and the crew were long gone, they had left by the actors' entrance. I made my way out of there. And I have been waiting for word ever since.

*

Outside the cemetery and I get to thinking: Fleming is wrong. They must know by now. At very least they must have an idea who it is they want. It won't hurt to swing by, let them know I was passing and just wanted to enquire if there is any news. That's right, Laura. Be courteous and polite. Showing my face can't do any harm, if anything it will further demonstrate my enthusiasm for the cause. And without giving the matter another thought I proceed toot-sweet as far as the Town Hall.

'Where are you off to?' I hear Camilla the Hun call out when I pass through the lobby doors and make for the stairs, not stopping until I am inside the bar.

'Hi, Emily. Has Stephen been around at all?'

For a second, Emily looks at me as though she hasn't got a clue who I am. I am about to repeat my question when she decides to speak.

'Oh, Laura. Hi. I think he was in. He might be around somewhere. I haven't seen you since . . . the audition.'

'It was quite the day.'

'Yes, it was. I don't remember seeing so many audition-ing before.'

'That is because everybody knows we were getting to perform for a master. I wonder where he is. Is he in the studio? I can wait outside if he is.'

'Hmm. I'm not sure, Laura.'

I have stopped listening to Emily when the young woman I have seen in Stephen's company on one or two occasions high-heels up to the bar and collects a coffee.

'Cheers, Emily,' she says and walks away again, in the direction of the rehearsal studio.

'Who was that?'

'That's Mia,' Emily says, busying herself at the coffee machine even though no one bar myself is present. 'I think they are planning to let people know very soon – about the auditions. You're probably better off waiting until they get in touch.'

'Thanks, Emily. I'll do that.'

I wave goodbye and leave the bar. Ignoring the stairs, I round the turn and continue towards the entrance to the rehearsal studio. Already, I can hear voices. Then the studio door opens. It's Camilla the Hun, and before she spots me, I duck into the nearest available toilet.

It's the men's toilet. I let myself into one of the two available cubicles, close and lock the door after me, flip down the toilet lid and sit myself down.

Moments later, or maybe it is much later, I'm not fully sure, it feels as though I have been drifting, nodded off even, I can hear a voice. A man's voice. I don't need to tune in for too long to realize who it belongs to. He seems to be on the phone. And it is obvious he is quite keen on whoever he is speaking to . . . *That's right. Yes. We're all set, I think. Yes. We're letting them know tomorrow.* Water flows as he chats some more. At some point he lets his phone drop to the floor, and it slides partially under the door of the cubicle I'm inside. With my foot I nudge it out of there, hear him gather it up again. Within the cubicle I bide my time, flush, tidy-up and nudge the cubicle door and peer through the gap I allow myself. It's him. My director. He has put down his phone, is washing his hands.

'Hello,' I say, stepping over to the second sink.

'Jesus Christ! My heart,' he says, clutching himself.

'It's me. Laura. The actress. I did an audition for you the week before last.'

'Oh, yes. How could I forget.' He brushes his dripping hand across his lips.

'And here I am.'

'So I see.'

'I suppose I just wanted to find out is there any white smoke yet?'

'In the men's toilet?'

'Well, it's really an accident I ended up in here. But here we are. So, I thought I may as well ask.'

'I can't tell you anything. Except to say we're contacting the successful actors very soon.'

'Great! How soon?'

'Very soon. If you don't mind . . .'

He indicates that he would like to pass by me and be on his way. But I am not quite finished.

'I just want to let you know that I am ready. You might have heard about my mishap last time out. But I am as good as new again. I want you to know that you can count on me.'

'I'm glad to hear all that . . . Laura. Can I go now?'

'Aren't you forgetting something,' I say, leaning against the sink and gesturing with my eyes. He looks uncertainly at me. 'Your phone.'

He turns, picks it off the washbasin. I stand aside, and without another glance in my direction, he leaves. I take a quick look in the mirror. A shred of toilet paper dangles from the side of my head. Doesn't matter. He remembers my audition. I made an impression. And what was the line I overheard?

*We are letting them know tomorrow.*

Well. It looks like I have some big news to look forward to. It won't be long now. I will be the one cosying up to our illustrious director in the front rows of the auditorium. I will be the one accompanying him on harbour walks, through the streets, along the canal, talking through the possibilities for my character. He'll be so impressed with my suggestions he'll insist we take it back to his for further exploration. He'll offer me a second nightcap, a third, fix himself some while he's at it, make himself comfortable beside me. Of course he'll now be a little distracted – the short skirt and strappy top I am wearing are interfering with his concentration. He'll move himself a little closer to me, allow his hand brush against my hip and I'll have to remind him that we are here to read over some scenes from the play. And for the next few minutes he'll stick to the drill, be on his best behaviour. Another nightcap or two in, however, it all gets the better of him, he can no longer contain himself, and now he is all wandering hands and foraging fingers while in the throes of declaring me the most remarkable acting talent he has ever been around, and well, oh my, Stephen, do you really think so . . . We are getting really into it when Billy the Lush walks into the toilet, interrupting my pleasant scene-making. Not to worry. It is safe to say that I can now call it an evening. No need to linger. After all, there will be plenty of evenings days nights to look forward to in the company of my director. I make my excuses to Billy (girl's gotta go, Billy, doesn't matter where) and skip happily out of there.

## 23

The following morning I check my emails. Nothing as yet, but it's still early. I should give them another hour. A couple of hours even. That's not too much to allow them on this momentous day.

Is it, Laura?

Why, of course it isn't, Laura. I think we can afford to be a tad forbearing at this point.

There is, however, something from Imelda. Of course, there is.

*Dearest Laura, how are you? Me? I think I might just have to pinch myself. Falstaff knocked on my bedroom door earlier (Falstaff! What did I tell you about disturbing me before noon?), entered and then presented me with an open copy of* Total Film. *Look, he said, gesturing wildly while prancing about the place with the elan of a frenzied chicken. Look, Imelda! Look! And there he was. Marty. Telling the whole world that he has finally found his lead for what insiders are mooting as his movie swansong. (Swanson swansong!) That's right. It's official, no longer a secret. Tell everyone!*

*You should read the press release. Imelda Ebbing is a screen icon in the making. So why shouldn't she play one of the early greats. That's what Marty said about me, Laura. Oh my. I started crying. I really did. Blubbering all over the wonderful image of myself adorning the front cover. (Don't you just adore monochrome?) Falstaff didn't know what had come over me. And with nothing better to do he started blubbering too. Then my phone started going and it hasn't stopped, Laura. It has not stopped.*

*Just as well I am on location this week and next. Rome. Vienna. And then Budapest. It's this television show I've been asked to do. Did I mention it? I know, I know. After all we said at acting school. Television! Bah! But I suppose I will admit to there being – how shall I put it? – an extra incentive for my taking the part. And something tells me you have already guessed his name. That's right. Ennio. Things have been moving pretty quickly on that score. He's touring with his opera (my word, you should hear his Rigoletto) – and it just so happens he has performances scheduled in these very same cities. Actually, he was under the covers when Falstaff arrived into my bedroom brandishing that film magazine. I could feel his fingers dancing up and down my thigh while Falstaff was talking. He was so happy for me he insisted on whisking me off to his villa in Tuscany*

*for the remainder of the weekend. ('I can rescue
you some more!') I can think of worse ways to pass
time until Marty needs me.*

*Have you done any television? Is that why I am
not hearing from you? You are involved in some
epoch-defining saga that will be talked about for
years to come? I actually had half a moment to
myself last night and tried googling your name.
Nothing much came up. For another half-moment I
was a little worried. Surely, my good friend and
favourite understudy hasn't packed it all in. Surely,
she hasn't turned her back on the theatre and all
those adoring fans just waiting for a glimpse of her
talents. Or could it be that you have changed your
name? Or haven't been well? And now you are on
the mend. Soon to be as good as new. Because on
no accounts should someone with potential like
yours call it a day. On no accounts! Tell me I'm
wrong and I will refuse to attend the Academy
Awards next February. What am I saying? With my
schedule the way it is these days I'll be lucky if I get
to the airport. Oh my God! I almost forgot. My
stalker. He turned up outside my gate last night.
The creep actually pinged stones at my bedroom
window. Luckily, Ennio was here. He wasn't long
sending Mr Creep packing. Now, please. Get in
touch! If you don't want to write, give me a call.
Kiss, kiss. Bang, bang. You're dead! Mel. x*

This time she has attached the front-cover image of *Total Film*. And there she is. A slightly off-centre headshot captured in the smoky darkness. And a tagline that reads, *All right, Mr Scorsese, I'm ready for my close-up*. Well, bully for you, Imelda. It so happens I am expecting some exciting news myself. So, if you will completely pardon my French (or is it Italian?), kindly shove that *potential like yours* up your *panini*.

Downstairs, I am greeted with the announcement that mother has volunteered me to look after Little Juan for the day. Jennifer needs to travel to Dublin in order to administer a no-nonsense bollocking to someone at the Mexican Embassy who is holding up urgent documentation for her latest work contract. This bollocking, she feels, may also serve as tangible evidence as to the matter of her existence now that she has sourced the Mexican bank official in constant denial about her. At first, Jennifer seems reluctant to make the trip. Her throat is niggling her, she's already been to see Doc Harper (of course she has). Then she considers taking Little Juan to Dublin with her. Mother encourages her to go alone, to leave Juan with us. Laura will entertain him. We both will. Off you go. It's only one day. We'll be fine.

'Why don't you take Juan to the circus?' mother suggests after she has helped facilitate Jennifer's departure.

'What circus?'

'What do you mean, what circus?' she says, laughing. 'You can practically see the tent from the front window.'

I go see and, like mother, allow myself a little laugh upon

glimpsing part of the blue-and-white marquee. I am only too happy to spend some time with the little fellow. Of course we can go to the circus. We can visit the arcades, play the stalls, chomp candyfloss 'til it clogs up our ears. After all, this is going to be a good day, a momentous day, a day to remember. It is going to be the day I get to tell everyone that I'm back. Jennifer, I got the part. Mother, I am returning to the stage. Talk to me, Fleming, tell me some of these television ideas of yours. Play your cards right, I might even star in them. Most of all, I can't wait for my next cemetery visit so as I can let daddy know. Already, I can see the press release I will read aloud for him.

*Laura Cassidy to play Blanche DuBois*
*in Khaos Theatre production of Tennessee Williams classic*

And maybe I should get in touch with Imelda. Let her know that she is right. I am all set for a significant moment in my career. Who knows? In the not-so-distant future she can expect some company over there in West End London. A rival for all those parts thrown at her. And, hey! Maybe the two of us will get to tread the boards together. Pit ourselves opposite each other. Wouldn't that be interesting?

Yes, it will, Laura.

Yes, it most certainly will.

First things first, then. A day at the circus with the little man. Bright lights and good company. Not a bad combination when word from the theatre comes through. Not bad at all.

If his excited little face is anything to go by, Juan already knows all about the circus. As does Fleming, when I message him to meet up.

'OK, little man,' I say, making sure my phone is fully charged. 'Off to the circus we go.'

*

We reach the bridge and I lift Juan onto the wall. Gripping the little fellow, I turn him towards the water and ease him into a sitting position. I point to the swans, some seabirds and to a Hooker making its way into open sea. I look about for Fleming. Presently I hear the familiar voice calling up at me from his back-to-the-wall perch.

'Hello, Beggar,' I say without looking down. 'Today's the day.'

'Is it now?'

'This time tomorrow you'll be addressing a leading lady.'

'And I hear Walt Disney is going to sail into the harbour with Donald Duck. Who's the sprog?'

'This little fellow?' I say, as Juan starts vigorously scratching himself. 'This is Juan. He belongs to my sister, Jennifer. She bought him at a flea market in Mexico.'

'I once knew a woman from Portugal. Make him say something.'

'He speaks in tongues, Beggar. Spanish. Gibberish. Other stuff.'

'He's met his match in you so.'

I look at the Beggar's blackened hands, his scratched

skin, his bitten nails. The tufty beard on him. The gone-to-hell-and-back teeth. Two men, suited and in a hurry, pass by. A woman wheeling a buggy. Someone drops a coin into his cap. I watch him reach out and claim it, hear him whisper a curse as he confirms its value.

'How much do you make, Beggar?'

'Mind your business.'

'Little Juan here wants to know. Go on, tell us. How much do you make in a week? Not much, I'd say. Any time I'm on the bridge your cap is empty.'

'Who are you looking in my cap? If you must know I used to be this town's top-earning beggar.'

'Isn't it amazing how fortunes can so quickly turn around?'

'Do me a favour, will you? Turn your head around to the water and amaze yourself somewhere else.'

I do as I am told. 'Breathe in some of that sea air,' I tell Juan. I inhale heavily for his benefit and he laughs and, draping my arms about him, I make a shield of my hands around my eyes and stare out over the bridge. To my left, a few terrorists mooch by the Arch. Clusters of youngsters sit on the grass near the quay. Pisser Kelly loiters. Seabirds screech. I look around for Fleming. The river roars its way into the harbour.

'She's in a bad mood today, Beggar.'

'That one is always in a bad mood.'

'If anyone should know, it's you, Beggar.'

'You should have heard her last night. And stop calling me Beggar.'

'Someone goes in there they are not coming out. That's what I think. Chew you up and spit out nothing.'

'You just make sure you hold on to what you have,' Beggar says, and I pretend-tickle Little Juan's ribcage. He kicks up his feet and for his benefit I squawk like a frightened bird. He laughs, heartily.

Again, I face the surging water, grimy and petulant, roaring its way into the harbour, the waves ragged and every which way, with no clue as to the direction they should be taking. I watch them clash against each other mercilessly, the ferocious banter of them, the hell-to-pay bluster. Relentless they are and furious and individual, every lick without allegiance to the one coming before or after, every madcap rise looking for a way into carnage, every chop and charge part of a gathering storm.

A gull swoops low and close enough for Little Juan to see its unpitying face. It screeches right at him. I summon a matching glare and screech right back. Little Juan laughs some more. 'Those seabirds are losing their minds,' I tell him, and below me I hear Beggar's phlegmy cough.

'Yes, indeed. It has the makings of a wild one. What do you think, Beggar? Is it going to be a boy or a girl?'

'I care less what they call it.'

'I think we're at G. Storm Gloria has a good ring to it.'

'Storm Gloria sounds like nothing more than a wheeze in a paper bag.'

'Maybe not, Beggar. Tell you one thing, though. This wind is going to drive everybody mad.'

'You'll have company so.'

*

I have lifted Juan down from the bridge and am about to message Fleming again when I spot him coming towards us, his bobbing stride throwing him a few inches into the air.

'Look who it is,' he says, as soon as he reaches us, already crouching down in front of Juan.

'Remember this crazyman?' I tell the little fellow. 'He's going to hang around with us today. Is that OK with you?'

Fleming pokes Little Juan gently in the ribs. Little Juan grabs my hand and leans into my leg.

'He's a brave boy,' Fleming says, now going for Little Juan with both hands as he chases after him around my legs.

'Don't mind me,' I say, producing a rollie from my pocket while frisking myself for a lighter. By now, Juan is squealing with laughter,

'So what do you say, little man?' Fleming goes on, kneeling down again. 'Fancy hanging out with your uncle Fleming for a few hours. Yes? Come on, then. What say you and me begin our adventure with a knickerbocker glory?'

Little Juan slaps his hand off Fleming's, the two of them now the best of friends all over again.

'Hey!' I call after them. 'Wait up.'


And here we are. Me holding Little Juan's hand. Little Juan licking the ice cream Fleming has bought for him. Fleming providing a running commentary. The three of us strutting our stuff along the river walk. The sun has come out and I'm feeling pretty good about things. Working with my new director. Opening night at the Story House. And after that . . .

'So, little man,' Fleming says. 'What do you like to do when you're out and about? Catch a movie. Go to bars. There's an exotic-dancing place that's just opened up down near the harbour.'

Fleming mimes his way through his list of ideas and Little Juan grins and gives us a happy nod of his curly noggin.

We pause at Middle River and watch a lad in boxer shorts snorkelling in the not-so-deep water. He plummets and rises up and plummets again, each time taking a moment to inspect the coins he has swept off the riverbed. He then tosses them onto the pile steadily accumulating on the grassy bank. Thinking they might come in useful, when he dives again I reach down, grab a fistful of the liberated coins and pocket them. As though he cannot believe what he is seeing, Fleming covers his eyes with his hands. Little Juan laughs and copies him.

And we're walking again.

A little further on fishermen cast their lines and hope for the best. Fleming coaxes Little Juan over to the riverside railings for a closer look. Jennifer messages from wherever she is. *Hope you're having fun.* Still nothing from the theatre. Not to worry. It's not even eleven o'clock.

'Tell me something, little man,' Fleming says, when we're walking again. 'What do you think of Laura's chances? Do you think she's got the chops? Is she convincing enough? You know. If you were the director, would you tell everyone else not to bother? Hello, everyone, and goodbye. The part is taken. Know what I mean? Aw, man! Don't shake your head so vigorously.'

I take another roll-up out of my skirt pocket, light up, take a drag. Fleming pulls a doobie out of his shirt pocket, lights it and drags. 'Hubba bubba,' he says as two young women, high-heeled and miniskirted, walk towards us. One look at Little Juan and the pair of them are cooing and aahing and hunkering down to say hello.

'Is he yours?' Pink Miniskirt asks me.

'He certainly is,' I say, patting the little man's curls.

'He has your mouth,' says Yellow Miniskirt.

'So everyone says.'

'But not your hair,' she continues.

'No. Definitely not that.'

'Nor your colouring,' the first one decides to contribute.

'He gets his colouring from his father.'

'He must be very striking.'

'I'm the fairy godmother,' Fleming says, dragging on his doobie.

The two women look at Fleming, then at each other. Then they return their attention to Juan. To milk the moment I pat the little fellow's curls again.

'What's his name?' asks Pink Miniskirt.

'He has three names,' I say. 'When it's sunny we call him Rafa, as in Raphael. When it's wet we call him Paddy, as in Patrick.'

'But mostly we just call him the Abomination,' Fleming adds with a smirk.

The Miniskirts reach out their bangled arms and scold

Fleming good-naturedly. They smile and coo and aah some more, and make some other strange-sounding noises that may even be words from another language.

'This little fellow speaks Spanish,' Fleming says.

'Really,' says Yellow Miniskirt.

'I love Spanish,' says the other.

'Say something in Spanish for your new friends,' I say.

I take a drag of my rollie and smile at the little fellow, basking in all the attention. To my surprise and to the delight of his admirers he even starts talking.

'What's he saying?' asks Pink Miniskirt.

'He's saying you have the most supple lips I have ever seen and I want to leap inside your eyes,' Fleming says. 'He's saying you two are the second and third most beautiful women in the whole world. He's saying I am on cloud ten when I look at both of you.'

'You mean cloud nine,' says Yellow Miniskirt, reaching out again and squeezing Little Juan's jaw.

'No, he means cloud ten. Cloud nine is for another woman,' Fleming says.

'What's he really saying?' ask both Miniskirts at more or less the same time.

I shrug my shoulder and let Little Juan talk away. He's probably telling them all about how he hasn't had anything proper to eat since breakfast and about the unpredictable woman he has landed himself with and to cap it all she has been joined by a doobie-toking non-stop-talking madman while his woe-is-me mother gets to swan around in Dublin for the day.

'Well. Do you want to buy him off me?' I ask the Mini-skirts. 'An hour in this fellow's company and it'll be like you've known each other all your lives.'

But they've had enough of Fleming and me. They pat Little Juan, toss his curls and one last time solicit another of his irresistible grins. My phone goes off. I'm convinced it's Khaos, calling with the news, and I am about to answer when I see that it's my darling sister. No doubt it has hit her what she has done with her little boy and she is expecting the worst. Well, sister. He's in safe hands. No need to stress yourself. I let the phone ring out.

Juan and Fleming wander ahead of me, towards the harbour. Bobbing boats. Hazy light. Couples holding hands. Others drinking cans of cheap beer. Laughter and shouting. Further out into the bay and Little Juan is reacting to the cruise ship that has berthed for a night or two. Then a loud clanging threatens to smash my eardrum and when I turn to locate the source of the din I see that we are a stone's throw from the circus marquee.

'Hey!' Fleming says, hunkering down beside Juan and pointing at the marquee banner. 'Look at those lights. It's the circus. And not just any old circus. Duffy's Circus is in town. They do the best candyfloss. Bet you didn't know that? Follow me, little man. You're in for a treat.'

When I catch up to them, Fleming and Juan are standing before a shooting gallery, staring at the display of prizes. Furry ladybirds and elephants and dolphins. And there are footballs. Juan has spotted the football he wants, and he's watching the lad who is out to impress a statuesque brunette grip the rifle, take aim and blast the target into the middle of the next stall. The hotshot presents a pink bear and, his spadework done, guides the brunette swiftly out of there.

Step right up! the shout goes out, and with the coins from Middle River I pay over a few shots' worth and Fleming takes the rifle in his hand.

'Did I ever mention I am a crack shot?' Fleming says, eyeing up the target. 'Oh, yes. God help any man facing the firing squad I am a member of. Tell me, what would you like, then?' he asks Little Juan. Juan points at a red football.

'The red football it is,' Fleming confirms and takes steady aim. 'Watch out.'

His first shot favours artistic impression over technical merit. He looks the part but misses by a country mile. His second shot is a mystery. So much so that I am not all that convinced the gun has actually responded when Fleming squeezes the trigger. Shots three and four are let off quickly and without much regard on Fleming's part for the intended purpose. I catch the little fellow's anxious eye and encourage Fleming to make an effort with his last shot. Nobody, not the attendant, not the couple patiently awaiting their turn, certainly not me, has any idea how this last effort fares. By now, the little fellow is regarding the red football as something that will never find a way into his toys room.

'You know,' Fleming tells him, as soon as I have hauled Juan forlornly away from there. 'You know back there at the shooting gallery. You know why I missed? It was a right-handed rifle. Me? I'm a lefty. A southpaw. Put a left-handed gun in my hand and I'll take out anything that moves.'

We pass a palm reader called Gypsy Teresa. Two sad-face clowns, a three-card-trick table and a quartet of tuxedoed stilt-walkers. A masked man dressed in a black-and-white prison uniform is dragging a ball and chain about the place. A ghost-face in a skeleton suit slides by.

Fleming looks back to the palm reader as though he has left something important behind.

'Come on,' he says, grabbing Little Juan by the hand. 'Let's hear what the gypsy has to say about what's in store for us.'

Gypsy Teresa motions Fleming to sit on the stool opposite her. Myself and Little Juan linger a ways off. Little Juan is curious, though, and he keeps tugging me closer.

Minutes later Fleming returns, beaming as though all his best days have arrived in one swoop.

'I'm going to be rich. I'm going to be famous. I'm going to be successful. She said I can go all the way – if that is what I decide to do. She said I have it within me to be a great man. Presidential. That's the word she used.'

'Did she say you could go to the moon?' I ask, remembering a familiar conversation from the first time we met.

'She didn't say I could *not* go to the moon. Then I asked her does she read the palms of little boys. And so . . . little man . . . you're up next. Come on, Laura. She said we could sit with him during the reading.'

Juan is initially scared of the wrinkled woman and a little coaxing is necessary. As soon as he is ready to let her, she takes the little man's hand, turns the palm upwards and starts to trace whatever line she seems drawn to. Little Juan is told he is going to be a sportsman and an entrepreneur. What sort of sportsman? Fleming wants to know and he is shushed. Little Juan is told he will see lots of places, break many hearts, that he must one day pay attention to a raven-haired girl named Carmela. 'Do you hear that, little man? Watch out for the black beauty,' Fleming says, and once again the gypsy woman hisses at him. Little Juan is told that, when the time is right, he will discover something important. Fleming nudges me, puts his mouth to my ear and wants to know do I think she is referring to Alonso. At which point Gypsy Teresa hisses a third time and starts speaking to Little Juan in Spanish.

'Her turn,' Fleming says when Little Juan is released, and points at me.

'I'm not doing it,' I say. 'I know my future.'

'Come on, we've all done it except you. Sit down and hear her out,' says Fleming.

Fleming hovers with little Juan. Gypsy Teresa makes no effort to begin, she even half-turns her back to me and folds her arms.

'I think she wants us to pay now. I think she wants *you* to pay, Fleming,' I say.

Fleming does as he is bid and Gypsy Teresa relaxes again.

'Now, clear off,' I tell Fleming. 'This is between me and Teresa here.'

Fleming and Juan move off, and Gypsy Teresa takes my left hand. She regards it for a moment or two, shakes her head in bafflement, then takes my other hand. Again, she regards it for a moment or two, shakes her head. Then she takes both my hands together. Then she tells me she can see not one but two futures.

'Would you like me to continue or stop?' she says.

'Thank you very much,' I say before she says another word and I go look for my companions.

A lollipop stand grabs Little Juan's attention. A kaleidoscope of large, sugary discs presents itself, and the woman flogging them has come up with the brilliant idea of individualizing the lollipops with personality tags. *Sour Puss. Drama Queen. Heartbreaker.*

There is a lengthy queue. Fleming offers to wait it out while the little fellow and myself sit at one of the bench tables near the lollipop stand. A woman with blueberry-streaked hair is sitting by herself, licking a *Moody Blue*. Little Juan points to her, whether at her despondent lollipop or her matching hairdo is hard to say.

While Fleming queues I spot my favourite terrorist couple. This time, in addition to the Virginia Beach baseball caps, they are wearing matching Aran sweaters. They too have been bitten by the lollipop bug, though from where I am sitting, I cannot make out what theirs say. 'Ah, so you found her,' I am about to holler over at Mr Virginia Beach, but I have been further distracted by just about the last person I expected to see wandering through the circus grounds.

Stephen Fallow.

'Wait here. I'll be back in a minute,' I tell the little man, and I am out of the bench table and weaving my way through the various clusters of people in my eagerness to get to him.

'Hello,' I call out, making a grab for his shoulder. He is out of reach. 'Stephen! Hello,' I say, a little louder, just as he rounds a Punch and Judy stand. The same woman – Mia – is with him.

I call out again. 'Stephen! Stephen Fallow!'

He half-pauses and looks back. I nudge people out of my way and give a little wave. He half-raises his own arm and turns away. 'Hold on,' I say, as he continues away from me.

For the next couple of moments I lose sight of him. Then I spot him – them – moving away from circus stalls and heading towards the green area near the water's edge where groups of youngsters sit around in circles, sharing bottles and cans. The scent of hash wafts through the air. Guitar music. My director and Mia continue towards the water, eventually pausing at the edge of the quay. I start towards them, just as my phone goes off, and, glancing down at it, I see Fleming's name flash up. Then I feel myself catching someone's legs and down I go.

'Watch it,' I hear someone say, a young lad, with tattoos where he should have hair and a helix of studs in either ear.

'You watch it,' I reply.

'Hey!'

'Hey, yourself.'

'OK, sister,' he says. 'Let's start again.'

'That's what I was thinking.'

'Live and let live.'

'Not a bad philosophy.'

I pick myself up off the ground. I turn to where I had last seen Stephen Fallow. There's no sign of him. I follow the line of the quay, all the way as far as the Spanish Arch. Yes. There he is.

My phone chimes through a couple of messages from Fleming.

*Where are ye?*

*I'm standing here with three lollipops.*

I message back as I hurry along the quay.

*Just give him his lollipop. Back in five.*

Seconds later my phone goes off.

'Fleming?'

'Laura? Please say he's with you. Because he is not here.'

'He's not with me.'

'Jesus Christ, Laura! Where are you?'

'I spotted Stephen. I want to ask him about the audition.'

'Jesus, Laura!'

'Where are you?'

'I'm still at this bloody lollipop stand.'

'Is he not there too? I left him at the bench. I told him to stay put. I was only going to be a minute.'

'He's four years old, Laura. Of course he's not going to stay put.'

'Aren't you the expert?'

'Laura! This is serious. We need to find him. Pronto.'

'Well, he can't have gotten too far. He must be there somewhere. Maybe he went back to the shooting gallery.'

'Right. Meet me there in five minutes.'

He hangs up. I look towards the Spanish Arch. Stephen and Mia are sitting on the nearby steps. As I start over towards them my phone goes again.

'Fleming! I'm coming. OK.'

'Laura?'

Flip. It's not Fleming. Flip.

Flip. Feck. Flip. Feck. Feck.

'Oh, hi Jennifer.'

'Hi. Is everything OK?'

'Sure, sure.'

'You sound a bit flustered.'

'No. No. I thought you were somebody else.'

'How are you getting on with Juan?'

'Great. We're out at the circus. We're having a grand time of it.'

'The circus. Sounds great. Put him on for a sec, will you?'

I hold the phone away from my face and wince. And now Fleming is trying to get through again. By the Arch, I see Stephen and Mia enjoy a long smooch.

'He's busy, Jennifer. Fleming is letting him have a go at the shooting gallery. Can I call you back in a few minutes?'

'OK, but . . .'

I hang up and connect Fleming.

'Where are you!'

'I'm on my way. Any sign of him?'

'No, Laura! There isn't. And I am getting very worried.'

He hangs up. Stephen has managed to separate himself from Mia and has sauntered over to the edge of the quay. By now, I have reached the Arch, just as a busload of terrorists is descending upon it. I make a beeline for my director. He turns as I approach.

'Hello, Stephen.'

'Hello again . . . Laura.'

'Don't suppose you have any news? I still haven't heard.'

'Actually, I do have some news for you.'

'Really? You do?'

'I'm glad I bumped into you, Laura. I have something I want to say to you. A suggestion, if you like.'

'A suggestion. About the part, you mean? About how to play Blanche?'

This is it. I knew it. My heart is picking up speed. Wait 'til Fleming hears. Wait 'til mother and Jennifer hear. Wait 'til . . .

'The way I see it – the way several of us see it, actually – is that you are – how shall I put it – a tad loud.'

'Loud?'

'A tad harsh even.'

'Harsh?'

'And I – all of us at Khaos – were wondering how you would feel about playing another part.'

'Another part?'

'Yes. We – that is to say, my colleagues and I – realize that – how shall I put it? – you have been away from the stage for a time. And perhaps now is not . . .'

Oh, I get it. He wants me to play the sister. He wants me to play Stella.

'Gosh, I don't know. I had my sights set on the Blanche part. I've been going over the play with only that part in mind.'

'Well, there are other parts . . . if you are willing to consider.'

'I know, I know. You think it's too soon for me to return as a leading lady. And if I am honest about it I suppose Stella isn't quite the lame duck she is sometimes portrayed as.'

'Actually, we've already cast the Stella part . . .'

Fleming's name flashes up on my phone again. I put it in my pocket.

'But, now that I begin to think about it, I can see how I may be suited to the role of Stella. In so many ways it's every bit as big a part as the other. Just as significant – in ways more significant, if regarded from a certain perspective.'

'Laura! Did you hear what I just said? Stella has been cast.'

'It goes without saying that it would be good to reclaim the play as a story of two sisters . . . And then there is that undercurrent at the end with Stella and Stanley . . . after what has happened to Blanche . . . you know, that suggestion of collusion between them . . . sinister, almost . . . Yes! Yes, I think I could be persuaded to go along with your suggestion. In time, I may even come to see it as an inspired call. I knew you were a good choice to direct. I knew it the moment . . .'

'Laura! The part is Eunice.'

'. . . I saw you . . . Eunice? Who is Eunice?'

'The neighbour. She lives upstairs from Stella. It's a small part I know, and I know you might think it's not a part you'd . . .'

'Eunice! You want me to play Eunice the neighbour from upstairs!'

Some terrorists by the Arch turn around to look. Across the harbour, I see figures walking along Nimmo's Pier and I wonder vaguely might Little Juan be one of them. Inside my pocket I can feel my phone vibrating. Stephen is talking again.

'Take it or leave it, Laura. It's all I have for you. And let me know soon, will you? There are others who would appreciate the opportunity.'

'Tell you what. I'll let you know right now, shall I? You can take Eunice the neighbour from upstairs and shove her where the sun doesn't shine.'

He walks away, towards the awaiting Mia, who has turned up again, bearing a pair of ice creams. I watch them walk off together, hand in hand, while a sizeable tour group drifts this way and gradually engulfs me.

Take it or leave it!

Loud and harsh!

Eunice! He wants me to play somebody called Eunice. How many lines does she have? About enough to be drowned out by anyone with a mild cough.

How can he ask me to play somebody called Eunice?

For the benefit of his audience, a tour guide has started into a story about the Spanish Arch and the shipwrecked sailors belonging to the Armada and where their final resting place can be found. I look through the crowd, so as to catch a glimpse of Stephen and Mia. And at last it hits me who our town's newest hotshot director has found to be his Blanche DuBois. She has only been hanging off his arm pretty much all day every day. 'Motherfucker!' I scream, as I stand there among the gathered crowd, unable to move. 'Motherfucker! Motherfucker! MOTHERFUCKER!'

My phone goes again.

'Laura! Get here and get here fast.'

I squeeze a way out through the tour group, cut down by the side of the museum and hurry back to the circus.

There is no sign of Juan at the shooting gallery. I continue through the throngs, past the Punch and Judy stand, passing the stilt-walkers and three-card-trick men, I even spot the fortune teller again, make yourself useful then, where is the little fellow?

By the time I reach the lollipop stand the only people I can make out are Mr and Mrs Virginia Beach, wedged into a bench table, happily licking their *Home Is Where the Heart Is* lollipops. Then I spot Fleming. Frantic, scanning the area all around him.

'Jesus, Laura! Have you seen him?'

'No, have you?'

'Jesus, Laura! I'd hardly be asking you if I had, would I?'

'He can't be far away.'

'He could be anywhere! Look at all these people. Someone could have nabbed him. Jesus, Laura!'

'Fleming, could you please stop saying that?'

My phone goes again.

'Hi, sis,' I say. 'You want to speak to Juan, right? Hang on, here he is.' And without another word I hand the phone to Fleming. He glares at me the way I imagine his brothers glare at him. Then he is all smiles and teeth and is instantly into a things-couldn't-be-rosier chat with Jennifer. At some point I think I hear the word *pizza*, and Fleming grins and nods at whatever is being said to him. All is well with Juan, he assures Jennifer in his best-friend voice and hands me back the phone.

'*This* is not funny,' Fleming says, watching me mimic his best-buds face.

*

Two hours later we still haven't found him. It's long past teatime. Light is fading, clouds have moved in, the rain is coming down and mother has messaged to say that Jennifer's bus is nearly in, we might want to think about taking Juan home, oh, and why am I not answering her calls? I'm on my way along the pier on the off chance he's come out here, though I really hope he hasn't. Fleming has been pretty much everywhere else, including a discreet visit as far as the house on another off chance Juan has been trying to find his way home – he hasn't. Fleming has now just caught up with me along the pier.

'Well?'

I shake my head. He covers his face with both hands,

sinks to his knees, and starts rocking back and forth. A couple of passers-by pause and ask me is he all right. I roll my eyes, assure them that all is well.

'We'll have to go to the cops.'

'Fleming. That we will not be doing.'

'Laura. We have to find him.'

'And we will – only without the boys in blue.'

'There's one over there. I'm going to have a word.'

'Fleming!'

## 24

I am in my room trying to figure out how to go about persuading Stephen to reconsider the casting. I'll do another audition. Pick a scene, I'll tell him, any scene, I'll do it, and there and then offer him my paperback copy of the play. I won't be loud. I won't be harsh. I'll do it exactly how he wants it done. I'll understudy the parts of both Blanche and Stella. I'll commit the entire play to memory and perform it for him start to finish if he wants me to. Anything he wants. Anybody, so long as it's not Eunice the neighbour from upstairs. I'm pacing around my room, running through my mind all these possibilities and more – *What would Lana and Barbara have done? What say you, Gloria? Veronica? Any advice you might like to impart?* – when Jennifer walks in and closes the door behind her.

For a moment or two she leans against the door, until I have stopped pacing, stopped muttering to myself, and she is certain she can enter properly into the room and say without interruption what it is she is here to say.

'Laura, what happened today?'

'Come again?'

She crosses the room and sits into my chair.

'Juan has a scratch on his arm. When I asked him about it he told me it was a secret. So I asked him why it was a secret and he said because no one knows about the scratch. Not even you or Fleming. And when I asked him how is it that neither you nor Fleming know he said, because they weren't there when it happened.'

She pauses and looks over at me. Clearly it is now my turn to respond. And by not immediately plunging in to discharge the getting-heavier-by-the-second silence, I can tell I have made a mistake. A big mistake.

'So?'

'So, what?'

'So, would you like to tell me what happened today?'

'He wasn't missing for long.'

'Missing! Why would he have been missing, Laura?'

'Missing is the wrong word. Exploring. That's probably a better way to describe it.'

'Did you let him out of your sight? Did you? It's my own fault. I shouldn't have trusted you with him. I should have known.'

'You always do,' I say.

'Jesus Christ, Laura! Wake up, will you? Anything could have happened.'

'It's only a scratch. To tell you the truth I didn't even notice it.'

Right there, Laura. Mistake number two. Keep it up.

'You didn't even notice . . . And his shirt was torn. I don't suppose you noticed that either!'

'If you look closely,' I say, putting on my calmest voice, 'you'll find six things that weren't there this time yesterday.'

'I don't believe I'm hearing this. And to think I was rooting for you with that stupid audition.'

'What audition?'

Mother has appeared. She's standing in the frame of the doorway, having quietly opened the door. Jennifer looks at her.

'Mother, could you please ask your younger daughter why she let my boy out of her sight today.'

For a moment nobody speaks. Jennifer stands out of the chair and stares out the window. Mother walks fully into the room and sits in the chair Jennifer has vacated. She looks at the pair of us, at a loss as to precisely what is going on between us.

'She needs help and lots of it,' Jennifer says, addressing mother and jabbing a finger in my direction. 'I said it a year and a half ago. Now, I'm saying it again.'

Jennifer remains by the window. Mother looks so sombre. I feel the dizziness coming on, my chest getting squeezed, and before I give myself a chance to think it all through, I have blurted it out.

'I did an audition for a new production. Today I heard I got the part.'

That gets their attention.

'Come again?' Jennifer says, giving me her best I'm-not-sure-I'm-going-to-believe-a-word-of-this-but-tell-me-anyway face.

'That's why I got distracted with Juan,' I go on, quickly finding my stride. 'I bumped into Stephen Fallow. The director. He wanted a fast word with me, and there and then he broke the news. I got so excited I took my eyes off Juan for a minute or two. I'm sorry, Jennifer . . .'

I cast about quickly to get a sense of any softening towards me. Jennifer wants to remain focused on what happened with Juan, at how I reacted when she confronted me about it, but I sense that a small part of her might be prepared to indulge me. Mother looks concerned, but wants to hear more. I'm only too happy to oblige. I give her a few lines about the new director and the Tennessee Williams production Khaos intends to put on, and I mention how it was one of daddy's favourite plays and so I couldn't resist going for the part, and wouldn't he be thrilled to know that I am going to be in it.

At that point I stop speaking. Mother is busy absorbing my extra piece of news, possibly arranging inside her head the precise wording of her concerns. Jennifer looks as though she has some more things to get out there. Before she has a chance, off I go again.

'I'm sorry, Jennifer. I saw the director and thought I would just be a minute. And actually, a couple of terr . . . tourists I know were watching out for him. I swear, it was a one-off.'

'A one-off?'

'Yes.'

'It's just that Juan also said something about the two of you being out on the pier together – sometime last week.'

'That's right. We had fun. Did he tell you about the swans?'

'It was the middle of the night, Laura! It was blowing a gale. He said the two of you were up on the wall.'

'The lights, Jennifer. I wanted to show him the lights.'

'What! WHAT LIGHTS? LAURA! Jesus Christ! Are you completely insane?'

She stands facing me, without saying a word. And I am waiting for her to turn to mother, *See, I told you. St Jude's, that's where she belongs,* when my get-out-of-jail-free card arrives. Little Juan has decided he wants in on our little gathering and, when he enters the bedroom, he walks right over to me and wraps his arms around my waist. Absolution indeed.

Jennifer reaches out her arms, claims her boy. Checks that he is OK. Then she looks my way again.

'I thought you were doing better. Even mam said you've been great company for her.'

'Saves you ever having to be around then, doesn't it?'

Whatever else Jennifer has in mind to say is going to have to wait. With Juan now present in the room, she is no longer so fast to condemn me. Mother, too, isn't saying much. Slowly, she stands out of the chair she has been sitting in and walks out of the room. Jennifer looks at me and follows mother, hauling the little man with her.

# 25

It was not long after the time Enrico the Magician came to town when I was first asked to talk about how daddy had died. It was more than three years since the accident, I had just turned fourteen, and for one night only Enrico was performing in the Town Hall. Myself and some classmates had snagged tickets. Mother decided to come as well. Jennifer and her friends.

In fact, the entire town must have shown up for the performance. Enrico came on and did a few card tricks, sawed up a few people, made melons disappear under his hat. Then he asked for a volunteer. He wanted to hypnotize someone. Without thinking about it I shot my arm up, leapt out of my seat and bounded onto the stage. Good girl, Enrico said. Then he tried to put me to sleep. You are getting drowsy, he said to me. Your eyelids are getting heavy, they weigh like full buckets. At any moment you will nod off. I couldn't have been more awake. Knew I wasn't going to be hypnotized. He could have hit me on top of the head with a mallet and I don't think I'd have shut my eyes for him. But he kept the routine going, telling me I was getting sleepier and sleepier. He turned to the audience and then looked intensely at me and I could tell he knew I was willing to go along with it, that I was happy with whatever it was he had in mind to do. Then for the next two hours he proceeded to make a gargantuan ass out of me in front of the entire town, and I was a willing participant.

I remember him asking me my name. What? I said. You mean my stage name? He chuckled, as did the packed hall, and I could see Jennifer and her friends laughing. Then he had me play all sorts of musical instruments. I was lead guitarist in a rock group. A classical violinist. A trumpeter. He gave me some superpowers. I could fly. Walk on water. Go invisible by clicking my fingers. I was very convincing. Then he wanted to have me executed. And he had the audience shout out their preferred methods of execution. Put her in front of the firing squad. String her up. Poison her. The audience was not shy. Tie the witch to a stake and burn her, I heard someone call out and I started to think it's time the show was over. Then I looked right into the audience and saw Jennifer and her friends load their rifles and shoot. I had to react and clutch my chest when the bullets landed and fall agonizingly to the floor and cry out my dying words. Then Enrico brought me back to life and I had to go through it all over again. I must have died and been brought back to life a hundred times that night. Jennifer and her friends, mother, the entire place was in stitches.

The icing on the cake was him getting me to pretend I was a lost little girl searching for her parents. Enrico gave me a countdown from thirty and I had to climb down off the stage, jam two fingers inside my mouth, and trawl through the audience in search of my mother. What I did was seek out Jennifer. I found her, sitting with her friends, and I plonked myself down beside them and put my arms around Jennifer as though to give her a hug. Then I moved my hands to her throat and started squeezing for all I was worth. How the audience gasped. And Jennifer was screaming and Enrico was fast-counting down, three, two, one, then he clapped his hands and hey presto I was returned to normality. Except I was no longer listening to Enrico's instructions. I held my grip. And it was all mother and some others could do to prise me away from her.

A couple of weekends later, mother sat me down at the kitchen table and told me about the head doctor she had invited around, while home-from-college Jennifer stood by the window, looking on. I didn't know for how long mother had been planning this. And I remember looking over at my sister and asking why she had to be present. Jennifer started to answer, but then the doorbell sounded, oh, here he is, mother said, I watched Jennifer go to let him in, and something stirred inside me, a gnawing resentment that she didn't have to go through any of this.

St Jude's aside, it was the only time I talked to anyone about daddy. I can still remember his words – after I had half-answered a couple of his questions.

*I want to tell you something, Laura. About your father . . . about the night he died. It was an accident, Laura. A terrible accident. It was the storm . . . it's not your fault, Laura. It's not your fault.*

Later, I remember mother held my left hand as she repeated the words. She held it with both of her own hands. I remember they were so cold. I remember her eyes imploring me to say something, to accept what had been said to me.

I ran out of there, not stopping until I had reached the boathouse and had scampered up the back-wall ladder onto the flat roof where I perched myself and tried to shut out everything around me.

And I was back to that wild winter night. Howling wind and crashing waves. I'm running towards the pier-end. I holler when I see him. *Daddy, daddy! Guess what? I got the part. At school.* He turns to me. He smiles. A wave crash-lands. And then he isn't there.

It's all I could see when I opened my eyes and looked out into the auditorium on opening night a year and a half ago. Daddy standing at the pier-end. There one moment, and then gone.

I often wondered if Jennifer knew I was faking it. That Enrico had failed to work his magic on me. And if she did know, had she asked herself why had I gone for her the way I did?

It's like I've got all these parts to me. Easy-to-see parts and long forgotten parts and parts I encounter in my problematic dreams. I have shadow parts. They do not wish me well. When I least expect it they tiptoe inside my skin, whisper awful things, needle my flimsy blood. Life is a series of ladders you have to climb, I remember the genius in St Jude's saying during one of our sessions together. Me? I don't go up ladders. I slide down snakes.

*

Someone is calling my name. Then gently touching me.

'Laura! LAURA!'

I open my eyes and Jennifer is standing over me.

'For a minute I thought you had fallen asleep and were having a bad dream. Are you OK?'

'I wasn't asleep.'

'Are you OK?'

She has turned on the lamp by the window. Now she kneels down on the floor, very close to me and is staring intensely at me. I clear the tears away from my eyes.

'Yes,' I say, taking the hanky she has offered and blowing my nose.

'What's wrong? Please, tell me.'

I clear my eyes some more, can feel her taking it all in. Middle of the night. Soup all over the floor. Distraught younger sister sobbing by herself in the kitchen dark.

When I don't answer she gathers up pieces of the broken bowl and she fetches a cloth and starts wiping up the spillage.

'Leave it,' I say.

'It's OK. It won't take a minute.'

'I said, leave it.'

'Laura. We want to help you. Please, let us help.'

I stand out of the chair and leave her to her cleaning up.

I leave the house, cross the road and walk the pier. It's cold but not as cold as it can be, and in the night sky I can even make out stars. I have no idea what time it is.

I wish myself back in time, back to the nights I was out

here with daddy, back to nights in the nearby hall watching the Claddagh Players in all their glory.

I think about the year they put on *Streetcar*. The last show daddy appeared in, the final part he got to play.

I stand at the end of the pier. Strain to make out the lights reflected in the water. They are so faint, scarcely make an impression on the darkness all around. The merest flicker, nothing more.

# Part IV

## *DON'T YOU KNOW WHO I AM?*

# GENE TIERNEY

November 19, 1920 – November 6, 1991
aka Laura

**Inducted:** February 8, 1960
**Star address:** 6125, Hollywood Blvd
Discovered aged seventeen while on a tour of
Warner Bros Studios
After her first movie declared she sounded like
'an angry Minnie Mouse'
Struggled with episodes of manic depression
For twenty minutes stood on the ledge
of a Manhattan high-rise
Fled one institution after 27 shock treatments

(*note to self:* do not end up in a jam like that)

# 26

So, daddy, it's been almost a month since my audition, the play has been cast, and rehearsals are well and truly under way. I keep checking my phone on the off chance there has been some kind of mix-up at Khaos, that Stephen has seen the error of his ways and here he is pleading for a chance to make amends. *Oh, Laura. We have made a horrible mistake. Of course you are perfect for the part of Blanche. I was blind. We were all blind here at Khaos. Please accept our apologies for this terrible misunderstanding. The part is yours. It always was. It's here, waiting for you. Please, please come back to us.* But every time I look all I see waiting for me is another alert from Imelda, detailing the latest from her stellar life. Location shoots. Photo-shoots. Her mug on the cover of glossy magazines. Her operatic love life. Her lecturing me about my potential. Potential, daddy! And if I hear another word about Marty and this Gloria Swanson biopic I really do think I'll rock up in London and tell her face to face exactly what she can do with her *role of a lifetime.*

Still. It's got me thinking, daddy. About Khaos. Stephen Fallow had his reasons for not giving me the part I was after, he even tried to explain them to me before offering me that other part. But by then I wasn't really in a listening kind of mood and, amidst all the confusion with Little

Juan, maybe I was a little fast out of the traps letting him know what he could do with his idea. That's another thing. Jennifer has been very slow letting go of that particular incident. Even though Fleming found the little fellow safe and sound, happily enjoying the company of a pair of terrorists who were plying him with the largest pizza I had ever seen. My, my, was Jennifer mad. You should have heard her, daddy. Yelling to all and sundry that I need locking up, that my head needs prying into. She even started raving about my taking Little Juan out along the pier. You would think I was intent on dropkicking him into the bay the way she was going on. All I wanted to do was give him a look at the lights – just like you used to do with me. It got so bad that mother had to intervene to calm her down. And all this before I made the blunder of not only telling them about the audition, but that I had in fact gotten the part. Call it a spur-of-the-moment kind of thing, an impulse on my part to divert attention away from my faux pas with Little Juan. And something to do with the wonderful time of it Imelda is having. So, as of right now, daddy, the way things stand I am going to have to crawl hands and knees back to Stephen Fallow and tell him, *Sorry, old chap, I was a tad hasty earlier. Thank you for the offer and here I am to accept the part of Eunice the neighbour from upstairs.* Otherwise, that sister of mine is going to interpret my behaviour in this matter as further evidence that I belong back inside St Jude's. If you have any suggestions as to how I find my way out of this bind, daddy, now might be a good time to present them to me.

# 27

*Dearest Laura, greetings from Budapest. More specifically, from my almost splendid hotel suite – oh but, Laura, you should see the Danube at sundown. In a word: paradise. Alas, it's my last night. And I'm having to spend it all by myself. Ennio was supposed to swing by after his concert performance, but – horror upon horror – his wife has found out about us. Did I mention his wife? She's Russian. A cellist. Quite well known by all accounts. Her name is Svetlana and I hear she is quite fond of archery. Just as well I'm flying to Los Angeles next week! Anyway, the entire farrago is all down to that pest of a stalker. He had his camera with him the night he came prowling around, and he managed to nab himself some choice balcony shots of Ennio and myself sharing a moonlit moment. And of course the pics have been plastered all over the place. What a bore, Laura. What a bore!*

*Roll on Los Angeles. A fast visit for a pow-wow with Marty, a meet-and-greet with the producers, drinks with the cast and crew. I think I'm going to posture a bit. You know. Like the great woman herself. Gloria. What a name! I've been watching*

*footage of her. Talk shows. Interviews. Did you
know she was a health freak? Some kind of
macrobiotic diet. Tell you one thing, it worked. She
looked great. I'm enjoying going through her back
catalogue too. All the silent movies. Have you got a
favourite? I think mine is* Sadie Thompson. *A
woman of the night seeking a fresh start becomes
the obsession of a religious extremist. What a pitch!
Marty loves that one too. He'd never do a remake,
would he? I might say it to him, and in such a way
that allows him think it's his idea. Listen to me!
Get this biopic in the can to begin with, Imelda.
Then we can worry about remakes.*

*Marty FedExed me a draft of the Swanson
script, actually. Oh, Laura! It's amazing. The
supporting cast is pretty interesting too. You'll never
guess who they've lined up – obviously I am sworn
to secrecy, but I will reveal that it is someone you
and I used to swoon about at great length.
Someone about whom you devised an elaborate
kidnap plan – to do with keeping him locked away
in a certain boathouse. Ha ha! He's coming to
Europe to have a look at me in action – in the TV
show, I mean. Maybe I'll let him have me in other
ways too – now that Ennio is indisposed!*

*Now let me tell you one thing I am most
definitely going to do when I get to LA. Make time
for a stroll along the Walk of Fame. I well
remember how you used to go on and on about it.*

*Like the broken proverbial, you were. I'd give you a
name and without blinking an eye you could give
me the exact location of their star. I'll be thinking
of you as I make my way along it. Might even take
some pics of my own.*

*By the way. I had Falstaff look up that theatre
group in your town. Khaos. What a great name. It
looks like you're putting a production together. I
assume you're involved, though I didn't notice a
cast listing and there weren't any headshots. You're
probably up to your neck in rehearsals. Though I
have to say I am at a loss to understand why my
former understudy isn't chomping at the bit for a
smidgen of advice from someone as well placed as
yours truly. Don't say you are too proud to ask! So,
then. Let me hear from you. Something, however
brief. Otherwise I might just have to make a detour
on my way to Los Angeles. Gotta fly! Kiss, kiss.
Bang, bang. You're dead! Mel. x*

She hasn't enclosed any links this time. No images of that
Danube sundown or moonlit moments with Ennio. Just
more quack-quacking from planet Imelda. Bad enough she
has it inside that inflated noggin of hers that I was her
understudy. Now she thinks I am in urgent need of her
advice. Well. Here is a piece of advice. From yours truly to
yours truly: Never listen to a duck in a thunderstorm.

*

I spend the best part of the week in my room. Staring at the walls. Making small talk with Lana and Barbara and Veronica. I watch *The Killers*, *Night and the City*, *Mildred Pierce*, *Criss Cross*, *Pickup on South Street*, *Stranger on the Third Floor*, *The Woman in the Window*, *Scarlet Street*, *The Big Combo*, *Key Largo*, *Dark Passage*, *Shadow of a Doubt*, *The Third Man*, *Angel Face*, *Sweet Smell of Success* (twice), *Where the Sidewalk Ends*, *Gun Crazy*, *Murder, My Sweet*, *The Glass Key*, *This Gun for Hire*, half of *Laura*, *Touch of Evil* (three times) and *They Live by Night* (note to self: watch this one again with Fleming). But mostly I just want to drift into a sleep that lasts for quite a long time.

At last, Jennifer seems to have gotten over what happened with Little Juan. If not, she does a remarkable job pretending she has. When she is not on the phone to the Mexicans, to her boss, to the airline, and now Doc Harper about her worsening throat, she expends an inordinate amount of energy trying to coax me out of my room. She deploys all manner of temptations. Cinema. Shopping. Coffee and cake. A trip out of town, to Dublin, out to Connemara, anywhere. 'Come on,' she says, 'Juan wants to spend some time with you.' And so every time she appears I hold up my copy of the play I am pretending to be poring over, and without even looking at her, utter the words, 'Sorry, too busy.'

Mother shows up too, knocking on my door before entering. Here, no doubt, to remind me of her own concerns regarding my behaviour with Little Juan, grill me about my meds (I've missed a couple of appointments with the Doc), and while she is at it, harp on about my return to the theatre, not that it matters one whit what she has to say or how vehement she is with it. Like Jennifer, her tactic seems to be to lure me into a false sense of security. She asks about the play, and about my part. She is even ready to heap kudos on me. I have given myself time to get over what happened before, heeded all the advice given to me, this new opportunity could be the best of things. When all is said and done, it is what I love, am passionate about, and who is she to pour cold water on what I most want to do. Next she proceeds to pass on well wishes from Yoohoo Lucy and Dolores Taaffe, 'and Odd Doris wants you to get her a front-row ticket,' mother says, now throwing in a laugh. 'And Peter is delighted for you. He reckons this is the start of something. Something really good.' I smile at her and everything she says. Part of me even wishes I could believe her. But all this well-wishing is too good to be true. It has to be a ruse.

That right, Laura?

'Thank you, mother. Now please,' I say, once again grabbing that oh-so-useful paperback and holding it aloft. 'I'm preparing for my part.' For a moment or two, she stands at the threshold, her thoughts suspended in another place. I am almost tempted to come clean, let her know that I did not get the part I auditioned for, that all I was offered and in no uncertain terms turned down was a token part no one even needs to audition for. Then she is talking again, a softness in her voice I haven't heard in quite a while. 'If only,' she begins, 'if only Frank was here . . . he would be so . . .'

Her voice catches as she utters the words, she finds it difficult to go on, and for fear of what will follow – tears, my
own as well as mother's – I do not utter a single word. I just
cross the room and put my arms around her. And we stand
there together like that for a little bit.

Then, as I knew was bound to happen, Fleming appears,
and of course he is not going anywhere until I have told
him precisely what is going on.

At first I don't say a word. For one thing, I am irked that
I have backed myself into this particular corner. For another
thing, I still don't have the energy to get into any of it. And
for a third thing, I don't think I want to see the expression
on his face when I tell him I have falsely told people that
my audition was good enough to get me a part; that having
wagged concerned fingers my way, everybody seems suddenly delighted for me, are enthusing over the imminent
night out my exciting news has provided, and really I do
not know what to do with all this too-good-to-be-true
behaviour. Gradually, though, his persistence chips away at
me and I tell Fleming everything. About the non-part in the
play and what I told Stephen Fallow to do with it, and
about Jennifer's reaction to our little misadventure with
Juan, and mother finding out I had an audition and then
my telling them that I had gotten a part just to . . . oh, I
don't even know at this stage why . . . shut everybody up if
nothing else.

'What are you going to do?' he says, when he has taken
a moment to absorb it all.

'Well, I should have thought that was obvious,' I say.

'It is?'

'Yes. I'm going to get ready for my part.'

'But, Laura, you don't have . . . a part.'

Neither of us says anything after that. We lie side by side on my bed, draping a light sheet over us, snuggling up close, resting a head upon an offered shoulder. And without uttering a word to each other, we lie there together through movie after movie.

At some point, to break the silence, Fleming shares with me his ideas for television shows. His concepts. I try not to listen, but his voice is gentle, soothing almost, and though it doesn't really matter what he is saying, gradually I find that I am actually tuning in. His pet concept involves his ongoing infatuation with American presidents. He even has a title: *Once Elected All They Do Is Watch Television*. For example, when Iraq and Iran go to war Ronald Reagan is watching *Little House on the Prairie* in the Oval Office. Next door, in the War Room, the generals are worried about a battle going off without them. They are bristling. But Ronald isn't budging. I'm not getting involved until *Little House on the Prairie* is over, Fleming has Ronald say in the script. And: Nancy, tell those boys in the War Room to keep it down.

In another episode, just as trouble is kicking off in Somalia, Bill Clinton is watching *The Simpsons*. Homer, Homer, Homer, Fleming has Bill say, with a finger wag and subsequent chuckle. Then, just before hell breaks loose in Afghanistan, George W. Bush is watching *The*

*Sopranos* – with his father. Hey pops, have you any idea what's happening? Fleming has George W. ask his father, who is sound asleep.

'I think you should shorten the title to *Once Elected*,' I suggest when Fleming asks for my opinion.

'Laura, I could kiss you,' Fleming says, beaming on the bed beside me, and goes on to tell me how each 'president' in *Once Elected* is based on someone from his own family. Ronald is his kind-hearted but forgetful grandfather. Bill is his incredibly bright but can't-keep-it-in-his-pants older brother. And George W. is his sister.

'You have a sister?' I say to Fleming.

'Oh yes,' he says. 'I wish she was more reflective.'

'Which one is Fleming?'

'I'm thinking Obama.'

'The visionary.'

'Got it in one, kid.'

'And what TV show is he watching?'

'I haven't decided yet,' Fleming says to that, but this time I think he is trying to dodge the question. 'For how long do you think you are going to stay in this room?' he says next.

That puts the kibosh on this particular get-together. I turn to face the wall, and a few minutes later, when he sees that I have opted out of our conversation, he leans over, squeezes my shoulder and quietly leaves. I hear him talking with Jennifer and mother downstairs. I am about to tune in to the nonsense they are doubtless plying him with, when Little Juan comes knocking on my door.

'Come in,' I say, and he tries to coax me downstairs to

watch something, to have something to eat with him in the kitchen, to join him on a trip out to the front garden deck-chairs. 'We can make a movie,' he says, 'Lana and Bogart.' 'You can stay here if you want,' I tell him, 'but I am not leaving this room.'

*

I wait until late into the night to eat, tiptoeing downstairs so as I can have the kitchen to myself. I make fast work of two cans of spaghetti hoops. I watch *The Asphalt Jungle, On Dangerous Ground, Out of the Past*, the second half of *Laura*. I stare at the walls in my room until it feels they are closing in on me.

Later again, when I am not sleeping and in the mood to be a little more communicative, I pass the time messaging Fleming.

**me:** you there?
**fleming:** just about
**me:** i was thinking
**me:** at next year's film fleadh
**me:** you should pitch your idea
**me:** the television idea
**me:** the one about the american presidents
**me:** you might need to come up with a few more characters
**me:** some wives. a mistress or two
**me:** wait

**me:** how about an intern

**me:** who is a pedal to the metal nutjob

**me:** i'll help

**me:** i'll even star in it

**me:** if i'm available

**me:** fleming?

**me:** you still there?

**me:** you getting all this?

**me:** fleming?

**fleming:** get some sleep, will you

**me:** well?

**fleming:** well what?

**me:** what do you think of pitching your television show?

**fleming:** i think it's late. i think i'm tired

**me:** that kind of attitude will get you nowhere

**me:** you need to think big, fleming

**me:** starry lights. the walk of fame

**me:** your name above the movie title

**me:** like my daddy used to say

**me:** fleming?

**me:** if you had to pick

**me:** lana or barbara?

**fleming:** i pick going to sleep

**me:** sleeping is for dead people

**me:** i know what we could do

**me:** we could watch the same movie right now!

**fleming:** it's four o'clock in the morning!

**me:** the blue dahlia

**me:** in a lonely place
**me:** all about eve
**me:** i haven't seen that one in ages
**me:** you on for that?
**me:** fleming?
**me:** you there?
**me:** fleming?

# 28

Eventually, so as to avoid further scrutiny – why isn't she at the *theatre* rehearsing? – and the ever-increasing waves of enthusiasm when Peter Porter and mother's friends swing by, I actually do go outside. I walk by myself. Around the harbour. Along the pier. Along the canal. Along the river all the way as far as Menlo Castle whose crumbling ruins sprout out of the bushes and bindweed. More and more I find I like walking by myself. Thoughts come and go. Some I quickly forget. Some I abandon once my galloping mind settles down again. Some I am afraid of.

It is thoughts of what I think ought to happen to Stephen Fallow I am particularly afraid of. I place us together in close proximity, rerun the scene where he breaks it to me about the part he has in mind for me to play. Lana would not stand for shabby treatment like this. Barbara would purr and give it to him right in the gut. And Gloria would load up and make Swiss cheese out of the man who tried to tell her that the only part for her was Eunice the upstairs neighbour.

I continue along the river, sticking to the dirt path cutting through the waterside plants and the trickle streams that feed them. Here and there I pick some wildflowers, link them together until I have several chains, and as I walk

I hang them off jagged brambles and low-down tree branches, place them on one or two nice-looking rocks along my path. I follow the path, not stopping until I arrive at the old jetty, where I plonk myself down to spend time with the view. Here the river splits in two and moves either side of a little tree island. Then it's gobbled up by the lake. They say the lake is bottomless and that way down in the murky depths scream the souls of all the boatmen who have perished. I was little when I first heard that, out on the lake in a rowboat with daddy, and I leaned over, put my ear to the water but could hear nothing. Oh well, I remember thinking at the time. Maybe my ears hadn't fully formed.

I toss the last flower into the water, watch it float away from me. When I can no longer make it out, I eat a bag of Chocolate Emeralds and try not to think of Khaos and Stephen and all the rest of it. Then the swans appear, and I lay down at the water's edge.

Eunice the upstairs neighbour. Must be a way to make it more than the bit part it is. Somehow wrangle more out of it. Now could be the time to get in touch with Imelda. Ask for some of that advice she seems very keen to impart. See what sort of tricks she has up her sleeve after her stint in West End London. Before I do any of that I'm going to have to go crawling back to Stephen Fallow, let him know that on second thoughts he doesn't have to shove Eunice where the sun doesn't shine. I will take the part and thank you thank you thank you for the opportunity.

*

Later that same evening. I'm outside the Town Hall where rehearsals are still going on. Another hour at least, Emily lets me know when she is leaving the building. That's OK, I can wait. No you cannot, Camilla the Hun comes back with, and she threatens a lot more than Billy the Lush on me if I don't put plenty of distance between myself and the building. What does she think I am going to do? Storm the aisles? Set the place ablaze?

Besides. There are other places I can wait.

On my perch on the boathouse rooftop. I smoke a few rollies and drink a carton of orange juice. Though I try not to, I think of times being out here after daddy died, thinking to myself: one day I will be out of here. I will leave behind all my clothes, my most treasured things. I will step outside of my brittle skin. I will leave no footprints and I will hop, skip and jump nimbly into another life. I will introduce myself to high society. Impress with my flawless ways. A millionaire will want to marry me. A movie man will hire me on the spot. They will marvel at my speaking voice. I will be an ambassador for amazing things. Find a way to be in many places at one time. Everybody will invite me to their parties. I will be the talk of the town, where it's at, the centre of it all. There she is, they will say. A legend in her time.

After a while it starts raining and I shelter under the Spanish Arch. The usual suspects are milling about, swigging out of their cans, one or two are already tucking themselves in for the night, and of course one or two are pissing up against the Arch's medieval stone.

'Boys,' I tell them, 'you should drink something else other than those cans. You wouldn't have to go so much.'

Pisser Kelly, their spokesman, halts mid-flow and turns to me.

'Do you want to spend the night with us?'

'That's a beautiful offer, best I've had all evening, but I've made other arrangements.'

'Suit yourself,' he says, turns back to the Arch and resumes his pissing.

On Shop Street, I lean against a shop window and listen to Goodtime Ray. Tonight, he has his guitar with him and his idea of a good time seems to be singing about the rain. He has just introduced a number called 'Persistent Drizzle'. 'I like this town,' he caws in between his guitar chords. 'It reminds me of a sad story. Let me share my sad story with you beautiful people.'

My mind drifts back to Stephen and to his leading lady and other things besides. Mia. I should make friends with her. Help her go through her lines, tell her everything she wants to hear, encourage her to spunk up her part. She'll squeal at my suggestions so delighted is she with them. We'll meet again and again. Become close friends. Swap stories about our lives beyond the theatre. I have a sister, I'll tell her. You remind me of her. Is she an actress too? No, she's a miracle worker. Ha! Ha! And we'll arrive at that lovely moment where she lets me know she'll be more than happy for me to perform on the night – should she be unable to do so herself.

Goodtime Ray is talking again.

'I realized something when it rained,' he caws, idly strumming his guitar. 'My girl no longer had the hots for me. Let's sing a song about the girl I lost.'

There is respectful applause from the non-existent audience as he launches into a burdensome number called 'It's Raining in My Heart'. At first, it's just a localized shower. Soon, it becomes a torrential downpour. By the time the last chorus comes around, the whole world is underwater.

My phone goes off. Mother. I don't answer.

Jennifer calls. I don't answer. She leaves a message that I don't bother listening to.

Fleming messages. Mother messages. I don't reply.

Jennifer calls a second and third time, and I switch off my phone.

Goodtime Ray reaches the end of his song and is talking again.

'I realized one last thing in the rain,' he caws to his devoted following, plucking at his trusty companion. 'A guitar and a six-pack – that's all I need. This is my last song. One of my happy songs. It's called "I Hope It's Raining on the Day I Die".'

I look around me so as to ascertain the extent of the audience. It comprises myself and a long-hair shouldering a guitar. By now it has occurred to me the lad in Little Mary's made an interesting point: I'd love to hear what Badtime Ray sings about.

When the song finishes, Long Hair crosses over and has a quick word with Goodtime Ray before walking away.

'What did he want?' I ask Ray, as he is packing up.

'He said I should be playing other venues.'

'Really? Like where?'

'The far side of the moon.'

I stop by the new theatre. They are putting in a night shift, the hoardings have come down, and I am just in time to see the last letter of the venue name raised high. As soon as it is hoisted into position, someone throws a switch and to an abbreviated round of applause the letters light up. I stand a while, staring up at the bright letters, shining like a friendly welcome in the rainsoaked night.

## STORY HOUSE

I swing by the bridge for a chat with the Beggar Flynn. I pour coins into his cap and ask him has he eaten anything decent recently. I gesture to the water and ask him has Dolores turned up yet. I turn away from the west wind, and ask him does he want to go to the movies. He grunts and tells me to go and take a running jump.

I switch on my phone. Flick through more messages. Fleming wants to know where I am. Another message from mother. *Please come home.* Another message from Jennifer. *Laura? Where are you? Are you OK?*

I'm thinking I should go and speak to daddy, but it's not that long since my last visit and he won't want me pestering him again so soon.

The rain comes down again and harder. The wind blows me every which way.

*

I am on my way back towards the Town Hall when I spot them in the street. The two of them huddled together beneath an umbrella. I call out his name. He looks up, and though I'm sure he has seen me, he doesn't stop. He steers Mia across the street. I follow, waving my arms while calling out to him. He doesn't seem to hear me. I call a little louder.

'Stephen! Stephen Fallow!'

This time he pauses. He and Mia have reached the junction of Cross Street and Middle Street. The rain seems to gather force as I approach them.

'There you are. I thought there for a moment you had gone deaf.'

'What can I do for you, Laura?' he says, glancing at his wristwatch.

'I'll wait for you inside,' Mia says, and she hurries into Little Mary's.

'It's about *Streetcar*, Stephen. I want to let you know that I have decided to accept your suggestion. I will play the part of Eunice – the neighbour from upstairs.'

'What?'

'The part you offered me. I accept,' I tell him, adding, 'I was a little rash before.'

'Laura. It's too late for that.'

'Too late? What do you mean it's too late?'

'I mean I've already cast the part.'

'What? But you said . . .'

'I didn't hear from you, Laura. I waited. But you . . .'

'Is there someone else?'

'I beg your pardon.'

'Someone else. There must be someone else I can play. Is there? Anyone. A street vendor. The Mexican woman selling flowers. *Flores para los muertos.* The nurse at the end who helps escort Blanche to the nuthouse. Anything, Stephen. I'll do it.'

'I've cast *all* the parts, Laura. There is no one left.'

'Stephen. Can I talk to you? Can I please talk to you about this?'

'Here, Laura. Take these. I have to go now. Goodbye.'

I stare at the already rain-damp theatre passes. Then watch Stephen Fallow at the door of Little Mary's. He pauses to shake out and fold down his umbrella. One or two smokers engage him in small talk. Laughter and good cheer all round. For the first time I feel my sodden clothes sticking to me, raindrops dripping off the tip of my nose, the ends of my hair. A pair of youths skip drunkenly either side of me, continue down Quay Street, brazenly belting out the words of a vaguely familiar song . . . *Oh the rain comes lashin', splish-splashin', down the town in a Galway fashion . . .*

Into Little Mary's I stride. Straightaway I see Stephen. Carrying drinks to the corner table crammed with the theatre crew. One or two I recognize from audition day. Others I have not seen before. Stephen is soon holding court, the others hanging off every word coming out his mouth. I take a high stool at the far end of the counter. I turn towards Stephen and his animated crew. Some of the new faces I assume have been cast in the play. I don't care to speculate as to which parts.

From my pocket I remove my purse, unzip it and spill coins onto the countertop. Save for an oldtimer with a long face and small ears sitting further down the counter, I have it all to myself.

'What can I get you?' asks the not-so-old barman with a spade for a jaw and cut-glass cheekbones.

'You're not my barman. Where's Gerry?'

'Gerry's on holidays.'

'On holidays! Gerry never takes holidays.'

'What can I get you?'

'Gimme a pair of whiskies, ginger ale on the side, and don't be stingy, baby.'

'Can I see some ID?'

'What did you say?'

'I'll serve you as soon as I see some ID.'

'Don't you know who I am?'

'No, and I don't really want to know.'

I have a good mind to rise off my stool, lean over the counter and – appealing or not – crack open this young teapot's head. But something warns me off. Relax. Take it as a compliment. Show him what he's asking for.

'You can see anything you want,' I tell him, warming up my flirty eyes and I root in my purse and toss him my medical card.

'A pair of whiskies and ginger ale coming up,' he says, handing back the plastic.

'And a pint of Hooker while you're at it. Send one of the whiskies down to the oldtimer.'

I half-spin around on my stool, take in the gathered theatre troupe. I am tempted to let out a hearty growl, tell them all where to go. Then the oldtimer pipes up.

'Haven't seen you in here before.'

I take up the little bottle of ginger ale and stare at it.

'Every man has seen me before, somewhere. The trick is to find me.'

Oldtimer cackles, swishes around his whiskey. Over my shoulder I can hear the others. They are in no hurry. That's OK. Neither am I. I have all the time in the world. I turn to Methuselah at the end of the bar.

'What are we drinking to?' I say. 'To feeling better? Is it desperate drinking in order to forget, be less ourselves? Or would you say it is something else entirely? Want to know what I think? Life is the search for the impossible via the useless. Bottoms up and down the hatch.'

Oldtimer cackles again. He finishes the whiskey and I shout him another.

'I'm an actress,' I tell him. 'I'm preparing for a role as we speak. And actually, my director,' I say and jerk back my head for effect. 'He's right there. Want to hear some more lines?'

Oldtimer looks to the barman and rolls his eyes. I get it. A hard-to-impress type. I should tell him something about myself no one else knows.

'You know, with my brains and your looks, we could go places. Ah! That got a smirk out of you. Come on, then.

Drink up and I'll buy you another one. Hey! Bar boy! *Garçon!* Pour the man another.'

The barroom fills up. Stephen's entourage expands. Soon there is standing room only. Spellman from the *Advertiser* and Hawkins from the *Tribune*. Emily is there. She gives me a little wave when she spots me. Camilla the Hun shoves a drink at her. From his best-seat-in-the-house perch Stephen is talking and waving his arms with gusto.

Mia is now on her feet, standing tall amongst the men gathered closely around her. She is gesturing as she speaks, throwing an arm here, touching a sleeve there, her big eyes and serene mouth providing all the dazzle her audience needs. They are smitten with every word that passes through her lips, totally under the spell she is casting. Not taking my eyes from the developing scene before me, I adjust my barstool, am just in time to hear Spellman wish Mia good luck and what a great choice she is. And Hawkins is busy with the dangling camera. And Stephen is smiling her way, as the others politely enquire if she is looking forward to the experience. Yes, I think I am, she replies in her smooth-as-silk voice. And she is fast into a speech about how excited she is to be playing the lead. A part like this doesn't come along every day, she says. Blanche DuBois is most likely at the top of every actor's wish list, she says. I wince when I hear her say the name. And a face on her that says, Look at me, I have won a trip to the stars.

I need to set her straight. I need to set everyone straight. The part isn't hers. It . . . belongs to . . .

'Excuse me,' I call over to them. 'There is something I

need to say.' No one pays any heed. 'Excuse me,' I try again, louder this time, slipping down off my barstool, the pint of Hooker in my hand. Mia turns to face me, an expression somewhere between confusion and amusement. Stephen touches her arm.

'Do I know you?'

For a moment I stand opposite her, scarcely believing my ears. *Do I know you? DO I KNOW YOU!* And just when I need them most no words will come. I spin around and move as fast as I can out of the barroom.

I stomp into the toilets. Stare at the graffiti written across the wall where the mirror should be.

## JUST ASSUME YOU LOOK LIKE SHIT

I turn on all the taps, press down the stoppers, lean on the metal disc of the hand dryer. And I let loose.

Raaaaaaaaaaaaaaaaaaaaaaaaaaaaaaaaaaaaaaaaaaaaaaaa aaaaaaaaaaaaaaaaaaaaaaah!

When I return to the barroom, Mia is getting cosy beside Stephen. On his lap she more or less sits. In her tinsel dress. Beaming. Legs confidently crossed. The glowing hair, which is given a two-handed flick every couple of minutes. Every part of her pointing the way ahead. She whispers something which has Stephen in raptures.

Then the lummox starts singing.

For Stephen's benefit, no doubt. And, once again, there is a general hush around the bar, as she belts out the song's melody. It's a familiar song, I know I have heard it before, and don't particularly care for it. I don't particularly care for her singing voice either. It's jaunty and slight, way too chirpy-chirp. Already, it's making me dizzy. Everyone present seems to be in love with it, though, at least they pretend they are. Stephen most of all.

I have heard enough. Dizzy I may be but up onto a barstool I stand, clutching my pint of Hooker.

'Ladies and gentlemen, I have a song I would like to share. A story actually. A sad story. About a little girl who had a dream. A silver-screen dream, a dream of seeing her name written in bright and dancing lights. This dream was a gift from her daddy and the little girl was only too happy to accept it. And she kept it tucked safely away inside her every minute of every day of every week of every month of every year. Until she had her chance. Her moment has arrived. Opening night and she is all set to wow her audience. Except it doesn't go the way she has always imagined it will. And she feels so bad for having messed it up. She feels bad for having let her audience down. For having let her daddy down. And how can I make it up to you, she wants to know. Then she has an idea. She will make another dream for herself. A comeback dream. She is to be the lead in a play. A play daddy himself had a starring role in. And this time she swears to herself and her daddy that she won't cock it up. She will show the audience what they had missed out on last time. She will show the theatre world what she is capable of. She will make her daddy oh-so proud. And she pictures the look on his face come opening night. So happy. And this time nothing will go wrong. There will be no last-minute nerves. No sudden collapses. And that is precisely how it plays. Every moment of every scene . . . And there . . . See her when the curtain comes down. Hear her name reverberating around the auditorium. The calls for her to take another bow. The deafening applause . . .'

Silence in the barroom. A cough or two. Someone snorts. I scan vaguely for Stephen, eager to see his face, detect some kind of reaction. But the dizziness has taken over and everything about me has become a blur.

'If you have a song to sing, sing it for Christ's sake,' snarls a lad cradling a banjo. 'I want to get home sometime this year.'

The heart is clapping inside me now, I'm struggling to take in air. I summon a half-smile for my audience, raise the pint of Hooker, and with a brief bow and curtsy, up-end it over myself. Then I clamber down from the barstool and bolt for the door out of there.

# 29

On the street, a short ways down from Little Mary's. The rain has eased. The streetlights reflected in the puddles about my feet. For company I now have a naggin of brandy. Pisser Kelly has joined me. I offer him the naggin and I watch him untwist the cap, and then gag down a mouthful. He hands it back and I wonder aloud where his dirty lips have been. 'Where have your own been?' he cackles back at me. 'Touché,' I say to that, raise the naggin in his honour, gulp down a neckful and present what's left to him for keeps.

I close my eyes, but as soon as I do an image of daddy at the end of the pier presents itself, and so I open them again. People, drunk and leery, leave the bars they have been inside. I allow them distract me. Boozy couples, all jibber-jabber and walking crooked lines. Clusters of young men and women. One woman is sobbing and another is pouring her heart out to no one in particular and another has chosen the wall I am leaning against to heave up her guts. I look towards Tone Bridge, can hear the river. Two youths are in the midst of yanking a bicycle away from the pole it has been locked to. They manage to get it loose, over the bridge wall it goes, and the ensuing splash is greeted with a loud cheer.

At last they appear. Arm-in-arm. The one leaning into the other. Look at her. In her tinsel dress. Linking his arm and letting him steer her wherever he wants. All high heels and tittering. A peck on the cheek, a giggle, a squeeze of his fleshy parts. That's OK. I can bide my time. For now she can have her fun.

They lurch, giggling and wobbly together, towards where I am standing, towards the harbour. Then they pause, and turn around as though they have changed their minds and are contemplating returning up town. Then they continue towards me. Halfway down Quay Street, Stephen pulls her into Druid Lane. 'Come on,' I hear him say, as I narrow the distance between. 'I want to show you something.' As soon as they have disappeared into the alley, I follow.

A couple of moments later they have emerged out the other end, have zigzagged their way, and are now standing outside the Story House, admiring the same letters I had earlier.

Taking Mia by the hand, Stephen moves around the side of the building. 'This way,' I hear him whisper. After them I go.

They are huddled together directly beneath the looming letters of the new theatre. Stephen spreads wide his arms and audibly gasps. Mia giggles and wanders out onto the road in order to better stare up at the building. Stephen joins her and they both stare together.

Hush, Laura. They are talking.

'You'll be the toast of theatreland after this show.'

'Oh, I don't know about that. I've still got a lot to learn.'

'You're a natural. Trust me. I know what I'm talking about.'

'Why, thank you, kind sir.'

'I'm just stating the obvious. Now get over here.'

Stephen is now leaning against leftover hoarding, against the poster announcing his imminent production, while Mia glides about, offering token lines, throwing her arms for effect, all of which has Stephen slapping his knees.

'I'm travelling over to London after opening night. I'm seeing some important people. You should come along.'

'I'd love to.'

She slides past him, reaches down her arms and raises her dress a few inches up her thighs. Stephen lunges for her but she evades his reach, skipping a few steps away from him before offering a wiggle and beckoning Stephen towards her.

'Come and get me, Mr Theatre Man,' she says, all pout and quiver-lips. Stephen doesn't need a second invitation. He reaches out with both arms and this time there is no evading his lunge and she allows him clutch her tight and then twist her around and that dress is quickly raised and his corduroys are dropping down, and for an anxious moment he is floundering about in his attempts to get at her.

'Come and get me, Mr Theatre Man,' I call out from my discreet spot.

'What was that?' Mia says, looking round her.

'I have no idea,' Stephen says, looking searchingly about him. 'Let's get out of here,' he says, and they are not long tidying themselves up and skedaddling.

I'm on the street behind them. Arm-in-arm they are, the one leaning into the other, all love-dove and already into a fast stride.

They cut down by Lynch's Castle and make for the Weir Bridge, and then on towards the canal. They stop outside Stephen's place, tugging at each other as Stephen looks for his keys. They disappear inside.

I walk to the end of street, turn left and enter the laneway running along the ends of the houses. I pause at the back of Stephen's place. Getting over the wall is a fool's errand. I push against the wooden gate and at once it gives. I stumble through the dark and itty-bit garden. Reach the vague light thrown up in front of me. I peer through the window. I can see them on the sofa. A little laughter. A little canoodling. A sip of a drink. A fondle here, a nibble there. More laughter. With my fingernails I start tapping on the window. Then I stand back, look down at the ground. Pick up some stones and lob them at the window. Plink, plink, plink they go. No reaction from the lovebirds. I reach for larger ones. Stephen is walking across the room. I duck behind some wheelie bins. He pulls a curtain. Again, I move right up to the window. I can just about see. Stephen has his shirt off and is helping his guest out of her dress. His fingers, hands, lips, face smothering what passes for her fleshy bits. Again, I stand back and hurl another stone. His hand reaches in under her dress. His other is tugging open his corduroys. While Mia reaches over to lend a hand. I hurl another stone. But director man is in no mood to hang about. He slides fully out and rubs himself into Mia's pelvis, his shiny buttocks rippling before my eyes. Not the best time to grab his attention, Laura. Ha! Ha! That's OK. I haven't planned on sticking around. I stand further back, reach down, pick up a rock and watch it crash through the window. Glass scatters. Mia screams. Somewhere a dog starts barking.

*

I make my way to the pier-end and stand at the very edge. I lean into the sea-breeze. Taste salt on my tongue. Listen to the water below.

And look out there, Laura. Can you see it? Look. A cruise ship. Passing this way. Actually, it looks like it's anchored down for the night. Passengers will want to be ferried ashore. Well, if they chop-chop they will be in time to catch one of my bespoke walking tours. I wonder where they all came from. The other side of the world, most likely. The always-sunny side. California. San Francisco and Los Angeles. Hollywood types! Yes, of course. Oh, where is Fleming when I need him? Because you know what we could do? When they come ashore we could cadge a lift out to the cruise liner. We could stash ourselves somewhere. Out of sight. Know what I mean? And when we look again . . . I can see it all . . . A warm sun greeting us when we arrive in Los Angeles, City of Angels. There will be some press commitments and my publicity people will be keen for me to show my face around town. A reception to attend, a gala banquet in my honour, and that's good, we can make time for all of that. Can't we, Fleming? But before any of that, you know what I am going to do? I am going to nab my driver – Conrad, his name will be – and his limousine for an hour, and get him to take me for a spin along Sunset Boulevard. A balmy evening and I roll down the window and angle my head and let the fresh breeze play with my hair. A warm feeling beginning at the base of my stomach ripples all the way through me. I will almost wish I was a singer. And for a few minutes I'll think about the song I could write along this drive through movieland, how good it makes me feel. At some point we'll happen upon a drive-in cinema. To my delight they are showing *In a Lonely Place* or maybe even *Sunset Boulevard*, and I plead with Conrad to pull in. Conrad tuts and points out the time and so I dispatch him to the busy popcorn stand while I sit up in the front seat of the limo for a better view of the screen. On our way back I'll ask Conrad to pull over where Hollywood Boulevard meets Vine Street. I'll step out, and for a block or two, pick my way among the star-studded pavement. At some point, perhaps because he has received a call summoning me back to base, Conrad will join me on the footpath. 'Oh look,' I can hear him say, pointing at a star I haven't noticed. 'It's your star.' And there I am. All over the path before me. My name among the stars. Won't that be grand?

Indeed it will, Laura.

Indeed it will.

*

I'm standing outside the front window of the house, peering through the gap in the curtains. They are all in the sitting room. Mother and Peter Porter. Jennifer and Little Juan. Yoohoo Lucy. Fiona French. Odd Doris and Dolores. One or two others I vaguely recognize. And Fleming. Music and laughter. Dancing. Now a collective hush. And someone has dimmed the lights. And now a candle-lit cake. And the song. *Happy birthday to you.* And Little Juan is encouraged to offer the Spanish version. *Cumpleaños Feliz. Hip, hip hooray. Hip, hip hooray.* Cheers and applause. Popped bubbly. The birthday girl is in tears. Mother is in tears. Little Juan and Fleming put on their party hats and blow streamers. They whoop and holler. The music is turned up. Fleming grabs Jennifer and Little Juan and together the three of them form a dancing circle. Mother and Peter Porter join in and now the others and they all form a dancing circle around Jennifer. *For she's a jolly good fellow. And so say all of us.*

*

Barna Woods. Moonlight and dew and peace and calm after the rain. My friends the trees. I reach inside the hollowed oak and pull out the scrapbook, tear open the plastic bag. I reach in again and feel around until my fingers wrap themselves around the knife. I tuck it away inside my pocket. I seek the clearing I am so fond of. I grip the scrapbook and rip out its first pages. Then the next and the next. I tear and shred and toss ribbons of paper into the darkness around me. I gather pages into a tidy pile, flick my lighter and watch them burn, burn, burn. Movie faces. Favourite scenes. Lines of dialogue. Names of characters. Pasted-in clippings. I watch it all come apart before my eyes, see my words become flames and take to the air. Drift, flutter, spark hither and thither, softly land on the ground around me. All the movie parts and all the movie lines. An entire movie world's worth, flittered into thin air.

*Do I know you?* Well, Miss Come-and-get-me Tinsel Dress. By the time your opening-night performance comes around you'll know me.

That you can be sure of.

I drop spread-eagled to the ground, seeing stars, listening to my own laughter. I slip my hand inside my pocket, dance my fingers along the knife. I watch the silent branches, discern grotesque patterns, watch the gnarled trunks transform themselves into familiar faces. I settle in for a long night of secret conversation. I start singing out the names of my trees. I have fallen asleep before I get very far. And as soon as I wake up I know exactly what it is I am going to do.

# GLORIA SWANSON

March 27, 1899 – April 4, 1983
aka Norma Desmond

**Inducted:** February 8, 1960
**Star address:** 6750, Hollywood Blvd (movies);
6301, Hollywood Blvd (television)
Screen debut at age 15
Made and spent eight million during the 1920s
One Golden Globe, three Oscar nominations
and six husbands
Icon of the silent era. 10,000 fan letters a week
**Real name:** Gloria May Josephine Svensson

*'Writing the story of your life is
a bit like drilling your own teeth.'*

# 30

For a time, brief and by-and-large untested, when I was very little I used to think I could walk through walls. I could float, drift, hover wherever I liked, when the mood took me. I could haunt people that bothered me, show up when least expected, say boo! I could make different shapes of myself, fit through cracks and narrow openings. I could slide, swish and sway. I could be here and not here. Walk on water, dance through mountains, tiptoe my way in the spaces between tall buildings. These were things I could do because I had decided I could.

I used to so enjoy imagining the world around me through the eyes of others. Strangers. Foreigners. Long-ago people. People yet to live. Dream people even, floating forms caught in a no-man's-land between this life and another, slipped inside my skin to register an experience and then out again and away back to their place of origin.

I would so easily lose count of the number of different people I became.

*

In their own particular way, everyone has been communicating as to my no-show the night of Jennifer's birthday.

Fleming knows better than to ask. Jennifer is acting as though it doesn't matter. Little Juan tells me over and over again all the good stuff I missed out on. Mother, though. Mother knows something is off. And it is bugging her because she can't quite alight on precisely what it is. She has tried coming at it from an angle. She has tried the direct approach. And she is not fully buying my line that, on the night of Jennifer's birthday, we were rehearsing until the early hours of the morning. Suffice to say that for the past couple of weeks she has been watching me very closely. That's OK. A couple of evenings ago I came up with an easy way of dealing with this unwanted scrutiny. And I am doing something I thought it unlikely I would ever get to do – I have moved in with Fleming.

All is well – for a day or two. Fleming rustles up a hearty meal or three. He doesn't pry too much. I even get to meet the brothers, who make a great show of being on their best behaviour.

The evening before opening night, I receive a rather interesting note from Imelda.

*Dearest Laura,*

*You are not going to believe this. Call it an impromptu decision on my part. Something, no doubt, to do with the attitude certain bigwigs are adopting in relation to some suggestions I have for the Scorsese project. Rewrites I have deemed necessary for my character. Plus an issue I have with one or two of the shooting locations. (If the movie significantly references Sunset Boulevard I don't see why we cannot film there. Marty reckons we can do it all in his beloved New York, but I'm not so sure he is right on this occasion.) And cue the clamour for an urgent conference call in order to resolve these sudden bumps in the road the moneymen seem to think I am causing. Me! Imelda J Ebbing. The single most important reason this project is getting off the ground in the first place. Don't they realize I have better things to do with my time, that I need to get into character for this once-in-a-lifetime part? That's what I had to say to Falstaff when he came for me, like the tap-dancer of doom he is fast becoming. And so I had to interrupt my morning sleep in order to indulge some infantile whimsies drummed up in a boardroom half a planet away. Martians, Laura. It's the only word for them.*

*Come on, then, I said, once seated at my desktop. Let me have it with both barrels, I told the moneymen, a uniquely baffling quintet, seated in line at a table so large it was clearly meant to intimidate me but instead merely dwarfed the suited numbskulls behind it. And* quelle surprise! It was *not the rewrites I am insisting on they wanted to talk about, nor my vigour for a Hollywood location shoot. What was most pressing is the myriad stories concerning my dalliance with Ennio, stories that seem to be readily available to just about anyone*

*who is bothered – along with a variety of suitably
compromising photographs. Lurid shots taken in
hotel rooms, according to one of my interrogators,
a bespectacled boor who would better serve the
world by making ice cubes at the South Pole. This
is going to be costly, declared another, frantically
pointing to Exhibit A, a gutter-press tabloid I
couldn't quite make out. And why, a particularly
odious one of them was very keen to ascertain, have
I declined to mention anything of this?*

*Yes, but you see, I said, now that it was clearly
my turn to speak, I thought we had gathered at this
unearthly hour to scale the heights of artistic
endeavour. I will say this, however: Ennio has the
most captivating mouth. And so, to borrow a
sentiment from my favourite actress, go hump
yourselves! Now please, if any of you screwballs
has anything worthwhile to contribute, say it now.
Otherwise this call is at an end.*

*Of course the spineless jibber-jabbers didn't
particularly care for being dictated to like this.
They'll be in touch, they said, before I had a chance
to say anything else, and that is the last I have
heard from them. No doubt they have gone away to
chatter amongst themselves, big-boys' style.*

*Let them. Let them chatter. Let them pussyfoot.
They'll come crawling back. They always do. And
that is when they will realize what a mistake it was
interrupting my beauty sleep.*

Meantime, the gutter press are hot on my heels, determined not to permit me a moment's respite. Some of them have even set up camp outside the gates of my home, zoom lenses at the ready. There's even a rumour that Svetlana the cellist is lurking in the vicinity. Goodness! I hope she hasn't brought along her bow and arrow. Falstaff suggested that I vanish off the grid, lay low in some no-name backwater nobody has heard of – until the entire ludicrous affair blows over. And this is when I came up with an absolute winner of a plan, dispatched Falstaff to make some calls and la-di-da I am coming, Laura. I am coming to see you!

My people have set it all up. I googled that theatre company you may or may not be involved with, and lo-and-behold it turns out that a certain opening night is imminent. Falstaff has already booked me a front-row seat. Against his will, Sir Henry is coming too. I'll drag him kicking and squealing if I have to. So, Laura, please say I am going to see you walk out when the curtain goes up. Afterwards, we can catch up properly. I'll even let you show me around that little harbour, you can point me out those starry lights you used to labour on about all the time. OK. I must dash. Falstaff is going to whisk me cloak-and-dagger style to the airport. Sooo exciting! See you at the theatre. Kiss, kiss. Bang, bang. You're dead! Mel. x

At first I'm tempted to panic. Last thing I need is made-it-big Imelda showing up on opening night. Making a fuss. *So, then. Where is she? Where's my favourite sparring partner?* I dwell on it for a bit, then begin to realize that her coming all this way may not be such a bad thing after all. In fact, it might actually work out in my favour. And the more I think about it the more inclined I am to see how her appearance might be of use. After all, it is none other than yours truly she has come all this way to see, it is yours truly she will be talking about when she turns to Mr Super-Agent sitting in the front row alongside her. *There! What did I tell you?* It is yours truly she will insist on when it comes time to cast . . . Oh my, Laura. Think of the possibilities.

*

It's almost light out. A clear light – sharp and golden, a world away from the cloying, grey light that usually accompanies the November rains. Fleming and myself are squirrelled away inside his shoebox bedroom. Beyond the thin walls we can hear his brothers take turns barking at each other and cat-calling at us. They have been at it all through the night. At long last things reach breaking point, one of them says the wrong thing and the fighting breaks out.

'You know what we should do,' Fleming says, tickling my neck. 'We should get out of Dodge. Leg it, once and for all time. You and me.'

'Go on,' I say.

'Under cover of dark we'll do it. I'll take the brother's car. I'll meet you at the harbour bridge. And we'll drive the hell out of here and not turn back.'

'Where will we go?'

'We'll just keep driving. Across rivers and streams. Up and down the mountains. Around the bottomless lakes. We'll stop when we have to. We'll take a boat when we need to. And when we reach the other side we'll point ourselves towards the nearest open road and on we go.'

'And how will we live?'

'We'll live off the land. Off our wits. Off the strangers we'll meet. Hell, we might even strike it lucky somewhere and get taken in by a dying billionaire. We'll end up landed gentry if we're not careful.'

Fleming smiles when he says that bit, as next door a bottle crashes off a wall.

'You'll be lord of the manor,' I say.

'You'll be a lady.'

'Oh, my. Pass me the soup, darling, would you?'

'Why, of course, my lady. Tell me, how are the quails?'

'Divine. Absolutely divine. By the way, sweetness. What do you think of my laugh? I think it needs to be more superior.'

Fleming chortles at that. It's a pleasant fiction he has conjured. Who knows? In another life I might even have taken him up on his offer.

There is a loud yelp from next door. Someone gets called a thundering bollox. Another bottle crash-lands.

'Here we go,' Fleming says next.

'What! You mean to say they're only starting *now*?'

'They're warming up now. That was a good party you missed the other week.'

'What party would that be?'

'Jennifer's birthday. We were all wondering where you were.'

'I don't remember.'

'I'd say you do.'

'Well, then. You don't need to ask.'

Another bottle lands, this one against the bedroom door, quickly followed by an alternating combo of Tarzan yelps and chest beating. Someone gets called a bad case of the plague. A herpes-laden fuckwit. A stale ballsack. An evaporated prick.

'They're getting closer,' I say.

'Still warming up,' Fleming says to that. 'Have you figured out what you're doing about this play?'

'Jesus, Fleming. Questions. I came here to get away from all that.'

'I'm just saying. Today's the day, you know. Opening night. In fact, in about twelve hours' time the curtain will be coming up.'

'And?'

'And? What do you mean, And? You do realize your mother is going? She told me so herself. Herself and Peter Porter.'

'You better not have said anything.'

'I haven't. But I think *you* should.'

'That won't be necessary.'

'Why not?'

A prolonged wolf-howl emanates from next door. Some-one gets called a crossbreed's leftovers. Someone's head is compared to a bull's testicle. I'm tempted to offer some assistance towards the name-calling.

'I told you before why not.'

'Would you mind telling me again.'

'Because, on the occasion of this opening night you've been banging on about non-stop, if people are expecting to see me onstage then that is precisely where they are going to find me.'

'But . . . Laura . . .'

The bedroom door swings open and three or four – it is difficult to tell precisely how many – of Fleming's brothers fall into the room. They scuffle with each other, chant random and by-and-large indecipherable swearwords, someone unseen throws a bottle that spins through the open doorway and lands among them.

For a moment they cease what they are doing – as though this rogue bottle has it within its powers to quell the ludicrous posturing. It is only then that I notice they are all scantily attired, among the garments on show are three socks, two string-vests, and canary-yellow Y-fronts. One of them has inked the letters DESTROYER across his chest. The one in the canary-yellow Y-fronts has decided to smear himself in something that reeks of Deep Heat. Are these lads for real? I am about to ask Fleming when the main event begins. I'm not fully sure what it is, but it seems to be some sort of homoerotic display that requires lots of pawing and slapping and groping for whatever bits of flesh can be gripped and twisted into hitherto unknown shapes. Fleming looks at me as if to say, happens all the time.

'I'm going now, Fleming,' I say. 'I have a part to prepare for.'

## 31

So, daddy. Today is the day. The Story House opens its doors for the very first time. And Khaos Theatre gets to strut its stuff in its new home. It's a beautiful day, I cannot get over how clear it is, somebody must have handed over a king's ransom for the wind and rain to pack it in. And here I am to tell you that I have come to a momentous decision. I am getting the hell out of here. Once and for all. I need to grab some things, pack a going-away bag. Possibly, I should leave a note for mother. Let her know of my plans, that I have been offered a wonderful opportunity in London, that in actual fact I am leaving immediately after this opening-night performance, and that there is no time to say goodbye in person. Mark my words, daddy. A rollercoaster adventure awaits. I really don't know why I didn't think of it sooner.

It's Imelda I have to thank. Since moving to London she hasn't put a foot wrong. In her own inimitable way she's been on and on at me to get over there. To London, I mean. She has made lots of contacts and it's pretty obvious she'll be able to help me out. I'll probably stay with her until I am settled and ready to look for my own place. Imagine, daddy. Little me lighting up Shaftesbury Avenue. Imelda's going to be in town this evening, actually. She's coming to whisk me out of here in person.

First things first, though. I have some unfinished matters with Khaos Theatre, matters I intend to see through before travelling across the pond to where my talents will be more appreciated. So don't worry, daddy, I am not going anywhere just yet. And before I do scarper, I will come say goodbye, let you wish me bon voyage. For now, all that remains to be said is fasten your safety belt, it's going to be a bumpy night.

## 32

This is where I need to be very careful. I need to get inside my room. Pick something to wear. Do my face. And I need to do it all unseen. Don't want mother and Jennifer involving themselves in my opening-night preparations. I can imagine what that will entail. Jennifer hauling me in front of the bathroom mirror, deliberating at length over what to put on, over what shade goes with what. *Oh, that colour tone. Oh, and your hair. You look like a star, Laura. You really do.* While, downstairs and out of earshot, mother puts in a call to St Jude's, lets them know I am ready to go back.

I move along our road, and tra-la-la, there is a white van parked outside our little gate. So here they are, hell or high water all set to cart me out of there. Back to St Jude's by special delivery. They hardly think I'm going to fall for something like this, do they? They try something like it on Gloria Swanson in *Sunset Boulevard*. And, of course, at the end of *Streetcar* Vivien Leigh, of all people, is led rightly down the garden path, thinks she is on the arm of her knight in shining armour, while all along she is being escorted to the nearest funny farm. Well. I can do a little play-along myself. They are not going to make a mung bean out of me. Not this time.

I stay well out of sight as mother opens the front door. 'At long last,' I hear Jennifer call out, with a ridiculous laugh. She walks out to talk to the lad getting out of the van. A shake of the hand and hello, how are you? *Yes, I'm her sister. Yes, this time it's pretty bad. We might need the jacket with straps after all.* They move around the side of the van. A door slides open and – lo-and-behold – Jennifer's luggage emerges. Arrived after all this time from whatever round-the-world adventure it has been on. No straitjacket for me just yet, then.

And then someone I do not expect to see appears. Fleming. My leading man. He's helping Jennifer with her bags. Who keeps dying and making him the good Samaritan? Look at him. All schmooze and banter. Jennifer laughing at everything out of his mouth. She thinks he's the funniest lad in the world. Listen to them. I do not like this. I do not like this at all. I close my eyes to counter the dizziness. By the time I open them again Jennifer's luggage has been taken inside, the white van is gone, and Fleming is leaving the house. I duck well out of his way.

\*

I move around the side of the house. I can hear them in the kitchen and so I hold back near the open window. They are at the kitchen table. Mother and Jennifer. Jennifer is sitting down, allowing mother draw out and caress the long strands of her hair. Occasionally mother holds on to a few strands and brings them to her face, inhales and sighs pleasantly.

For I don't know how long I stand there and watch mother close her eyes and breathe in the scent of Jennifer's hair and release it only to grab another portion and clutch it to her face.

I wait for talk of St Jude's and what delights I have to look forward to. But they are not talking about that. Jennifer's and Little Juan's well-being seems to be the topic of conversation. And Alonso gets a mention, and as soon as he does the tears arrive, along with lots of sniffing, and the handkerchiefs are fast running out. 'Do you really have to go back?' mother asks. 'Could you not call them and post-pone the next contract?' Jennifer mentions having to see it through now that she has committed, and for the next minute she sniffs and blows her troubled nose, not stopping until mother has offered all manner of reassurance and help.

Jennifer says something else, but I cannot fully hear. I lean into the open window and can see mother holding Jennifer's hand.

'But I thought . . .' Mother's reaction when she gets a chance to say something. There is that softness in her voice again, resignation too. '. . . I thought that you might stay, make a go of it over here.' Barely has she begun than she stops again. And for a minute, long and silent, there is no talking.

I am tempted to make a grand entrance and wish my darling sister a hearty bon voyage back to whatever corner of the world she is headed for, when mother starts again.

'And, Laura? What am I going to do with Laura? Doctor

Harper has been on to me again. She's missed another appointment.'

'I wish I could be of more use,' Jennifer says. 'I wish I knew what magic button to press.' And I see my mother, her lips pressing hard together, her eyes welling up, nodding slowly at every word.

'I know I shouldn't say this,' mother says as soon as she can speak again, 'but she is starting to really scare me. What if something had happened to Juan that day at the circus? Or out on the pier? And this obsession with the theatre . . . I often wonder how she would have turned out if Frank hadn't . . .'

I am no longer listening. I am my ten-year-old self again. At full pelt along the pier. Not paying a bit of heed to the gusting wind. Not stopping until I reach the end of the pier. And daddy standing there . . . dark night and the swirling rain and the seawater roiling so strong is the wind . . . In time to come I would try not to think of him standing out there on his own, would often wonder what might have been his final thought, in the very last moment, in the seconds between when he is still a presence, standing on the lip of the pier, and when he is no longer there.

Mother is speaking again.

'I remember you being so upset afterwards. Calling out his name in your sleep. But Laura. She hardly said a word. By herself up on that boathouse. In her room staring at those movie posters. It was as though she had gone numb.'

They are both silent for a bit. They lean forward and hug each other, allow the embrace have its moment. Then

Little Juan – who else? – turns up and he is wrangled into the hug and this gesture of togetherness seems to magic up some good energy because they are now on their feet and fussing about him, and now the phone is ringing. It's Peter Porter, and my, my, is that the time, come on, come on, we have to eat before the show, and they disappear out of the kitchen and after a flurry of getting-ready activity the three of them leave the house and, at last, I have the place to myself.

\*

I'm now in the spare room upstairs. Going through Jennifer's luggage. She has some nice things. I hold them up to the mirror. An array of flirty skirts. Sleeveless tops. Look at all the colours. Mellow green. Happy yellow. Contemplative turquoise. Oh, and here's a saucy mauve. Very saucy indeed. And the dresses. Ah, yes. I should have guessed. Short and fitted all the way. So light I bet I could sit down on a coin and tell if it's heads or tails. Skimpy thongs too. Ooh, and fishnet stockings. These I can definitely stretch into. No matter a little tear here and there. And what have we here? Hippy-dippy sandals. Thank you very much, sister. Now, you're talking my language. Yes. They go well with my feet. And now the skirt. And now one of these tops. I think the mauve. And are these silk gloves the length of my arms? And what have we here? A box of jewels. I need something to show off my soon-to-be glistening complexion. Ring. Bracelet. Pendant to go around my neck. Oh yes.

They are all a perfect fit. And what is this? Shadow for the eyes. Rouge for the lips. White powder for the face. Everything that will make me look the part for my performance. Oh, and sunglasses. In the shape of octagons. Perfect. I can move incognito.

Back in my own room I stand before the mirror.

Well, would you look at that. A completely different person.

Goodbye, Laura Cassidy. Has-been. Also-ran. Never heard of you. Nobody.

Hello, performer extraordinaire.

Critics' darling.

Fans' favourite.

Legend in her time.

Superstar.

At last, worth a million dollars.

Isn't that right? I say to my crew on the wall, and they nod their heads in collective agreement.

*

First things first. A little toddy for the body. A pre-performance cocktail. Or three. To take the edge off, so to speak.

I scour the place, pull out what I can find in the line of booze, procure glasses, a carton of juice, ice, haul it all outside and set everything down on the coffee table I drag out into the front garden.

I put my menu together. Cocktails for everyone. Heroes

and villains. Friend and foe. Bimbo and genius. Assassin and victim.

Here is my Killer Queen. A hearty combination of Bombay gin, lemon juice, sugar syrup, topped with a generous measure of fizzy wine and garnished with a bursting-at-the-seams raspberry. Here's to you, Lana.

Here is my Femme Fatale. It's the same as the Killer Queen, only with twice the amount of gin and fizzy wine. And a strawberry instead of that other thing. Bottoms up and down the hatch, Barbara.

And this one I think I will name Trouble Is My Business. Guaranteed to take the enamel off your teeth. In honour of my good friends, Gloria and Veronica.

I position the deckchair. Sit myself down, slip on my sunglasses, reach for my drink and sip away.

Fifteen minutes later I am on my fourth. Slouched into the deckchair. Middle of the front garden. Sunglasses. Harbour views. A tall glass with an umbrella and a straw. I've tossed in measures of this, that and the other. Not bad at all, if I say so. Not bad at all.

Yoohoo Lucy passes by.

'Hello, Yoohoo Lucy. Isn't it a lovely day? All of Spain would be glad of a day like this, don't you think? I was just about to make myself a Scourge of the Street. Will you join me?'

She's never heard of a cocktail called Scourge of the Street. I'm making it all up as I go along, Lucy. Here, try it. No? Well, what about this one? It's called a Build My Gallows High. Sandpaper rough and redolent of burning tractor tyres. Though I might have gone a little heavy on the grenadine. Look at this instead. I call it my Kiss Tomorrow Goodbye. Puts me in mind of rotting fish. Hmmm. Too much lime in that one. Oh, you can't stop. You're off to the theatre. See you there!

Juan. I should organize a cocktail for him. A very special little-man cocktail. And here comes a very dressed-up couple. Haven't seen them around these parts before. 'Hello there,' I call out. 'Step this way. Have a drink with me.' They look at me as though a set of feet has started growing out of my head and they hurry on.

Glick Nolan and his missus pass by. Half-pausing, they look my way. I raise my glass. 'Cheers,' I say. 'Next stop Broadway.'

They look at me as though that set of feet has started to sprout daffodils. They continue on their way.

I don't blame them in the slightest.

I wonder where Peter Porter has taken the others. I bet my second Oscar that they are plotting. Planning to catch me off-guard. Let the loony booze herself up, then, when she least expects it, we'll bundle her in the van and away with her to St Jude's, out of our sight for the foreseeable and good riddance. Fleming better not have said a word to them. Otherwise I will lift him up by the ankle, pour cooking oil all over him and strike a match.

Well. If the crowd won't come to the party I will just have to move this party and performance a little further up town.

Won't I, Laura?

Yes, you will, Laura. Yes, you will.

# 33

On the bridge I count five, seven, eight couples all set for a gala event. Dress suits. Black ties. Gowns straight out of a period drama. 'What says the town's top-earning beggar, you fancy going to a party?' I say to the Beggar Flynn, flashing my theatre passes, and notice he is not where he has been for just about every day since I care to remember. Dolores Taaffe must have finally turned up. Another dressed-up couple passes me. I fall in behind.

I move on from the bridge, follow the bend of the road which has been closed off to traffic. And still more people, in their finery, moving in the same direction, towards the familiar location. Of course they are. This is an event nobody wants to miss.

And there it is. I never thought I would see the day. The Story House. In all its glory. At long last ready for business.

A few people are milling around outside. A few? Make that a couple of hundred. In their finery. Photographers. Journalists. TV crew. A few talking heads surround a portly man adorned with a weighty-looking chain. Red ribbons surround the entrance doors. Matching carpet on the front steps. Why wouldn't there be? It's opening night. Anyone who thinks they are anyone is here for the occasion. But

Fleming. He keeps messaging me. *Laura? Where are you? Laura, you're not going to do anything stupid, are you?* Silly boy. I really hope that mother and Jennifer have not put some kind of hex on him. I turn off my phone and throw myself into the horde.

'Make way, make way. Actress coming through.'

The gathering crowd parts before me like the waves did for that demented old codger in the Bible. I unfurl my gloved arms so as to claim more room. I nod and smile for those who stare at me. Make way, make way. Actress coming through. Everyone obliges. Of course they do. A star in the making is among them. Need an autograph? A lock of my hair? Some wise words? Oh, there's the photo-man from the *Advertiser*. And the journo from the *Tribune*. I'm so sorry. Is it OK if I answer questions later? Now, where is my director? I can do a small scene for him. Right here on the red carpet. A taster for what's to come.

Along the red carpet I sashay. The people cheer me on. One or two whistle and applaud as I pass by. The photographers are snapping good-oh. Look this way, Laura. And over here, please, Laura. Oh, my. That camera flash is exceedingly harsh.

By now I have reached the top of the steps and I turn around to take in my fans. My adoring fans. They are all applauding me. Thank you, thank you. Thank you all for coming out. Without you, none of this would be possible. And now, if you will excuse me, I must go inside. I need to find my director.

There are more people inside the foyer. Drinks to hand. Nibbling food bits. Falling over themselves to compliment the new building. A kiss on the cheek. And another. And how are you? I haven't seen you since forever. And don't you look absolutely stunning? And where did you get that dress? Oh, this plain-Jane rag? I picked it up when we were passing through Venice. Or was it Cannes? Cruelty-free, you know. And doesn't that colour suit you so? And that chain. And your hair. Is that cruelty-free too? Oh, you look wonderful.

Everybody looks wonderful.

Wonderful, wonderful, wonderful.

Don't they, Laura?

Absolutely, yes they do. Absolutely.

My head is spinning by the time I spot him coming through the crowd. Stephen Fallow. My director. His strong chin. His manly hands. A purple scarf whipped twice around his neck. Stepping up the red carpet and inside the shining new building. He is probably thinking: where is my leading lady? And I am thinking: I should make an effort to say hello.

Mia is on his arm.

I push through a circle of powdered mannequins, help them spill some drink, elicit a how-dare-you look or two. 'Make way, make way. Actress coming through,' I squeak. 'Yes, it's me,' I reassure them as they look my way. 'Should we know you?' a giraffe-like thing asks me. 'No, we shouldn't,' says another one of them, guffawing like a ferret.

I mingle among the ever-gathering crowd. Oh, hello to

you. And to you. Oh, don't mind me. I'm just hanging with my fans before curtain call. Meet good people, drink bad wine. That sort of thing. Or is it drink good wine, meet bad people? I can never remember. I really can't.

On the steps someone is starting into a speech. The crowd hushes to tune in to the talking head, that chain weighing him down. Everybody wants to hear his words. I drift further into the lobby, make my way towards what I assume is the entrance to the auditorium. It is unmanned, the door gives, and inside I go.

It is everything I thought it would be and more. The velvet seats, rows and rows of them. The wall-to-wall decor. Balcony and brass. And, oh my, the drawn curtain. Everything in place. Everything in order. Just as I imagined. I walk the length of the aisle until I reach the stage. I clamber up, not stopping until I am standing front and centre. I turn fully around and take in the auditorium. Soak up the dark-lit atmosphere. I am about to take a peek behind the curtain when I hear a faceless voice calling out.

'Hey! You there. What are you doing?'

Someone is pounding down the aisle towards the stage.

'Step this way, young lady,' the voice booms out in the low light, and moments later, a firm-arm grip is turning me and then making attempts to guide me towards the exit.

'Unhand me,' I say, summoning as much indignation as I can.

'And why should I do that?'

'Because I am one of the performers,' I yell, as he quick-marches me out to the foyer.

*

My theatre pass is good for middle of the third row from the end. As yet, no one has claimed the end-of-row seat. I flop right in.

People trickle into the auditorium. They pause here and there to admire a feature of the new building. Comment as to its impressiveness. Pose for pics. I spot some familiar faces. Doc Harper arrives with his good lady. Yoohoo Lucy Garavan arrives in a fluster of giddiness, and once she has figured out the seating system, greets Dolores Taaffe and Odd Doris with an elaborate wave and proceeds swiftly towards the front rows. Then I spot mother, on the far side of the auditorium. Peter Porter is with her, though there is no sign of Jennifer and Little Juan. They move all the way towards the front. I've started to wonder about Imelda and her fanfare arrival when Fleming turns up, and not wanting to be seen, I slide down in my seat and shield my face with my hand.

'Excuse me, I think that's my seat you're in.' It's the giraffe from outside earlier. She is standing over me, slapping the programme into the palm of her hand.

'Oh, really? How completely incompetent of me,' I say. 'But can I ask . . . you see, I have this condition. I cannot sit in any one place for long spells of time. I may have to vacate my seat at some totally unsuitable moment, and I would hate to think I might be the cause of someone missing out on a key moment or wonderfully rendered gesture while clunky me clambers past them. Would it be at all possible for me to claim this seat?' For added effect I start rubbing my backside.

She looks at me, uncertain, but I have one last card to draw.

'Look,' I say, elaborately waving my own pass and at the same time gesturing towards the middle of the row. 'You'll have to agree. It is a much better seat.'

I allow her a moment to absorb the fact that what I am offering is entirely in her favour. Naturally, she doesn't want to appear too obliging, but I can tell that my work is done. Moments later she has agreed to my proposition, has seated herself and has spotted someone with whom she can jibber.

The five-minute bell sounds. An announcement urges everyone inside, and the auditorium quickly fills.

An old lady claims the seat next to me.

'That is a lovely outfit you have on,' she says to me once she has settled herself, a task that involves gnashing down a half-packet of Silvermints and reaching for a needle and wool.

'Why, thank you,' I say. 'It's getting its first outing this evening. What are you knitting, may I ask?'

'Mittens. I have a feeling we're in for a long winter. I knitted an entire scarf during an exhausting performance of *Who's Afraid of Virginia Woolf?* a while back.'

'Oh, yes. I caught that one as well. Exhausting is the word.'

Portly-man-with-chain marches out on stage and continues from where he left off outside on the red carpet, welcoming everyone, complimenting everyone, booming his voice through the auditorium until he is certain everyone is aware of his involvement in the historic evening. Camilla the Hun walks out and welcomes everyone and in her no-nonsense way points out the emergency exits and tells everyone to turn off their phones. Enjoy the performance, she says and exits stage left.

The lights dim. The audience settles down. An anticipatory hush descends.

'This is momentous, isn't it?' croaks the old lady beside me. She clutches my arm as the curtain rises.

The set looks great. It is cramped and lively and not nearly as sordid as Blanche herself would lead us to believe. A jazz piano trickles through the midnight-blue lighting. I sit back, make myself comfortable.

It starts off reasonably satisfactorily. The early scenes, in particular. Stanley is a quietly menacing presence. Stella is perfectly adequate as the lame duck. Mitch I am impressed with. He is a winning blend of awkward charm and fatalistic resilience. Blanche, though. I'm not sure that she is hitting her notes. The accent is a little forced. She seems to think her sole purpose on stage is to out-spar Stanley with witticisms. And the way she keeps throwing out her right hand every time she delivers one of these witticisms is very distracting. I make little effort to suppress my boredom, while those seated beside me glare my way.

The interval arrives after scene six. Everyone hustles their way out into the lobby to collect their pre-ordered drinks, scoff more nibbles. I bide my time and wait until the auditorium has emptied. For some reason the old lady beside me doesn't seem in any hurry out of there. She is busy with her knitting, her hands going good-oh. I leave her to it, vacate my seat and walk into the lobby. I can see mother and Peter Porter standing outside, on the steps. Fleming is with them. The three of them in thick confab. Mother and Peter Porter no doubt wondering when I'm due onstage. Fleming doing his best to let on he is none the wiser. I jostle my way to the busy bar and order the largest glass of red wine Emily will give me. Keep pouring, Emily, I tell her. And she is kind enough to do precisely as she is bid.

Then I see him. At the end of the bar. Smiling at well-wishers, pressing hands. Glass of wine to hand, I jostle over to him.

'Hello, Stephen,' I say loud enough to ensure I get his attention. 'Are you enjoying the show?'

'Oh, hello . . . eh . . .'

'Eh . . . what does that mean? Don't tell me you're not enjoying it? Your own show!'

'Eh . . .'

'You're probably kicking yourself for not casting yours truly. So?'

'So?'

'Are you kicking yourself for not casting me? How many times have you kicked yourself? Ten? Twenty? Go on, tell me. I won't say anything.'

'I have to get back, Laura.'

'Oh, don't mind me, Stephen. I'm just trying to yank

your chain. Off you go now. Wouldn't want you missing the second half.'

\*

My favourite moments have come and gone. Blanche telling Mitch of the fate of her early love. Her talk of the rainy New Orleans afternoons. Of the searchlight that had been turned on the world going out. For that moment I could feel the tears rolling down my face, as the old woman beside me let go of her needles and held my shaking hands.

And at last. We have arrived at the pivotal scene. Stanley is togged out in his special-occasion pyjamas. Any moment now he is going to pounce. He is going to back Blanche into the bedroom. And suspecting the worst, Blanche is going to reach for a broken bottle to ward him off.

An anticipatory silence envelops the auditorium.

'Would you excuse me for a moment?' I whisper to the old lady beside me and I rise from my end-of-row seat, walk down the aisle and take the left-hand-side stairs up onto the stage.

I look about me. Mia is standing stage right, a quivering waif of vulnerability and calculation, a broken person who is somehow clinging to the last vestiges. I have to admit that, after the better part of two hours on stage, she finally looks like a genuine Blanche DuBois. 'Doesn't she?' I say out loud, turning to face my audience. I examine some of the faces immediately below me. Mother is in the front row.

More or less directly below me, alongside Peter Porter. Practically the best seats in the house. Fleming is there too. And mother's friends are close by.

I take in the entire auditorium, and as soon as I do, the various faces start to wheel about me, now in, now out of focus, it's already difficult to concentrate on any one of them. Tut-tut. The show must go on. I clear my throat and join my hands.

'Hello everyone. I have an announcement to make in relation to this evening's performance. Unfortunately one of the actresses is unable to carry on and I have been asked to stand in. I will be your Blanche for the final scenes this evening.'

Billy the Lush has moved slightly out of the wings, Stephen Fallow is there too. I move across to Blanche, who is still gripping the broken bottle. 'Look at this plastic thing,' I say, relieving Mia of the bottle prop. 'This is what you need,' I say, and I reach inside the pocket of my skirt and remove the knife.

Mia flinches and backs away from me. A collective gasp issues throughout the auditorium.

Good. I seem to have everyone's attention.

'So, tell me, Mia,' I say, waggling the knife in front of her. 'Do you know me? Would you like to know me?'

There is no chance for her to reply. Someone wants to cut into our little get-together. Stephen Fallow. Our director. And not before time.

'What kept you?' I say, as he joins me onstage.

'What are you doing?' he says.

'Yes, you're quite right. I think this scene calls for a little direction,' I say. 'So, then, Mr Director Man. Give me some.'

'What? Give you some what?'

'Listen to you. The hotshot director all the way from Broadway. Come on, then. Let's have some direction.'

Now someone else wants to cut into our little get-together. It's my leading man. And about time too.

'Where were you earlier?' I say, as he takes to the stage.

'Laura! What are you at?'

'Fleming! You of all people should know the answer to that. Look around you. See the gathered crowd.'

'And?'

'What do you mean, *And?* This is my *stage*, Fleming. This is where I was born to be.'

'What are you doing with the knife, Laura?'

'Fleming, are you listening to a word I'm saying?'

'Same question.'

'Fleming, please. I did not invite you up here for an interrogation.'

Stephen Fallow is gesturing to Mia to stay calm. In the wings, Billy the Lush is watching every move, edging his way onstage. The audience looks on, spellbound. Fleming is talking again.

'Will you let me take it? The knife?'

'Tell me about your TV show, Fleming. The one about the American presidents. The one I helped you with.'

'*Once Elected.*'

'Yes. *Once Elected.* And all they do is watch television. So what show is loofah-face watching?'

'Laura. I don't think this is the time . . .'

'Fleming! You are absolutely right. We need to wait for Imelda.'

'What? Who's Imelda, Laura?'

'Imelda is my friend. My acting friend.'

'What friend? What acting friend?'

'Imelda Ebbing. Imelda *J* Ebbing. Don't tell me you've never heard of her, Fleming.'

He holds out his hands and shakes his head at me. I half-turn to face the auditorium, at the same time jabbing the knife in Fleming's direction, mock-smiling as I go. 'Hear that, folks. He's never heard of Imelda Ebbing.' I turn back to Fleming.

'Imelda and me go way back. All the way back. We were like that,' I say, twisting together the middle and index fingers of my spare hand. 'She's made it big in London. She's coming here tonight. As soon as she sees me perform, she's going to whisk me away.'

Fleming takes a deep breath. 'Laura! I don't think that's going to . . .' There is pleading in his voice. Layers and layers of it. Well, why shouldn't there be? After all, he is my leading man.

'Now where could she be? She said she was going to be in the front row.'

'Where could *who* be, Laura!'

'I told you. Imelda.'

'Laura! What are you talking about?'

'Daddy knows who she is. He liked Imelda from the

very first moment. He said someone with a name like that
. . . is going . . . all the way . . .'

Fleming looks at me, a flicker of something – recognition –
passes across his face.

'Laura. I think it's time to call an end to this.'

'You want to know something else my daddy told me
when I was little, Fleming? Life is just a few moments.
That's all. Me? I just wanted a part. To be a part of something. That wasn't too much to ask for. Was it, Fleming?'

'No, Laura. No, it wasn't.'

I look to the wings, to the stagehands that have gathered
there, one or two busy talking into mobiles, the others
watching my every move. Fleming looks from me to the
knife. I clutch it closer to me.

'Laura, please,' he says, reaching out an arm. 'Let me
have it.'

He takes a step towards me. I turn away from him, and
again I face the auditorium, see mother standing out of her
seat, hand to her mouth. And now the dizziness comes on.
And Stephen's expression catches my eye. A mix of mirth
and contempt and who-do-you-think-you-are upsetting my
opening-night spectacle. Mia, too, is watching me, her gaze
flicking from my face to the knife. Go on, her smirking face
implores, I dare you.

I make to pretend-lunge at her and, not-so-steady on my
feet, stagger forward. Stephen throws himself between
myself and Mia. The audience howls and others rush
onstage. I loosen my grip on the knife, let it fall onto the
stage floor. Oh my! Is that blood I can see on the blade?

And everything is dark. And I am outside. Salty air and chill of night. I am standing at the end of the pier. The west wind hushed and not a stir. Someone is talking to me. A gentle voice, familiar and reassuring, so, so easy on the ear. Come, Laura, I hear it say. Stand beside me. I do as I am told. Look out there, Laura. Tell me what you see. I do as I am bid and look out into the black water. Tell me what you see, Laura. And, yes! I can see it now, daddy. So, so clear. Stretching out before me like never before. 'I can see it!' I cry out, taking a step over the edge. 'I can see it I can see it I can see it.' The star-studded path. All the famous names in glittering letters. I take another step. And another. And another. And I can so easily see the way. No need for assistance, no need for the arms reaching out to me. And I step fearlessly onward, and I hear the collective gasp from the audience, and at last all the walls have dissolved, every single last one of them, and I am walking among stars.

# FINALE

I remember the first time I was inside a theatre – it was more of an old hall, the one they would restore and call the Story House. The Claddagh Players were putting on a production of *The Playboy of the Western World*. Daddy had the lead role, and I had begged him to let me tag along. As soon as the performance began I couldn't take my eyes off the stage. Was instantly transported. And there and then I knew it was where I belonged.

After the performance daddy took me backstage and I met the other actors. Laura, this is the Widow Quinn, daddy said, affectionately jabbing the woman he had been sparring with all evening. And this is Billy the props man – singlehandedly built the entire set. They were all there, the actors, cracking open cans of beer and popping bottles of fizzy wine. They clinked glasses and toasted each other, proud that they had pulled it off. I felt proud of them too, and I listened to their verdicts on the show, the various performances, what could be done better, their satisfaction at a particular moment or gesture. Good job, beautiful work. The Abbey would be hard pressed to emulate what we just did. Next stop Broadway! I was in thrall to everything that was said, hung off every word.

And gradually the talk moved away from their own play and on to other plays, plays they would love to put on in the future, plays they had put on in the past, plays they had seen and admired. Did you the see the movie version? someone asked and the conversation then swayed in that direction. Movies they had seen recently and movies they wanted to see, and movies they had seen long ago and wanted to see again. They talked about the stars and who they liked and who they were not so keen on and those they thought were under-appreciated and overrated. Who do you like, Laura? I remember Billy the props man asking me. I didn't need to be asked twice. I like Lana Turner, I said. Do you now? Billy said, and tell me what have you seen her in? And without a pause for breath I mentioned *The Postman Always Rings Twice*. *Madame X* is good too, I said, and I like her in *The Bad and the Beautiful*. Who else do you like? Greece McLoughlin asked me. Barbara Stanwyck, I said. Especially *Double Indemnity* and *The Lady Eve*. Veronica Lake is really good too. And so is kick-his-head-in Jane Greer. And fasten-your-seatbelt Bette Davis. They couldn't believe the names coming out of me and what I knew about them, and they laughed some more when I threw out a line or two from whatever movie daddy and me had watched that week. Most of all I like Gloria Swanson, I declared, and they all stopped talking and looked my way. Did you know, I asked them, that at the end of a private screening of *Sunset Boulevard* Barbara Stanwyck knelt down and kissed the hem of Gloria Swanson's skirt? And in an instant I was Norma Desmond living in a mysterious mansion along with the butler I was once married to. My pet monkey has just died and we are about to bury it when the handsome stranger pulls into my driveway. He's on the run and needs to hide out from the moneymen he owes big time. You're Norma Desmond, handsome says when he gets a proper look at me. You used to be big. *I'm still big!* I howl back at him. *It's the movies that got small.* By the time I was finished they were slapping their knees and jabbing each other good-oh and hooting like there was no tomorrow. At which point daddy and me eyed each other and smiled.

Later at home that night, daddy asked me had I chosen my star name. I knew he was going to ask me and I was ready with my answer. Of course I have, I replied. It's Imelda. Imelda Ebbing.

Imelda Ebbing, he repeated after me, rubbing the tip of his chin with his thumb and forefinger. I think I like that. I think I like it a lot.

\*

And so, against all the odds, I have landed back inside St Jude's. I'm on the third floor, in a ward with several others. Sharing a room with a woman called Margaret. She keeps getting out of bed and packing her suitcase, every few minutes announces that she is going somewhere. Where are you going, Margaret? the nurses ask her. Then she unpacks and gets back into bed. The other day she took off without bothering to pack. The nurses said she does it at the same time every year. Like a swallow flying south for winter. Now that the climate is changing they don't know what she is liable to do.

Next door to us is Rita. This week, she has been accusing everyone of sprinkling dishwashing powder into her chilli con carne. There's an aftertaste, she says. A nurse told me it's the only way to get anti-depressants into her. Angelina Jolie is here too. 'Hello,' she said to me when I rocked up. 'My name isn't Sharon Fyffe, it's Angelina Jolie.' She has started writing her life story. And she wants Helen Mirren to play her in the movie version. Fleming was very interested in this piece of information, wanted to know does she look like Angelina Jolie. No, I told him, she looks like the Bride of Frankenstein.

And then there is Sandra who is always hogging the radiator. Stole money from her husband's mother. She won't say how much or what she did with it. She told me she's been married for fifty years. Once for twenty-two years. Once for ten years. And three times each for six years. She says her love CV reads very well. And that an acute sense of responsibility leaves her in a state of permanent unrest. I've seen her try but she is unable to do anything for herself. They haven't decided yet precisely what is wrong with me.

There are three Kitties and a Katie. One of the Kitties is eighty-eight. She is not responsible. On Thursday she saw fireworks for the very first time. You should have seen her face light up. She won't let us turn on the TV. It affects her asthma. Tomorrow, she's leaving. In a helicopter. As soon as she transfers the insurance from her car. I'll miss her but at least I'll be able to watch *Better Call Saul*. That's right. I have started watching television shows. Won't mother and Fleming be thrilled?

Any chance I get I go outside, roll a ciggie, light up. Every time, a man hobbles up and stands alongside me. He is tall, gaunt-looking, trying to grow a beard. He holds his arms out in front of him. His hands tremble. Around here he is known as the Thief. He steals anything he can get a hold of. Cigarettes. Flower vases. Pillow slips. The first time he stood beside me I offered him the rollie I had just made. He took it, looked intensely at me and said, 'You are four great people.' 'Only four,' I said right back to him. We have been smoking together ever since.

Stephen Fallow is well on the mend. The knife barely grazed his arm. But I hear he is considering a move. Another outfit is keen to avail of his services – as soon as he is ready to take to the stage again. I wonder what Khaos will do after his departure. I wonder if Mia is going with him.

Doc was around to check in on me. He was happy to sit down and listen to me talk theatre and movies and television. And once I mentioned her, he was especially keen to hear all about Imelda. When was she discovered. The name of the hotshot director dying to work with her. Her middle initial. He smiled at everything I told him, as though I was confirming lots of stuff he already knew. And so I asked him straight out how much he did know. He was silent for a moment, and when at last he did decide to speak, he said it was his turn to ask a question. But by then I didn't want to play any more.

Who in their right mind calls themselves Imelda Ebbing anyway? Fleming's words when he swung by. Next time, he suggests I come up with a better name, and I am not inclined to disagree.

Jennifer and Little Juan have been in. To everyone's relief her existence has finally been confirmed by the Mexican bankmen. And so her cards are finally working – now all she needs to do is persuade the same bankmen that she had nothing to do with the series of transactions responsible for more or less depleting her account. If you stuck to not exist-ing you were home free on that score, I said to her and she laughed. There is still no sign of Alonso. I really know how to pick them, don't I? she said. Sign me up if you need him taken out, I told her and she laughed again. Her new con-tract start date has also been given the OK. She and Juan are leaving in a few days and so her luggage turned up at a very timely moment. I returned the bits and pieces I had taken. She laughed, was chuffed even, that I had deemed them useful. She insisted I keep the octagonal sunglasses and smiled approvingly when I tried them on again. Juan has a present for you too, she said next. And the little man handed over a multipack of Chipsticks.

The three of us were still chomping away when mother and Peter Porter arrived. Mother pressed my hands and stared intensely at me, as though eventually she might be able to see inside my head, spot the bad part and yank it out once and for all. Peter Porter drew up a chair for her alongside my bed. Then he mentioned the trip he and mother are planning. Guess where to, he asked me, and winked. As soon as you're better, Laura, mother added. I told them not to delay their trip on my account. If you do, I told them, I am going to find a way out onto the rooftop and stage a sit-down protest. Mother didn't like the sound of that at all, and I had to reassure her I was joking. I even got out of bed and threw in a hug for good measure. She didn't want to let me go.

And, as I said, Fleming has been by. Has been on a daily basis. What did she have that you don't, he asked me after I had told him all about her – Imelda, that is. I shrugged my shoulders and fed him lines about talent fame beauty success. Not much, then, he said.

Today he lies up on the bed beside me. All he can talk about is the result of the American presidential election and the surprise victor, or maybe not so surprising. I find myself listening to everything he has to say. I even start quizzing him about his television show, the one that features American presidents.

'So, Fleming. *Once Elected*. And all they do is watch television. What show *is* loofah-face watching? You never told me.'

'I've decided to leave him out of the show,' he replies.

'Oh? So he doesn't watch television?'

'No. He plays golf and tweets.'

'Do you think that's a good idea, Fleming? I mean that loofah-head is such an imbecile. Think of the possibilities . . .'

'I know . . . but some people aren't worth the effort. Know what I mean?'

'. . . and Obama. You never said what TV show he's watching either. It's a really good idea, Fleming, maybe you're on to something after all with this television malarkey.'

He nods, smiles at what I am saying. His eyes look so blue. And until this precise moment I've never realized how fine his hair is. Cutting it could do wonders.

'So? What show is Obama watching?'

Fleming smiles my way – it takes years off him – leans into me and whispers the name of our show.

Apparently we're starting dramatherapy tomorrow. Which suits me perfectly as I have something rather special I intend to share. It concerns a girl who wants more than anything to be a star. There is plenty at stake. Lots of characters – both from my own life and from the world of movies. I have even started casting. Rita is perfect for Lana Turner. Sharon Fyffe I think has the makings of an excellent Veronica Lake – provided, that is, she can get Angelina Jolie out of her head. Margaret has already confided in me that she fancies herself as a bit of a Gloria Swanson. And I might try one of the Kitties as purring and conniving Barbara Stanwyck. It's going to have everything. Thrills. Spills. Jeopardy. Suspense. Highs and lows. Sadness and joy. Hope and despair. I fully intend to both direct and play the lead role. Though I might seek some consultation on some of the finer points in the script. I can't wait to tell daddy all about it. Already, I have a title. It's a good one. It's called – well, perhaps I'll keep it to myself until I speak with daddy. It's going to be a big hit, I just know it is.

# IMELDA J EBBING

---

July 16, 1991 –
aka Melly Dearest

**Inducted:** February 8, 2030
**Star address:** off-Hollywood and Vine
Father drowned when she was ten
Discovered performing monologues while
gigging as a tour guide
Held her director at knife-point during
an opening-night performance
Fan of Oatfield chocolate emeralds and
Chef brown sauce
Oscar glory for Martin Scorsese musical *Glorious Gloria!*
**Real name:** Laura Cassidy

*'A girl can't always have the fairy tale.'*

# ACKNOWLEDGEMENTS

Once again, thanks to Ansa Khan Khattak for inspired involvement on this one, and to Paul Baggaley and everyone at Picador.

To Aoife Casby for an early read; to Cormac Kinsella, Davy Adamson and Jamie-Lee Nardone; to Ivan Mulcahy.

A shout out also to Padraig Stevens for kind permission to use a lyric from his wonderful song The Streets Of Galway.